Dog Men Dream of Magic Things

By Lee Dresselhaus

PublishAmerica
Baltimore

© 2008 by Lee Dresselhaus.
All rights reserved. No part of this book may be reproduced, stored in a retrieval system or transmitted in any form or by any means without the prior written permission of the publishers, except by a reviewer who may quote brief passages in a review to be printed in a newspaper, magazine or journal.

First printing

All characters in this book are fictitious, and any resemblance to real persons, living or dead, is coincidental.

PublishAmerica has allowed this work to remain exactly as the author intended, verbatim, without editorial input.

ISBN: 1-60672-140-2
PUBLISHED BY PUBLISHAMERICA, LLLP
www.publishamerica.com
Baltimore

Printed in the United States of America

Young birds dream of lightning wings,
To flee the fears the daylight brings,
In Moroccan sands a night bird sings,
And Dog Men Dream of Magic Things.

A rich man dreams of simpler things,
While young girls dream of golden rings,
The stars belong in Dog Man Dreams,
For Dog Men Dream of Magic Things.

At dawn the light wakes with gentle touch
A dreamer who to sleep's mantle clings
While in that sleep he's learned so much
For Dog Men Dream of Magic Things

1

No Talent or Ambition Will Get You....Sent to Morocco

I was lucky. If it had been up to my talents and my abilities to make it happen, it never would have. I didn't have any then talent or ambition or a desire to succeed and I liked it like that. But it did. It happened anyway. And it was good.

I'm one of the few who would ever know just what it was to live a genuine dream, and what it felt like to share dreams in a place known for dreams and legends. There had been a magic and beauty in it, and a sense of belonging like I had never felt before or since.

It was a shame it had to come to an end much too soon because of a damn possum.

I suppose I should explain that, so I'll do my best to tell you what a Dog Man is and how I was lucky enough to become one. Stick around. You'll like this story.

I've always had an attitude problem, or at least that's what various ex-wives, miscellaneous bosses, and a hefty slice of the general population have told me from time to time over the years. I don't understand it, really. Or at least I didn't in my younger years. My philosophy was that the world was filled with incompetent idiots and that was a cross I had to bear, being one of the few who were enlightened enough to understand that most people were pretty hopeless. Looking back with the benefit and relative wisdom of age, I can see how some people had considered me an arrogant jerk. At the time, though, I preferred to consider myself an independent thinker no matter who it pissed off. And thinking independently, which really consisted of not listening to a damn thing anyone had to say even when they were older, wiser, and just plain smarter that I was, is what kept getting my young self into one brush after another with much despised authority figures, who would often tell me, the all wise and all knowing seventeen year old, how to live my life.

In keeping with my absolute refusal to listen to anybody, especially authority figures of any kind, I decided to quit school at sixteen, and on the day of my seventeenth birthday I forced my reluctant mother to take me to the local military recruiters. I had decided that I wanted to be a Marine. When my Uncle Ralph found out what I was doing, he offered me guidance.

"Don't do it, dumbass," my Uncle Ralph, a veteran of two combat tours in Viet Nam, said, "You don't like following orders, and they don't like people who don't like following orders. They'll eat you alive, boy."

"They'll eat who alive?" I asked with my usual cocky inability to accept advice of any type.

"You, junior. They'll eat you alive. Those drill instructors are some very tough boys. And they will not swallow your line of bullshit." My uncle knew me well.

I was determined, though, and said so, "I'll make it fine. I can handle it," I told him.

"You'll hate it." He hesitated for a moment then looked at me quizzically, "Tell me something? Just how tough do you think you are, boy? You weigh every bit of a hundred and forty pounds soaking wet and less than that if you cut off all that goddamn hair, which they *will* do as soon as you get there."

Well, I wanted to get away from home and that seemed to be the way to do it and when I wanted something I had the ability to ignore logic and reason with the best of them. I saw our family homestead as having nothing to offer my future but hard labor. And being the way I was, hard labor and I just did not get along.

"How tough can it be?" I asked my uncle in my usual cocky manner.

He looked at me and shook his head, "You've seen too many movies. All right, go ahead, have at it. Just remember this conversation."

He was right. I hated it. They cut off my hair right down to the scalp—with hot clippers, too—and I hated it, so he was right on both counts. As with so many things in life the idea of the whole thing was so much different than the reality. And reality had hit me right between the eyes.

When I joined in '71 I scored high on the battery of entry tests, which qualified me for a four-year aviation guarantee. I figured that an assignment to a Marine Air Wing would keep me out of the mud and keep me from being shot at by people I didn't know, and I congratulated myself for being clever enough to avoid these things and still get a ticket away from that Indiana farm. There was only one small problem before I could start my new career with the Wing.

They call it "Boot Camp."

Boot camp, of course, was a nightmare for me. Well, it's a nightmare for everybody except the idiots who enjoy that sort of thing, but it was a special hell for the likes of me. Totally unimpressed by my lack of response to their tender guidance the drill instructors, Smokey Bear hat wearing lunatics that make a living destroying personalities like mine, when they tired of screaming at me and calling me names I had never even heard before, would insist that I was a communist agent intent on destroying their Marine Corps and the American way of life in general.

"You're a Russian spy, aren't you, Dillon?" one of the drill instructors, a pin headed sadist named Smith, would yell at me. His eyes were bright blue and would shine an even brighter hue when he was enraged at me. He was a spitter, too, and I would often get the full benefit of his rage in the form of mini facial showers as he screamed at me, which I would not dare to wipe away, "You can't possibly be this stupid! You should die! They sent you here to destroy my beloved Corps, didn't they?"

"Sir, no Sir!" I would scream in my best robot recruit voice.

"Bullshit," the knuckle dragger would roar, "I think you're here from Moscow. You're a fucking spy, you pig fucker!" Personally, I found it interesting that in the same breath I could be accused of being on a par with 007 and being someone who has sex with barnyard animals. That interchangeable logic could only take place in Marine Corps boot camp. Expressing that thought at the time, however, would have been unwise.

The other drill instructors, who seemed to loathe me every bit as much as Smith, would nod sagely and agree that I was probably either a spy or a complete idiot since I couldn't seem to grasp the simplest principles of recruit training.

"I don't think he's a spy. I think he's just an idiot," said one of them amiably.

The third chimed in with, "Nope. I agree. Nobody's that stupid. He's a spy. Has to be."

They then told me to do push-ups until I died.

Actually, I understood quite well what they wanted me to learn, but becoming a disciplined, highly trained fighting machine was very low on my to-do list. I squeaked through boot camp solely on the basis of my own stubbornness and my refusal to quit because I knew that's what the drill instructors wanted. They wanted me to quit. Or die, but barring that, quitting and going home to mama would do as long as I wasn't around any longer to contaminate their beloved Marine Corps. But since quitting was something that someone in authority wanted me to do I would be damned if I would give it to them. I decided I would die first. I made it through and graduated, much to the chagrin of my D.I.'s. They shook their heads the night before graduation, glaring at me, and predicted the end of democracy. Then they made me do push-ups all night long, again hoping I would die before I graduated. I didn't, much to their disappointment.

After boot camp and infantry training, the Corps lived up to their end of the deal and shipped me off to Naval Air Station, Jacksonville, Florida for an elite aviation electrician school. From which, after a few short weeks, I was unceremoniously booted. The official reason, according to my service record book was, "Lack of interest or application." The real reason was that I had quickly discovered how to abuse the hospitality of the local Navy Enlisted Men's Club. I spent a great deal of time playing when I should have been studying, which the Corps frowned upon mightily. I found myself a fake ID and spent my evenings in that club, studying the inside of endless pitchers of beer instead of in the barracks studying the electrical components that are contained in F-4 Phantom warplanes. The whole thing about responsibility and accountability was a concept that I was having a difficult time grasping.

So they kicked me out. I had accomplished my first great failure at seventeen. Of course, it was not my fault. I hadn't learned to associate a rotten attitude with getting kicked in the ass, and I blamed everyone but me, the school, the math involved in the course, the hours, the staff. I think I even blamed my mother. Anyone but where the blame squarely belonged—on me.

The next thing I knew I was drawing a pack, helmet, M-16 rifle, and a bunch of other stuff that I had hoped never to see again after boot camp and infantry training Then, in a daze, I was becoming acquainted with the culture (none) and atmosphere (hot and damp) of Second Marine Division, Camp Lejeune, North Carolina. My four-year aviation guarantee, it turned out, was based on me actually *succeeding* in my selected field. That hadn't occurred to me. Due to that lack of foresight on my part, the Corps decided that the infantry could put my reluctant services to good use and I was suddenly a grunt, my aviation contract vanishing in a puff of irresponsibility. The four-year enlistment commitment, however, did not.

I had discovered, much to my dismay, that in real life there are no guarantees. No matter what kind of papers you sign.

So that is how I came to be lying on my bunk in Mike Company, 3rd Battalion, Second Marine Regiment, a hard leg grunt unit that I hated with my every breath. I was hiding from my platoon sergeant and wondering how in God's Green Earth I was going to weasel out of an assignment to mess duty, which was due to begin the following Monday. I was to report to the mess hall at the unholy hour of 3:30 AM. At that time this particular duty was a joy that was shared by the lower three enlisted ranks, private, private first class, and lance corporal. Of which I was the second, a one stripe private first class who had somehow just managed to hang onto that much.

Mess duty was basically thirty days of greasy slave labor in the vast kitchen which mass produced the oh-so-yummy and, occasionally, unidentifiable food we were all forced to eat in order to survive between paydays. It was miserable duty, and my rank of PFC made me a prime candidate for the job. I would do anything short of actual physical self-mutilation with a hot iron or something sharp to avoid it, although that option had been discarded only after careful examination. Begging wouldn't work—I'd already tried that when the Company Gunny had first notified me that I had won that particular lottery. "Oh, come on, Gunny. Can't you get somebody else?" I begged. I had no pride when it came to avoiding mess duty. "Shut up, Dillon," he replied in a disgusted tone, "Just be there Monday, 0330." And that was that.

It didn't help that I strongly suspected that my hated platoon sergeant had volunteered me and it didn't look like I could squirm out of this one. I was good at squirming out of assignments, too, and racked my brain for an escape from this one to no avail.

At this point in my brief and unhappy association with the Marine Corps I had become an accomplished weasel. I didn't consider avoiding work as shirking my duty. Avoiding work *was* my duty as far as I was concerned. Weaseling was a challenge, an art I felt it was my obligation to master. I thought about feigning an illness to avoid the mess duty nightmare but I had just successfully done that to get out of night guard duty at the ammo storage bunkers. I really didn't think they would fall for it twice. Plus, I reasonably suspected that they might get more of an attitude toward me than they already had if I were to attempt it again so soon. Successful weasels must think ahead, you know.

So I was lying there trying not to moan aloud at the thought of a whole month of grim, unrewarding and worse yet, closely supervised work (close supervision not being my favorite thing) when my platoon sergeant, Sgt. Meyers came looking for me. I looked up and saw him standing there with that boy-did-I-just-screw-you-and-I-like-it-so-much look on his face. Several black Marines, who had been standing in a group near the end of the open bay, also saw Meyers and eyed him warily. They had been about to light up a joint rolled in a bright pink strawberry paper which disappeared like magic when he made his appearance. He was death on anything like that and they knew it.

Sgt. Meyers was one of those lean, hard, razor sharp Marines who lived his whole life for the Corps. His appearance was recruiting poster sharp. He lived and breathed USMC regulations and slept with the Uniform Code of Military Justice under his pillow. He was a credit to uniformed services everywhere, and would have been right at home in Hitler's Gestapo. In fact, I believe he would have excelled there. He certainly looked the part, standing over six feet tall, with close cropped blond hair, perfect teeth, and the bright blue eyes of a homicidal maniac. There was something behind those eyes, though, something dark and shifty, that made me distrust him even more than others in authority.

We had an understanding, he and I. I detested him, and he thought I was a blemish on the face of his beloved Corps that should be crushed out of existence and, if anything, he despised me more than I did him. He missed no opportunity to harass me and I missed no opportunity to make his life as miserable as I could. So it was in this spirit of mutual admiration that he delivered his announcement, "Hello, Dillon. I've been looking all over for you." The group of Brothers sauntered past Meyers on their way to safer pastures. One of them, a tall, thin Brother with a black power hair pick thrust into the back of his Afro, gave Meyers the Angry Black Man look as he walked by. That was bold or just plain stupid because Meyers liked to fuck with everybody. He was an equal opportunity prick except when it came to me, who he took a special joy in annoying. I waited for him to brace the Brother, but he just let him go by. Normally Meyers would not let such a challenge pass unanswered and would have had the Brother locked at attention while he read him the riot act, but he ignored the stare and focused on me. Uh oh, I thought.

This could not be good.

'Hi, Sarge. Been right here," I stretched and yawned to show him that I was unconcerned that he had been looking for me, although I was actually very concerned since I was supposed to be raking the tons of pine needles that have the nerve to fall daily onto hallowed Marine Corps ground at Lejeune. It was just another of the shit details that Meyers blessed my life with. Then I became incredibly depressed when I heard I was on top of the list to be sacrificed to kitchen duty, said, "Fuck this," dropped my rake right where I stood, and had moped to my bunk to sulk, leaving the detail without second thought. I had my priorities, you know. It didn't help that I was sure that Meyers had manipulated the mess duty list so that my name was number one. Vengeful bastard.

When he found me lying on my bunk instead of doing what I had been told to do I knew that Meyers could make things even more miserable for me, so I braced myself for the massive shafting that was sure to come my way. Meyers smiled the kind of smile that cannibals must use when they see a particularly plump, unarmed missionary, took a deep breath, and instead of telling me that he was going to write me up for leaving a duty assignment or tell me for the twentieth time that I was slime, a worm, a maggot, a disgrace to the Corps, etc., etc., blah, blah, blah, he just said, through those recruiting poster teeth, "You have orders in the First Sergeant's office."

That got my attention in a most unpleasant way. Sitting straight up I said,

"Orders? What kind of orders? To where?"

"Don't know," he sighed as though Miss June had just written him a love letter promising carnal thrills. Or in his case, maybe Mr. June. I'm never sure about guys like that. He made a show of examining his immaculate fingernails, "All I know is that Top told me to tell you to get your worthless ass to his office pronto, and that they were overseas orders."

This was not good news. In 1972 there was still a little thing in Southeast Asia called the Vietnam War going on. We were supposedly going to sign a withdrawal soon, or already had or something, but some of our ground troops were still engaged. Including some Marines, or so we heard. And, *supposedly*, they weren't sending anybody else but it was too near the tag end of the damn thing and everybody felt that it really wasn't over. Whenever anybody heard they had orders they always prayed it wasn't to one of the units who were still there or one that was poised to go back in after the South Vietnamese Army started screaming for help. Nobody, especially me, wanted to be the last to die in a useless, pointless war that couldn't be won, but nonetheless people were still dying while politicians stayed in luxury hotels in Paris and argued over the shape of the negotiation table. Meyers must have read my mind because his smile got even larger.

"Gonna do the due on the Z, Dillon?" The Z? His reference to the DMZ, the demilitarized zone that was the free-fire meat grinder between North and South Vietnam made my skin crawl, but I didn't give him the satisfaction of showing it. He went on, "I sure hope so. I think you'd make *fine* cannon fodder. You sure as hell can't do anything else. Or maybe it's Iceland. Like the cold, Dillon? I hear the nights are six months long there and it gets to thirty below. Not including wind chill. All the time. Heh. Now get your ass to Top's office most rikki-tik," he sighed that same irritating sigh, "Life is good. By the way….Just to let you share in the joy since I know you're very interested in my career, it looks like I'll be getting a commission. That's right, Monkey Boy. Some of us are educated enough to be officers. Unlike some high school dropouts who shall remain nameless and who may or may not have a body bag in his immediate future. Looks like my ship will come in about the time yours goes drifting right on by. So long, maggot."

Whistling the Marine Corps Hymn, which he always did whenever he'd done something particularly nasty to me, he sauntered off to gloat and fantasize about me getting shot, killed, stabbed, maimed or maybe even tortured in various horrible ways. Or working a guard post in sub zero weather.

Iceland? *Iceland?*

With deep sincerity I flipped him off to his back, straightened my uniform and headed downstairs to the First Sergeant and whatever fate had in store for me.

On the way downstairs I began to run my options through my mind and realized.... I didn't have any. If in fact I was headed to a combat zone I would just have to go. Oh, I could go to Canada or desert and live in a hippie commune in San Francisco or something like that, but those weren't really options. Neither was jail for desertion. And another thing. My family, the patriotic, loyal, all-American midwest types that they were, would surely disown me. Liberal rich kids from New York and California go to Canada. All they have to do is loudly espouse a cause and they will eventually be forgiven. Farm boys from Indiana go wherever they're told to go and do their duty. Even reluctant weasels like me. Unlike with the liberal rich kids, forgiveness would not be forthcoming from the families of people like me. No, I would go wherever they sent me.

And another thing, I told myself as I started towards the First Sergeant's office and whatever fate awaited me there, dying in the mud of some backwater, useless, dirty little country is usually the job of people like myself who couldn't even vote or legally buy a beer, not some bloated pompous wrinkled ass of a geriatric politician. On the way down the stairs I began to stew with these thought percolating in my head. And what the hell were we doing in Iceland anyway? *Iceland?* Jesus! Of all the useless postings in the world. What was there to protect? Who in their right mind would want to invade Iceland? What could they possibly want there? Ice? Tall, cold, smelly women? What? Just give them the damn place for God's sake and leave me out of it! The Russians could have it as far as I was concerned, and good riddance. I had worked myself up into a fine frothy state of mind by the time I reached the office of First Sergeant M.K. Johnson.

First Sergeant Johnson had been in the Marine Corps for nearly thirty years and was one of the last of the rare breed that had seen combat in the Pacific, Korea *and* Vietnam. I actually respected him a great deal, and that was rare for me. He had more battle ribbons than anyone I had seen before or since and I knew that he was not the man to whine to. My whimpering would not find a sympathetic audience with M.K. Johnson. I just straightened up, knocked on his door and said,"You wanted to see me, Top?"

He looked up over his desk, lowered his glasses and said, "Come in, Dillon. I'm sure Sgt. Meyers told you that you have orders." He shuffled through some papers then lifted one and examined it. I stood in front of his desk with my hands clasped behind my back and waited for the inevitable. For some reason, even though he knew I was a shitbird with a severe case of attitude, Johnson always liked me, although he probably would have chosen a sharp stick in his eye before he would admit it. Actually, the fact that Johnson liked me was the only reason Meyers hadn't been able to do anything really unpleasant to me like make me a permanent kitchen slave or mop floors till I died. And I respected and admired Johnson because he was a mud Marine and not a recruiting poster wonder like Meyers. Even though being a mud Marine was very low on my list of Career Things To Do, I knew one when I saw him. He was the classic physical example of what was meant by walking softly and carrying a big stick. I figured he would break the bad news to me gently.

Johnson put the paper back onto his desk and leaned back, clasping his hands behind his neck. He gazed at me for a full minute, just long enough to make me start to squirm but not long enough for me to open my big mouth. Finally he looked over the black rims of his reading glasses, and said, "You know-I've been in this man's Corps for a whole lifetime, and every once in a while I see something that I never saw before, or I see someone get something that they really don't deserve." I could agree with that. I certainly didn't feel I deserved to get shot at repeatedly by people I didn't know and hadn't done a damn thing to. Or freeze to death in some lonely, icebound hellhole, but I kept quiet, waiting for the brick to fall. Then he went on, "Dillon, I don't know how you managed to rate this, but you got orders to Marine Barracks, Morocco."

I stood stock still for thirty seconds or so, not sure if I had heard right. Morocco? Was that some place in Vietnam? Wait, though. I remembered old Foreign Legion movies like Beau Geste. Weren't they in someplace like Morocco? It began to dawn on me that I wasn't going to Vietnam. Or to

Iceland for that matter. Morocco was clear on the other side of the world, as far away from unfriendly people in black pajamas with guns as you could get, wasn't it? And it doesn't freeze there, does it?

The First Sergeant went on, "Apparently we have a very low key communications station on the Atlantic coast of Morocco. Or the Navy does. It's choice duty. And there are a few of God's Finest there to protect said Navy people and their families. You, Birdturd, will be one of those chosen few. You are to be in Marine Barracks, Philadelphia in ten days to be processed for your clearance and your passport. You will be on temporary duty there until all that is complete, then you will have your skinny ass on its way to Morocco via Rota, Spain. Any questions?"

I sat, my mind whirling. I was still processing the sudden change in mindset, and didn't know quite what to say. "Are we talking about the Morocco in North Africa, Top?" I managed to stammer out.

"Do you know of another one?" he replied, handing me the typed orders.

"No, Sir."

"Then you had better go get packed if you want to clear from my beloved Marine Corps Base in time to get a couple of days leave before you have to be in Philly."

Then I said what is possibly one of the stupidest things I have ever said, "But what about mess duty?"

Johnson stared at me the same way he would if I had just announced that I intended to staple my face to the door, then said, "I'm sure that mess hall will function just fine without your capable direction. Now, scat." I turned to leave and he said, "Oh, Dillon, I'm sure Sgt. Meyers will be disappointed that you won't be here for mess duty and that you're not on you're way to the Z. I think he somehow got the impression that you had orders there. Won't he be surprised? Like I said, I hear Morocco is very choice duty," I turned to leave again and he added," I haven't told him yet, by the way. Be careful when you do. Don't quote me on this, but he's a vicious little dipshit. He'll make a good officer. I'm just glad I'll never have to work under him, but I pity those who will. And if you ever run into him again watch him close. He won't forget that you slid out from under his thumb. Trust me. I know his type. Now, get out of here. And Dillon—good luck."

He was smiling and had returned to his stack of papers as I left his office.

I started to head back to my bunk area to begin gathering my gear to turn in, but then I thought, hey, first things first.

I turned to the company clerks, "Hey, any of you guys seen Sgt. Meyers?"

2

All Things Considered, I'd Really Rather NOT be in Philly

Philadelphia was everything I expected and less. I found myself disliking that place almost as much as I had hated Lejeune.

I felt like I spent a year there in the month I was actually there, like I had been caught in some weird alternate dimension where time slowed down, another personal, private hell. I was assigned to the temporary Marine detachment at Philadelphia Naval Yard which is, or was then, a vast grimy dock filled with dozens of empty, mothballed warships. I would walk along the piers in total awe of the size and numbers of these vessels. If you ever wonder what happens to all the money you give our government in taxes just go to one of these installations. You'll see.

My pay was screwed up so I seldom had anything else to do except to walk along these docks and marvel at the size of the ships. If it is at all possible to totally screw your life up the military will do so, and since I was almost totally without money wandering among those mothballed ships supplied the only form of recreation available. In the grandest traditions of the military service Someone Somewhere had misplaced an essential Something Important that was needed for me to get paid, and as a result I was flat broke for the first two weeks I was there except for what they would allow me to draw against whatever they felt they owed me. They call it 'health and comfort pay.' I can tell you that it may keep you healthy but there just can't be a lot of comfort on thirty bucks every two weeks. And they wondered why I had an attitude.

The walks I was forced to take as my only form of recreation were educational, though. If I was somewhat in awe of those ships, I was also amazed at the size of the mutant rats that hung around the docks, too, apparently with as little to do as I. They casually eyed me as I walked past, not bothering to move unless I happened to wander too close. Which I tried not to do since I consider football sized rats that aren't afraid of me to be quite intimidating. Sort of like officers. Besides, the way they lounged around I figured they must have had their pay screwed up, too, although judging from their size they ate well. So, because of a total lack of money I spent much of my off duty time wandering those docks, ship gazing and watching the giant rats watching me.

My on duty time was spent doing the mundane, meaningless things that the military sets great store by and trying to stay out of the way of anyone over the rank of corporal.

Then came what I called the Great Passport Experience. Since I was to be issued a burgundy colored Embassy passport, special documentation was required, which I filled out and submitted.

It was effectively, efficiently, and immediately lost. So I filled out another one.

They lost that one, too, somewhere in the short journey between Philly and Washington D.C. I was then ordered to hand carry the documents to whichever bureaucrat does such things, so I did. Upon arrival I was told huffily that they had my documentation already, and that I was to return my presumptuous self to Philly without hesitation and wait like everyone else.

The conversation went something like this:
Stuffy Office Geek: Can I help you?
Me: I have the documentation for my passport and clearance here.
Stuffy Office Geek: And who are you?
Me: PFC Lester Dillon.
Stuffy Office Geek: We already have your paperwork.
Me: They said you lost it and I was told hand carry this to you.
Stuffy Office Geek (now offended): I don't lose paperwork, so you can just return to Philly. When we're done processing your paperwork you'll be notified.

Me: And when will that be?

Stuffy Office Geek: When we're done. Now, go back to Philly.

So I did. And there I was again ordered back to D.C. because it turned out that they didn't have my stuff after all. The Stuffy Office Geek had been wrong. So away I went. Now, at this point you would think that most people would be pretty angry, but you don't really know what humor is until you've been hostage to total bureaucratic horror. After an initial bout of anger I thought it was the funniest thing I had ever been subjected to in that ridiculous, Three Stooges sort of way that only the government can achieve without really trying.

If you run a business like that in the real world, you get fired.

It was on the third go round of filling out the very same paper that I ran afoul of an overly efficient, self-important cherub of a second lieutenant, the direct supervisor of the Stuffy Office Geek. He glared at me through wire rimmed glasses when, for the third time, I approached the hallowed halls of his tiny office kingdom.

"Excuse me, Lieutenant," I said smiling in a relaxed sort of way. I figured I had been there so frequently at that point that I could ease up a bit with the formalities. He, the officious little prick, had a different take.

"First off, Private, wipe that smile off your face. Second off," he continued, "I'm getting just a bit sick of dealing with you." Like this whole stupid circus was my idea. "What is it this time?"

I maintained my composure but what I really wanted to do, after dealing with one senseless bureaucratic mess after another, was to hit him right in his round, shiny little face. Which, of course, would land me in jail, not Morocco, so it wasn't really an option.

"The same thing, Sir. They lost my papers again."

"They lost your papers again. Has it occurred to you that I have better things to do than to keep stepping and fetching for you and your paper work?"

I could feel my anger beginning to swell at the sheer authoritarian idiocy of the man. Careful, boy, I thought, what you don't need right now is a charge of Insubordination. Be meek, I told myself. Morocco awaits. "No sir, I'm sorry. I just have to get this done."

"Well, have a seat over there," he pointed to the same table I had seated myself at twice before. He stomped away and returned shortly with the now oh-so-familiar stack of forms. Again he acted as though everything was my fault, "Get these done right this time, Dillon. I'm not going through this again." He turned away, muttering, "He must think I'm some kind of clown."

I was steaming at his attitude by now, and helpless to do anything about it. Anyone who has ever been a Marine private knows exactly how I felt. All I could do was put my head down and start on those papers. He was wrong about another thing, anyway. I didn't think he was a clown. Clowns have a purpose in life.

So, browbeaten into submission by higher authority once again, I finished the documents. I was pretty sick of the whole thing by the time I finished. I managed to extract some measure of satisfaction by putting on one paper that I was six foot ten, and on another where it said religion I put "Jewish." It was between that and "Druid" but I stuck with Jewish. Actually, I was an Indiana German Lutheran who had "no preference" on his dog tags but I was sure that nobody really looked at all that stuff.

And then back in Philly during final waiting period, the ultimate nightmare: They tagged me for mess duty. Of all the lousy tricks fate could play. They got me. I had slid out of the clutches of Meyers The SS Goon and his damn mess duty assignment at Lejeune, only to be nailed with it in Philly. Somebody must have heard me in the Enlisted Club running my big fat mouth that I had never had to do mess duty time and they told someone else, because during the following morning's formation I was given the happy news. To this day, I don't know which one of the NCO's or officers besides the tubby lieutenant I managed to piss off in such a short period of time, but evidently I had succeeded in doing just that. Irritating authority figures is a talent that I have never had to work to develop, and this time it cost me. It got me stuck fast with mess duty. Try as I might I couldn't get out of it either, and reported for duty the next day at 4 A.M., grumbling sourly about my victimization the whole way. And of course the management of that fine dining facility, meaning a grumpy, disheveled Gunnery Sergeant who hated everybody, immediately recognized a young man with no potential whatsoever.

"Holy shit, what have we here?" he chortled after one look at my disgruntled face as I stepped into his slightly grimy, paper-strewn office. The place smelled like cooking grease.

"PFC Dillon reporting for mess duty, Gunny."

"You look thrilled to be here, Dillon. Well, whether you are or you aren't doesn't matter. You're here. And since you're here, listen up. These are the rules. This is a thirty-day assignment, or until whenever your orders come in, whichever comes first. You get one day off a week, maybe. Reporting time each morning is at 0330. There's a lot of prep work to do each day. You get off when I say. You'll keep your hands clean and your mouth shut and if you work out all right I'll put you on the serving line. That's about the easiest job here. Any questions?"

Damn right I had questions. 0330? I wanted to ask him if he was out of his fucking mind. But I didn't. For some reason I asked, "If I have gonorrhea, am I excused from mess duty?"

He looked alarmed, "You have the clap?"

"No, but if it gets me out of this shit I'll go get it. Tonight."

"Oh, I get it. An attitude problem. Well, PFC Attitude, I have just the place for you. SHORTY!" he bellowed through the open door of his office.

About five seconds later a small Marine appeared in the door. He wore a t-shirt that was wet and slightly grimy already at the ungodly hour of 0415 and was a towering five-foot-four. "Yeah, Gunny?" he asked.

"This is your relief. Take Mr. Attitude and show him all about your little world." He leaned back, produced a cigar from somewhere, lit it, and smiled.

Shorty looked at me, "Come on."

I followed him, hating every breath I drew in the care and feeding of the United States Marine Corps.

As soon as we were out of earshot of the Gunny, I stuck out my hand, "Les Dillon," I said. Might as well be friendly with my fellow peasants. He hadn't done anything to me. Shorty shook my hand with a grip that was surprisingly strong, "Shorty Callahan. Boy am I glad to see you. My orders are in and I'm supposed to leave tomorrow. I have today to get you broken in." Based on my sad experiences so far in the Marine Corps, phrases like that can be alarming.

I asked warily, "Broken in as what?"

We walked through a large door into a tiled room with a huge sink in the middle and several rows of pots ranging in size from large to huge. A big tub of some sort was mounted on a motor in one corner. The sink was full of steaming, soapy water. It smelled like grease, too.

"Welcome to the pot shack," said Shorty.

I looked around in horror. "So this is it," I whispered, "this is hell."

The potshack. For those of you who don't know what that is, I should explain. It's where one unfortunate individual (me, in this case) gets to spend ten or twelve hours a day scrubbing baked-on crud from the endless parade of pots that are used to prepare mass quantities of barely edible foods. And as soon as you get one clean some cook comes along, snatches it, and you get to start all over again as soon as he gets it as dirty as he possibly can. Oh, and you get to peel potatoes, too. That's what that huge tub on a motor thing was. It was a giant potato peeler. My joy knew no bounds.

I further endeared myself to the Gunny by dumping fifty pounds of spuds into the revolving peeler and forgetting all about them because I became engrossed in a conversation with Shorty who, it turned out, was also on his way to Morocco. In fact he was leaving the next day. He was a bit squirrelly but seemed like a good guy and we passed some time wondering about what Morocco was going to be like. Neither of us had a clue.

I asked him what he had done to get posted in the Gunny's pot shack because it was evidently not an assignment for rising superstars. "I break things," he said. I looked at him quizzically. "No, I mean it. I drop things, knock things over. I break things. I don't mean to, but it happens. I broke some stuff—two whole stacks of plates—so he put me in here. A tray of glasses, too." He waved a hand at the rows of gleaming pots, "It's tough to break those. Or the potato peeler."

"The potato peeler! Shit!"

I ran over to it and shut it off, but it was way too late. The fifty pounds of large potatoes had been reduced to about a pound of marble sized remnants in the turning, grinding peeler. The Gunny, of course, went nuts. Nobody besides Meyers had been that mad at me since boot camp, when my drill instructor grabbed me by the throat and began shaking me, hysterically screaming, "YOU'RE A DISOBEDIANT LITTLE SONOFABITCH AREN'T YOU!" That was a defining moment in my life in the Corps.

The Gunny finished his tirade, most of which I don't remember because it was the same old shit, and stalked away.

I looked at Shorty, "High strung type, isn't he?"

"Yeah. He acted like you'd ground up his mother."

"As if he had one. And if he did have one *he* probably ground her up." I could tell my time here was not going to be pleasant.

Then just a week of mess duty misery later, like a gift from Heaven, I was notified that my passport had arrived and that everything else was at last complete. I closely examined everything, every sentence, every word of the orders, looking for that final governmental blunder that would doom me to another endless delay, but it wasn't to be found. I was to be in Morocco in two days. With tears in my eyes I bid a fond farewell to the kitchen Gunny and managed to get out of the door just ahead of him. Evidently a sense of humor isn't required to run a mess hall. That same day I had turned everything in, collected my pay records, passport and orders packet and was on my way to an air base in New Jersey for a MAC flight to Europe, then on to Morocco.

I boarded the 747 feeling on top of the world. I had managed to land a choice duty assignment without even trying, my only qualification for it was the fact that I was breathing, had tweaked Meyers and the Gunny in charge of the grease mill in Philly, and had gotten away smooth. I patted myself heartily on the back for this and I told myself that I would make the very best of it, no matter what. A new beginning in an exotic country where nobody knew me, including the officers there. I told myself that I would take care not to irritate, offend, anger, annoy, confuse, confound, dismay, or piss off any of the upper rank in my new duty station. I would attempt to be a model Marine. Now there was a novel thought and I found it strangely satisfying, if uncharacteristic. Yep, I would leave all the attitude baggage that I carried around with me like a neon rucksack right back in the States where it belonged, and start out on the right foot in my new command. Honesty and Dignity would be my new credo. Upon arrival in Morocco I would be prepared to be a new man. On the heels of that thought it occurred to me that there were some other documents in the packets that I hadn't examined and in the interest of being interested, I decided to study everything.

As the airliner lumbered heavily into the air I began pawing through the packet. There was a small brochure containing information about the culture, language and customs of Morocco that I read with some interest. There was a security warning that I was not to reveal location, strength, mission, etc., of the bases. And then, at the bottom of the packet, was an envelope addressed to me from the Navy Chaplain at Philadelphia Naval Yard. Now, what in the world could this guy want, I wondered. I hadn't ever met him, mainly because I never went to church, and also because I generally like to avoid people who make other people feel guilty for a living. I'm not religious but I'm not an atheist either, I just don't get organized religion and belief in God mixed up and I have little patience for structured anything. Especially religion. Curious, I opened it and began to read, and if I could have jumped out of that plane at 30,000 feet I would have. The letter read:

Dear Private Dillon,

It has been brought to my attention after review of one of the information packets that you submitted that you are of the Jewish Faith. Since you are on your way to a strongly Islamic country I have taken the liberty of notifying the Base Chaplain, Lt. Commander Cooper, at Naval Training Command, Kenitra, Morocco, of your impending arrival. He has assured me that, although Morocco is an Islamic nation, they are extremely tolerant in their religious views and have a large indigenous Jewish population. He has arranged for an English speaking Rabbi to greet you on your first day in country. The Rabbi will introduce you to some of the local Jewish families so that you can worship comfortably and in the company of your own Faith. Cdr. Cooper tells me that the Rabbi is quite excited about your impending arrival, since so few Americans of your Faith get assigned to Islamic nations. I hope this makes you feel at ease and at home. Good luck!

Captain David Walsh
Chaplain USN

3

The Counterfeit Jew and the Caddy for Jesus

I made the crossing to Kenitra, Morocco full of apprehension because I knew that my smart-ass attitude was about to get me in a huge bind. All the way across the Atlantic I held onto the faint hope that they would forget this ghastly idea, or that the whole thing would be lost in some bureaucratic screw up. After all, if they could lose pay records and passport request documents with shocking regularity they could forget to communicate with a Rabbi two thousand miles away, couldn't they?

I stewed in my own misery for the three days it took to get to Morocco. It took that long because I had to wait in Rota, Spain for a hop to Kenitra, Morocco. I don't pray often, not because I'm a total pagan or don't believe in God—I do—just mostly because I recognize the hypocrisy of praying only when I need to beg for help, but I spent both of those days in Spain in one form of repentance another. I'd find myself walking along and mumbling, please, please, oh PLEASE let this whole thing fall through the cracks. I'll be good, I swear I will. I spread the prayers around, too, just to be safe. I either prayed directly to or gave passing consideration to God, Jehovah (which seemed appropriate), Allah, Jesus, Buddha, and Vishnu. I think I included Zeus and Thor the Thunder God, too, just to make sure I covered everything.

Rabbis are a notoriously intelligent bunch, and if in fact there was going to be one there to greet yours truly he would be friendly. Very friendly. He would want to get acquainted. That meant he would be full of questions about my family and me. Questions that, if I could answer them at all, I would have to be very careful with because not only was I not Jewish, I had only the faintest inkling about the Jewish religion and how it operated. I'm from Indiana, for chrissakes.

But, I couldn't tell anybody that the whole thing was a terrible mistake, the result of me just being a smartass. Because of the few things I remembered about the endless stack of papers I had filled out one thing stuck in my head—a warning that a false statement of any kind on those forms was a crime, and punishable by fine and imprisonment, neither of which did I need in my life. I desperately looked for wiggle room and became more and more depressed when I realized that for the first time I had outsmarted myself while trying to outsmart the Corps. There wasn't any wiggle room.

I could reasonably argue that I had accidentally put a six where the five should have been in that height block. But I didn't think they would buy that I mistakenly substituted "Jewish" for "Lutheran" during some momentary mental lapse. And the well meaning meddlers had gone to a great deal of trouble to accommodate me and therefore would probably be extremely resentful if I suddenly said, "Sorry, fellas, I was just fooling around." Possibly even resentful to the point of charges. And that just couldn't happen.

So—now I was a Jew. Well, howdy. I'll probably go straight to hell for that when it's all over, but what could I do?

So, now I had two choices. I could fall on my knees when confronted and confess to the whole stupid thing and hope for the best. Bad idea. Or I could try to bluff it out and hope for the best. It involved a lot of hoping for the best either way, and either way, I was screwed if they found out. So it was decided. I would take my chances and roll the dice. I would bluff it out until the end because I had no faith in the tender mercies of the United States Marine Corps when it came to people like me, who pissed them off at each and every opportunity.

I hadn't set one foot on Moroccan soil and I had already been forced to chuck my new "honesty is the best policy" credo in the interest of self-preservation. Go figure.

So I summed up all of the knowledge of the Jewish religion I had—which consisted of having read the novel "Exodus" by Leon Uris during class and study hall in high school when I should have been doing other things. And that imparts about the same amount of knowledge of Judaism as watching a St.

Patrick's Day parade does about life in Belfast. I decided to ride it out, praying that I wouldn't get caught.

And sure enough, there he was. When I finally reported to the processing station in Kenitra I barely had time to drop my sea bag when a young Lance Corporal with a civilian in tow walked up to me.

"Are you PFC Dillon?" the Lance Corporal asked, an expectant look on his face.

I nearly fainted because I looked at the civilian over his shoulder and knew the jig was up. Life as I knew it was over. Somehow I held myself together, "Yes."

"I'm Greaves. Chaplain's assistant. And this is Rabbi Trosclair." Here it was. The last minute of my life. Greaves stepped back smiling like he had just brought clothing to the shivering naked. The Rabbi stepped forward. I guess I had expected an older priest-ish kind of guy. This man was relatively young, thirtyish, and casually dressed.

He thrust his hand at me, "*Shalom, Torea Rashone* Dillon."

Here we go, I thought. *Rock and roll, baby.*

"*Shalom,* Rabbi," I said, taking his hand firmly and smiling like I'd just sold him a car. That one word was the total sum of my Hebrew—I remembered it from the novel "Exodus"-and I wasn't even really sure what it meant. I hoped it just meant hello. As for the rest of what he said, I hadn't a clue.

"Welcome to Morocco. May we show you around?"

That afternoon was a nightmare. Those two went everywhere with me as I checked in and did all the things the military requires when you check in to a new duty station. I was right, the Rabbi was full of questions about me, my family, and my religion. I played it fairly well. He didn't seem suspicious and before evening I was beginning to feel as though I might, just might be safe. I may have pulled it off.

Actually, instead of feeling good about having gotten over on the Rabbi, I began to feel a bit guilty as the day wore on. He believed me, you see, because it didn't occur to him to question even when I stumbled at such basic questions as whether I was a Conservative or Reformed Jew. I didn't know what that meant and managed to change the subject before he could nail me down and force an answer. Anyway, that day I had a relative degree of success in fooling people I had no right to fool and who didn't deserve it.

To make matters even worse, that little weasel of a chaplain's assistant had been assigned to escort me and the Rabbi around base while I checked in, and even went with us to some of the homes of the Jewish families that I was supposed to meet. I had no idea what to expect from those people because I was totally ignorant of their religion and they may as well have been Polynesian idol worshippers for all I knew of them. To my pleasant surprise they turned out to be some of the best people I have ever met. They lived in modern, clean homes, spoke French as a main language but did well with English, and welcomed me as though I were a long lost son. I was neck deep in the charade by now and couldn't have extricated myself if I had wanted to, so I played it by ear and hoped I wouldn't make too many mistakes.

I imitated whatever I saw. I know I blundered a couple of times, occasionally raising the curious eyebrow, but I managed to get by. I maintained an ongoing friendship with those people for the entire time I was in Morocco, too, a year and a half. Knowing those good people is one of the best memories of my life. The fact that the Robair family had two beautiful teenage daughters who spoke good English, Beti and Dani, helped to keep my focus. They and their families liked me and treated me well, and if I had been exposed as a fraud they would have been disappointed and hurt. That added sincere motivation for the upkeep of the ruse. I still feel guilty about deceiving them but I console myself with the knowledge that it was never meant maliciously. It was just survival. I could write a whole other book about my experiences as fake Jew so I'll get back to the main subject and leave that for another time.

The chaplain's assistant, a Lance Corporal named Greaves, was a problem. He hovered around me like a fly, taking to me the way losers and weirdos often do. As with Meyers there was something about him, some indefinable quality that I just couldn't put my finger on. I disliked and distrusted him right away but I didn't dare show it. I didn't need him to start resenting me. If he got mad he might get inquisitive, and I didn't want that.

He professed to be a student of religion and said he wanted to learn as much from me as he could since he didn't know a lot about Judaism. Great, I thought, just fucking great. The Rabbi had went away after handshakes, hugs, and slaps on my back, and had gone back to whatever it is Rabbis do, but Greaves stuck to me like gum to a shoe. I managed to steer the conversation away from Judaism whenever he brought it up. Sooner or later, though, he was going to ask a question that I should be able to answer and couldn't. I would be exposed as, of all things, a counterfeit Jew. He was lively, curious little creep with a strong streak of the old-school Baptist phony and I had no doubt that if he felt betrayed by me that same old school vindictiveness would surface. I was sure he would be on the batphone to the chaplain the second he smelled a rat. He talked incessantly about anything and everything religious and in a very short time I found myself having fantasies of strangling him. It was because he was so talkative, however, that I found myself a way to weasel out of my immediate situation.

The second day I was there we were walking back to my quarters and he was briefing me on the local situation as far as duty assignments were concerned. I still hadn't been posted to any particular duty, and Greaves had just told me that he was going to try to get me assigned to his office with him.

With a bubbly eagerness that made me want to hit him with a fireplace poker he described the duties of a chaplain's assistant.

"You get to maintain the Chaplain's schedule, coordinate services on different bases. Oh, and you keep his office clean. Oh, yeah! On Sundays you help with services, carry stuff for him. It's a really cool job."

"Carry stuff for him," I repeated, appalled. How could anyone think this was a cool job?

"Yeah!" he said

I feigned eagerness, "Like a caddy for Jesus!" I exclaimed.

"That's it! That's it!" I noted that in his religious fervor he forgot that I was a Jew. An ersatz one, but he didn't know that. "The Chaplain also likes me to help with ideas for his sermons. '*Being a Caddy For Jesus*'. He'll love it! Hey....I know. I'm gonna ask the Chaplain if he can swing an assignment for you......with us!"

He completely mistook the look of horror on my face for some kind of joy. I tried to speak, but he said, "No, no, don't thank me." He backed away from me, looking at his watch. "Maybe I can catch the Chaplain before he leaves the office!" With that he bolted, carried away on the wings of an idiot's enthusiasm.

This was great. Just great. I was ready to run screaming into the desert, fall down and flop around like a fish at the mere thought that this could come to pass. I would rather have pounded a nail into my forehead with the heel of my shoe than be stuck in a job where my every move would be watched and evaluated and the thought of being a glorified handmaiden to a chaplain was almost nauseating. I watched him running off and if I'd had a gun I think I would have shot the little bastard in the back.

It seemed that God would get me. It was destined. He was determined to make me pay for being a fake Jew. And for lying. And for having a dysfunctional attitude gene. And for praying to Thor the Thunder God. And for, well, just every goddamn thing else. It wasn't fair. I was going to be a Caddy For Jesus. Christ, that sucked!

Wait, now, I told myself. Easy boy. *Think*. There had to be a graceful way out of this religious quicksand in which I found myself sinking.

And then, like a smack of Thor's hammer it hit me.

Earlier in the day Greaves had been telling me about the various assignments for Marines here in Morocco.

He told me that there were actually three bases in Morocco. One was the main base, the Naval Training Command in Kenitra, where we were presently and where, if my luck didn't change, I was destined to join God's Country Club as one of the help. The second largest was about forty kilometers north. It was a communications jump station called Sidi Yahia and had about a hundred Marines, the First guard Company, assigned to the barracks there. He and the Chaplain went there frequently and held services.

The third was the smallest, Bouknadel. When he said the name, he got a dark look on his face, like he had just seen Satan in the church sanctuary. Bouknadel was located about 40 kilometers south of Kenitra. There were about sixty Marines assigned there, the Second Guard Company, but he shook his head, "You don't want to go there. Those guys are strange. They have no respect for authority and they're blasphemous. *Blasphemous*. They don't even have a chapel to worship in, and I don't even think they want one. The Chaplain went there for services and only three guys showed up. And one of them was drunk and kept yelling, "Take it off, baby," until some other guys came and got him. I was there once and it was kind of creepy. Those guys.... I couldn't wait to get out and I try not to go back if I don't have to. And those Dog Men..." He let it go there, like he had just accidentally mentioned the crazy aunt who lives in the basement. I had other things on my mind at the time and didn't pursue the issue.

Well, hello and hallelejuah brother, I thought as I remembered the conversation. Blasphemous, eh? And not just blasphemous. *Blasphemous.* Sounded like my kind of place. I belatedly grasped that Bouknadel, wherever that place was, was my ticket away from Holy Roller Greaves, the chaplain, and the kind but annoying Rabbi who would sooner or later expose me if I rolled the dice once too often.

I didn't know what Dog Men were, and it didn't make the slightest difference. They could have been the Werewolf of London for all I cared. Whatever they were, they could be any worse than being a Caddy For Jesus. Bouknadel sounded like heaven, and not the kind the little ferret Greaves liked.

I jumped to my feet and started toward personnel when I remembered what else he had said about just who was unfortunate enough to get posted to Bouknadel.

He said, "Sometimes it's just bad luck and new guys get stuck there. Sometimes the Colonel sends people out there who are problem children or troublemakers because it's isolated. It's kind of like our Siberia. Or you could go to personnel and volunteer, if you're crazy enough. They're always looking for volunteers."

"Not me, brother," I said, shaking my head, agreeing with him that it would be an awful fate, to be stuck out in the wilderness with the Godless.

I made a dash for personnel and asked to be assigned to Bouknadel. The female Navy person behind the counter gave me curious look but handed me an assignment request form, which I filled out. Correctly, this time.

The next morning I was on the gray Navy bus, headed south to Bouknadel. As the bus pulled away Greaves waved sadly to me, a victim of an unfeeling Corps who had somehow been unlucky enough to draw Bouknadel as a duty assignment. I waved back until I was around the first corner, changed the wave to the bird, and settled down to enjoy the ride.

"Praise the Lord," I sighed. There is absolutely no doubt that there will be a very special hell for me at the end.

There were a few sailors and Marines on the bus on the way to liberty in Kenitra, some of whom looked at me curiously but nobody offered conversation, then they all got off in town leaving me the only one to continue south to Bouknadel. There had been no uniforms among the passengers, including myself, because there was no status of forces agreement with this country and our presence was very unofficial, so no uniforms were authorized when we were off base. Jeans and t-shirts were the order of the day whenever any of our people were off base and that, of course, suited me just fine.

As we passed through Kenitra I was amazed at the mixture of the modern and the medieval that, as I have since learned, is a standard in some Islamic countries. In the days before radical Islam reared its ugly head the black and white differences in the cultures were striking. One second you see a donkey loaded with branches to be used as firewood being led by a veiled woman in the long concealing kaftan, and a few yards away you see a beautiful woman in jeans working in an outdoor stall that sells radios. In Morocco you could see the faithful on their prayer rugs as the *muezzin* sings his call to prayer, while down the street a modern nightclub cleans up in the afternoon prior to the night's opening. Morocco, as I was to discover, is a relatively open and modern country.

Anyway, the bus finally turned off of the main highway onto a long dusty side road. In the distance to my left I could see two tall steel towers, thrusting like red needles into the clear blue sky. I would later learn that these two towers, called helix towers, were both eight hundred feet high and were part of the reason for our presence here.

Finally the bus approached a fenced compound, slowed and stopped at the main gate guard booth. A corporal in dress blues with a white duty belt and holstered .45 got on the bus and eyed me strangely, asking for my orders and ID. I provided them and he wrote my name down on a clipboard, then got off and waved the bus on. As the bus pulled onto the base I looked back and saw him talking excitedly into the phone in the guard booth.

At last the bus came to a stop. The door hissed open and I stepped off, seabag and orders in hand. Behind me was what appeared to be a small Navy Exchange, sort of a general store on Marine and Navy bases, and some sort of snack bar, a "Gedunk" in the Navy and Marine vernacular. Beyond that I could see the rows of neat base housing that were occupied by the officers and senior enlisted personnel who had their families in country with them.

This, I would learn, was the illustrious Brownbagger's Row, a place of pseudo domesticity combined with all the carnal antics that accompany military families wherever they go. Across the street from where the bus stopped was what was clearly a new, modern barracks, unlike anything at Lejuene. It was clean and new and nothing like I had expected, and as I looked at it I saw curtains suddenly drop closed in two different windows on the second floor. I got the distinct feeling I was being watched. A second later a ground floor glass door swung open and a Marine in the green utility uniform sauntered toward me. He had on dark glasses with his hat pulled low across his face, and his hands were thrust deep in his pockets, another of the many practices the Marine Corps frowns upon. I thought he was coming to greet me or assist me but he just sort of drifted right past me, headed for the gedunk. I cleared my throat, expecting him to stop or at least display some sort of curiosity toward the new guy.

He didn't, and I had to say, "Excuse me. Can you tell me where the company office is or where I can check in?" He never even looked back, just jerked his thumb over his right shoulder in the general direction of a sidewalk that ran alongside the barracks, made an abrupt turn and disappeared behind it. I watched him for a second more. Just as he opened the door the little snack bar he sneaked a glance at me, then vanished inside. I hoisted my seabag to my shoulder, wondering about the strange guy, and followed the sidewalk.

The company office was located behind the barracks. It was an old Quonset hut that set among several palms. I knocked on the door and was admitted by a tall Sergeant. He actually introduced himself, much to my relief, as Sgt. Piazza. Taking my orders he told me to stand by and he would let the major know I was there. He went into an office located in the back half of the hut and closed the door behind him. I could hear the low murmur of voices behind the door then it swung open and Sgt. Piazza stepped out and said, " Major Moran will see you now, PFC." I stepped into the office, centered myself on the desk and with my eyes straight forward said, "Sir, PFC Dillon reporting as ordered, Sir."

The Major seated behind the desk said, "Stand at ease, Dillon." I assumed the proper at ease position, then looked at the major for the first time. I was a little startled by what I saw. He was tall and a bit thin to start with, but Major Moran looked like a man about to have a total nervous collapse. His eyes were sunk in his face and there were dark circles beneath both, as if he hadn't slept for days. The right side of his face had a funny little twitch to it and as he began to speak it seemed to get worse, until he actually put his hand on it to stop it. "Welcome to Bouknadel, PFC, er, what was you name?"

"Dillon, sir, PFC Lester Dillon." I was trying to get over the fact that he looked a little like a nervous, twitchy raccoon.

"Yes, well, welcome to Bouk. I hope you enjoy your time here. We have a serious mission here, and that's to guard the antennas that you see here in the the antenna field," he waved his hand at the blank back wall, then went on, "See Sgt. Piazza when you leave and he'll get you set up with a room and your issue." He took his right hand from the tic in his face long enough to offer it to me. I shook his hand and it was limp, clammy and warm. As I left his office and closed the door, I wiped my hand off on my trousers, and looked up to find Sgt. Piazza staring at me. I couldn't stand it.

I said, "Sarge, meaning no disrespect but, is there something wrong with the Major?"

He sighed and said simply, "Yep," then told me to follow him to the barracks. I stifled the impulse to ask Piazza more about the weird Major and once again shouldered my seabag and obediently followed him, glancing one over my shoulder at the now closed door to the Major's office.

As we walked toward the barracks I saw two more of what I assumed were Marines in civilian clothes, standing outside the barracks. Both wore dark sunglasses. As we approached them, the taller of the two, who was blond, turned to the shorter and said, "Hey, *Seesco*, we gotta gringo among us. Do we keel heem?"

The shorter of the two, a very muscular black guy, replied in the same Frito Bandito accent, "No, Pancho. How many times I got to tell you we are the *good* guys now. We don't need no *steenking* badges, but we don't keel heem." Then they both crossed their arms in unison and watched me approach. As I walked by they did an abrupt about face and stood with their backs to me as we passed. It was downright rude but I was too astonished to say anything. Sgt. Piazza didn't seem to notice them at all. I followed Piazza warily past the strange duo, glancing back at them a couple of times for the sake of self preservation. Piazza led me up a flight of stairs to the second floor.

We entered an air-conditioned foyer. It was carpeted and clean, with cheap motel type furniture lined against the walls. Having been used to the open squad bay type environment at Lejuene, I was impressed. As we walked through it we came to a large community bathroom, which was lined with neat blue tile. It was equipped with individual shower stalls and private toilets, mirrored sinks on the wall, and a large burro wearing a neat little sailor hat standing in the middle of it. I walked on past the door to the head at first because it really didn't register that I had just seen a donkey standing in the bathroom of a Marine Corps barracks. Sometimes the brain just refuses to accept certain types of input. I stopped, stepped backwards three steps, and stared. Sure enough, it was a donkey. And it was, in fact, wearing a white sailor hat. We called them "Dixie cups." Sgt. Piazza once again appeared not to notice and the donkey seemed quite content and ignored my stare. I said, "Er, Sarge. There's a donkey in the head."

He stopped with his hand on the door of one of the rooms and sighed, "Yeah. Flagg must have been drunk again last night. Whenever he gets really drunk he gets Fuzzy—that's Fuzzy, by the way—from special services and brings him upstairs to spend the night. Makes Flagg feel more at home," he turned and started to knock on the door of the room, then hesitated, turning back to me, "Flagg's from Texas," he said, as if that explained everything.

I was just assimilating the donkey and hat thing when suddenly a very tall guy with a shaved head came around the corner from the other side of the hall and walked up to me, stopping just a foot away. He looked at me for about five seconds then said, in a deep baritone, "How's it goin', new guy,," then thrust his face so closely to mine that our noses lightly touched, then continued with, "pretty good?" He then straightened suddenly, spun on his heel and waddled out of sight around a corner with a weird, Chaplinesque waddle. If Charlie Chaplin and a penguin had had a love child, it would have walked that way. I started to say something to Piazza about the odd lunatic but stopped before I said anything and stood with one finger up in the air because, again, Piazza seemed to fail to notice and did not comment.

Piazza knocked on the door and shouted, "Brunner! Hey! New guy alert! Get your ass out here and find him a bunk. And leave J.R. in there."

By now I was just about on sensory overload. J.R.? I didn't want to know who—or what—J.R. was just yet. I really needed a short break from the rather oddly unfolding situation. Piazza then turned to another room and pounded on the door. "Flagg! Get up and take Fuzzy home, you pervert." The door opened and a crew cut, stocky Marine wearing a t-shirt, boxer shorts, and cowboy boots emerged, scratching his crotch and yawning. He put a tattered cowboy hat on his head and walked past me, saying, "Howdy," took Fuzzy by the halter and led him outside the barracks and started down the steps. Fuzzy didn't seem to mind.

Piazza shouted, "Flagg, get some pants on, for Chrissakes!" and Flagg led Fuzzy laboriously back up the stairs, handed me his halter, and dashed to his room. He emerged a moment later in jeans and claimed his burro, thanking me like I had been a parking attendant. They left again. Piazza sighed another one of his sighs and said, "I hope the Major doesn't see that this time. He nearly stroked out the last time and wouldn't come out of his office for three days. Now, let's find you a room."

A flash of Quasimodo hanging from the church bell shouting, "Sanctuary!" flashed through my head. Yes, a nice safe room would be good right now.

I could hear a variety of music from several of the rooms on the side of the hall where I now stood. Country music, I think it was Conway Twitty, came from the room where the rumpled cowboy Flagg had just emerged. From the one next to it to the right came Black Sabbath, and from further down the hall came the unmistakable sound of Al Green.

I mentioned the mishmashed variety of music to Piazza, and he said, "Well, there's no TV here, unless you can speak Arabic, and the only radio is the Armed Forces Propaganda Network. Everybody has their own taste so everybody plays their own shit. So, if you want to be entertained I suggest you do like these guys and buy yourself a stereo and some tunes from the PX. They actually have a good variety of music."

He turned and knocked again on the door and shouted, "Come on, Brunner. The smoking lamp is out. Open this door, goddammit."

I thought, while waiting for that door to open, that no matter how bad or weird whatever was awaiting could be it could not possibly compare to the hell of being a Caddy For Jesus.

4

Something's Just Not Right

Reality, as a wise man once said, is an interesting concept. When you're submersed in the surreal, realty begins to flicker in and out of focus like an old black and white television, and soon the surreal becomes the real. I was standing in the hallway watching a cowboy lead a donkey from a U.S. Marine Corps barracks and had decided that it just doesn't get much more surreal than that, when the door to the first room that Sgt. Piazza had been knocking on swung open. A short, slim guy wearing yellow lensed wire framed glasses thrust his head out. He briefly eyed me with suspicion, the said to Piazza, "Hey, Pizza Man. What you got here?"

Piazza said, "New guy. Name's Dillon. Find him a bunk. In the barracks this time, if you please." I didn't know what that last part meant but it got my attention, my anti-being-fucked-with radar suddenly switched on. Piazza turned to leave and asked me if I had any questions. Boy, did I, but one question had been lingering in my head for the past few minutes.

"What's wrong with the Major?"

Piazza sighed and, ignoring a short snicker from Brunner, said, "Major Moran retires in just a couple of years, so he doesn't leave his office anymore except to go home at close of business, and he never comes over here. He figures that what he doesn't know won't ruin him. He just hangs around hoping that his career won't crumble until he gets back to the world. There are no other officers assigned here, although there's supposed to be an exec. The guy who was on his way broke his leg or some shit so for now there's just NCO's, a company Gunny and me. And I leave in ten days," he sighed again and I took note that he seemed to have been doing that an awful lot. Then, without another word, he just sort of drifted away, leaving me standing there with Brunner staring at me as if I were a slide specimen.

I stuck my hand out and said, "Les Dillon," and he shook it briefly.

"Timmy Brunner," he said, "come on in."

I grabbed my seabag and went into the room. It was large, with three bunks, two in a bunkbed setup and another that sat apart individually, and on it sat the odd individual who had drifted by when I had first gotten off of the bus. He still had the hat on, and the dark sunglasses. In the corner a stereo with green speakers played an Alice Cooper album. The tune was a song about insanity that seemed perfect for the moment, *The Ballad of Dwight Fry*, and the screaming refrain "*I gotta get out of here I gotta get outofhereIgottagetouttahereIgottagetottahere*" was filling the room. As I put my seabag down the sunglasses guy stood up and thrust his hands into his pockets. Again I stuck my hand out as he walked toward me, thinking he was going to introduce himself, shake my hand. Or some such civilized nice thing. He only paused briefly, glanced down at my hand like I'd just picked my nose with it, then slouched past and out the door.

Brunner watched him leave and closed the door behind him. "That's Henley," he said and for the first time I noticed a soft, almost aristocratic Southern accent, "He'll get used to you." Like I was a new pet or something. "He's a Dog Man," he added, again as if that was in itself an explanation for Henley's bizarre behavior, like being from Texas explained Flagg and Fuzzy. I didn't know what Brunner meant by Henley being a dog man and I didn't even ask. I just sighed, like Piazza, in acceptance and was being thankful that Brunner, at least, seemed relatively normal. At that very moment I caught a slight shuffle of movement near my foot and jumped back with a cry of, "Jesus, is that a *rat?*" I hate rats. Brunner stepped between me and the critter I was getting ready to stomp, then stooped and picked up the damndest looking thing I had ever seen. It was about six inches long, and looked like a mutant pygmy porcupine. "This," he said, "is J.R. Pizza Man doesn't like J.R., does he J.R.?" It made a peculiar snuffling noise that sounded something like Cousin It on the Addams Family as he cuddled it, and he then made the same exact noise back to it. So much for my premature supposition that Brunner was normal, I pondered. I was again dumfounded but decided to salvage as much of my dignity from this encounter as I could.

I started to speak but Brunner gave me a wounded look and said, "No, J.R. is not a rat. J.R. is a hedgehog. In fact, sir, J.R. is a prince among hedgehogs and I'll thank you to apologize to him for that insult. Now, if you please."

I was just completely at a loss. Apologizing to vermin is not high on my list of priorities and under normal circumstances I would have told Brunner exactly where he could deposit said creature. I was about to explain this to Brunner in my own tactful style when I caught myself. These were anything but normal circumstances. I hadn't figured out the lay of the land so to speak, and didn't know what offense might isolate me for the rest of my tour here. And eighteen months is a very long time to spend in a hostile environment. So I figured, what the hell, when in Rome....So I said, "I'm sorry I called J.R. a...." then stopped abruptly as Brunner shook his head violently enough so that the yellow lensed glasses became unseated and slid to one side, forcing him to adjust them with the push of a finger.

"No, no. Not to me. You must apologize directly to J.R., for you have wounded him greatly. A rat, indeed."

His Deep South accent seemed oddly appropriate for this encounter. I can adapt to anything but discipline. I looked the repulsive little varmint in his beady little eyes and said, "Sir Hedgehog, I apologize to you if I have spoken out of turn. I spoke from ignorance and no offense was meant," and do you know, that little critter actually made that squeaky Cousin It noise as I finished speaking. Brunner seemed pleased, and placed J.R. inside his shirt where it continued to squeak and move around as I asked Brunner about my bunk, the presumed safety of which I was becoming more and more eager to acquire. I asked Brunner, who seemed to have become more disconnected, a second time about my bunk when suddenly the door to the room opened and a half dozen guys came in, led by the sunglasses guy.

Oh, boy, I thought. *Now what?* It didn't take long to find out.

They surrounded me quickly, pressing close and all stopping within inches of my body. I thought I was about to get my ass kicked and I was wondering why. I really hadn't had time to offend anyone just yet. I glanced quickly around, looking for a way out. There was none. None of them spoke, just pressed closely around me. I braced myself and prepared to make as good a fight of it as I could then I felt something press against the back of my knees and suddenly I was sitting down in a chair with two of these guys on each side like guards. The others drew another chair up between the two bunks and, to my surprise, the tall guy with the shaved head sat down in it facing me. There was a moment of silence, then the sunglasses guy, Henley, spoke to me for the first time, "What's your name, new guy?"

"Dillon," I said, "Lester Dillon."

The black guy who had been doing the Cisco Kid imitation earlier said, "Did he say, 'Lester'?"

A big blond guy who looked like the All-American jock type said, "He did, indeed, say Lester." He had been half of the Pancho/Cisco act that welcomed me earlier.

"Yep," said another, a great hulking oaf of a guy with a potato face and very bloodshot eyes.

A really weirded out looking guy who stood to the right of the impromptu throne wore very dark sunglasses, a long dark trench coat and, I suspected, nothing else except the flip-flop shower shoes on his bare feet. He chewed vigorously on a toothpick, moving it quickly from side to side in his mouth, "Just what was your mother thinking, Lester?"

"I think," said Henley, "that she went into shock at the sight of little Lester and panicked."

"I think she was on drugs," said the muscular black guy who had been the other half of the Pancho/Cisco act.

I'm not really a familial kind of guy, but even *I* thought that insulting someone's mother on such short acquaintance was a bit rude, "Hey!" I said, starting to feel a slow burn.

Another black guy who had been standing quietly in the background spoke up for the first time. He had an Afro that stuck out about six full inches and a Fu Manchu mustache. In case you're wondering about the hair length, this being the U.S. Marine Corps and all and being sticklers about hair length, I should explain one small thing.

The Brothers, that is to say the black Marines, had a distinct advantage there over those of us of the Persuasion, as they called us. The Caucasian Persuasion, that is. They had developed a system to mat their hair down when they were on duty by wearing tight fitting stocking caps when they slept. This had the effect of smoothly mashing down the hair so that it would pass a casual glance from an officer or NCO. Then, come off duty time, they could take their hair picks and fluff out some fine Afros, which were the style in those days. It worked well for them, and I'm not criticizing. If we could have found a way to keep our hair long and get away with it, we would have done so in a split second. If anything—we of the Persuasion were a tad jealous.

Anyway, the Brother with the major 'fro spoke in a low, mellow tone, "Excuse me, my brothers. I have a question for this unfortunate young white man. Did you have anything to say about your name?" I didn't have anything to say in defense of my name because I had never liked the damn thing either. Being named Lester had caused me endless grief as a kid. When I didn't reply he went on, "No? Obviously, then, another should be chosen for you. Perhaps, brothers, we should offer our assistance and….rectify this mistake."

With that they all gathered around the shaven head guy in the chair in a huddle that was reminiscent of a Marx Brothers bit. There was a whispered, animated conversation broken up by the occasional burst of laughter or a pause for a thoughtful look at me. I sat there in a state of bemusement, the likes of which I had seldom found myself. I could have gotten up and walked away, or at least I thought so because I was reasonably sure at this point they meant me no harm, but this was becoming too entertaining to abandon just yet. My momentary flash of anger had subsided and I watched them with a wary, interested eye.

There was a sudden nodding of heads all around the huddle as they apparently reached some sort of agreement. The huddle dissolved as they all returned to their former places.

The one with the shaved head suddenly tapped a staff he had been holding. I hadn't noticed it at first, but it appeared to be about four feet long and as thick as a baseball bat handle, with a knob about half the size of a baseball on the upper end. I would later learn that the local countryside Moroccans used these as herding staffs and weapons, and that they were made of what is called ironwood back in the world, which is some nearly unbreakable, incredibly dense wood that can smash your brains out when used properly. Everybody shut up when the staff tapped.

"New guy," the shaved head guy said in that rumbling bass voice, "We have decided that, from now on, your name is Marshal. Get it? Marshal Dillon!"

I got it, all right, and I didn't like it too much, "Yeah. Gee, that's the very first time anyone's ever called me that," I said sarcastically. "I've heard that since the first grade. If I've got to be named, don't I have a say?"

This was apparently quite a joke, because they commenced to do some serious knee slapping, then suddenly stopped and looked at me straight faced.

"No"

"Nope"

"Nuh-uh."

"No way, Jose."

"Never happen."

"Finish it, Crow."

Crow, the guy with the staff, tapped the staff again and the room quieted. "We hereby christen you Marshal Dillon, and on behalf of all of us I just want to say, "Howdy, Marshal!" Which brought forth a chorus of howdys and shucks and several bad Chester and Festus imitations, along with a couple of quick draw showdowns, a la *Gunsmoke*. It was quickly apparent that my seal of approval was not necessary nor requested for my new nickname. It was done.

There comes a time when you know you can't win so I just shut up and grinned lamely, hoping the whole nickname thing would go away—and soon. It didn't, by the way, and for a year after I left Morocco I would find that during a casual introduction, I would introduce myself as Marshal Dillon, which would leave me grinning stupidly and the other person looking at me like I had an undiagnosed mental disorder after I had corrected my unconscious blunder.

The focus of the conversation then shifted to where I would find a bed. It seemed that nobody liked to stay with a new guy (the reason for this would soon become apparent) so, after an ensuing discussion it was suggested by Henley that I would stay with somebody they referred to as El Pachuco. This again inspired much debate, some saying that they would not inflict this fate on anyone, even a new guy, but others argued that all new guys must pay their dues, even one with such a cool new name as Marshal. This argument finally won out and it was decided unanimously that my new quarters would be with the questionable El Pachuco, whoever—or whatever—that was. For the first time ever I was assigned quarters by committee. My vote, again, was not solicited.

It was only after that little aspect of my life had been decided by people I hadn't even known a mere half hour before that they decided to introduce themselves. Again, it was done in a strangely ritualistic manner. They lined up in front of me, Crow first. He stuck his hand out, "Crow. Howdy, Marshal."

The next up was the powerfully built fireplug of a black guy, "Rock. Howdy, Marshal." I didn't know why the first guy had been called "Crow" but it was clear where Rock got his nickname from.

He moved aside. The really weirded out guy with the trench coat and toothpick thrust out a hand that I wasn't really sure I wanted to shake but I took it anyway, "Termite. Howdy, Marshal."

The All-American looking guy followed, "Cow. Howdy Marshal."

The huge oafish looking guy was next, "Animal. Howdy, Marshal." Besides Rock, I really hadn't been able to make sense of the other's names, but his absolutely fit the marquis.

The last was the soft-spoken brother who had decided to rename me. He had been standing slightly off to one side, quietly watching the odd ritual. He stuck out a thin hand, "The Deacon. But you may call me Freaky Deac." I shook his hand. In mid shake he changed the hand shake into the dap, a ritualized hand shake that involved much twisting and turning of the hands. I was surprised when he started it with me because in those days it was usually reserved for brothers only. Naturally I screwed it up. He stepped back and shook his head, then raised his hands as though in exasperation, "White people," he muttered, then looked over at Crow, "Are we done?"

"We are. Bye, Marshal."

"Bye?"

"Yep. Bye."

"Tootles."

"Au revoir."

"See ya."

"Don't let the door hit ya where the dog done bit ya."

I was abruptly and rudely dismissed.

So, with the impromptu court suddenly over, it was in this spirit of total uncooperation that I was hustled out the door in the company of Brunner. The door was slammed behind me, then opened just long enough for one of those thoughtful fellows to hurl my seabag and orders carrier into the hallway. I caught a brief glimpse of Crow pulling what appeared to be a long stemmed pipe from under the *jelaba* he wore, then the door was once more slammed in my face. Brunner, squirming t-shirt and all, told me to follow him.

As I picked up my seabag and began to follow Brunner, who was once again cuddling and talking to the snuffling J.R., I realized that I was sighing again. Suddenly a dark haired guy about a third again my size came around the corner. He stopped in front of me, blocking my path. He eyed me up and down, a disdainful look on his face. I hadn't seen him before and I thought at first it was just another one of the many weirdos in this place just having a go at freaking me out. But then I saw his eyes.

There was a genuine hostility in his eyes, a blank anger I had seen before. It was the anger of a bully, uncalled for and illogical, but dangerous in the way bullies are dangerous to those they think they can devour. I stepped back, casually maneuvering my seabag between him and me, "Howdy," I said.

He turned his head just slightly enough so that when he spat it landed a tiny bit to the side of my left foot. I fought the instinctive urge to jerk my foot back and held still, warily watching this sudden and unpleasant encounter develop. I decided that a direct approach to the impending confrontation was the best because that had usually worked with this type in high school and in the brief time since. Being slight of stature (scrawny actually) I had been through enough encounters with bullies to know that diplomacy doesn't work. There are generally two ways to deal them: Submission, which was not in my nature. Or pasting them right square in the nose with all you have. They may then proceed to stomp your ass thoroughly, but they generally think twice before approaching you again. I had learned to consider the ass kicking that sometimes followed my pre-emptive strike as an investment in future peace. Nobody is eager to get hit in the nose, even if they can kick your ass afterwards.

It was the second of the two methods I had decided on in this case. He wasn't that much larger than myself, at least not when compared to some others I had dealt with. I figured I could at least dissuade him from bothering me in the future.

I braced myself to slam him with the seabag I had positioned between us and follow through with what I hoped would be the end of the issue. Just as I thought, *let the games begin*, Brunner spoke up.

"Back off, Alfie," he said.

"Fuck you, burnout. Who's the faggot?" he asked without taking his eyes from mine.

"New guy. Marshal Dillon. Marshal, this is Alfie Morales."

I didn't even begin to extend my hand. Alfie stood and stared, his face slack and neutral but his eyes still hostile. He made a little *hmph* noise, turned, and walked away.

I watched him go, relieved at the end of the sudden unexpected encounter with hostility. "That was fun," I said to Brunner as my pulse began to slow, "What's his problem?"

"That's just Alfie," Brunner said, "He hates everybody," as though that explained everything. As the hostile Alfie turned the corner in the hall Brunner turned and opened a door. "Come on, this is your room."

I turned briefly to make sure the aggressive Alfie wasn't sneaking up on me. It had been a full and interesting day, and I had the feeling it would get more interesting as time went on, but I had no intention of being blindsided by a hostile lunatic.

The encounter left me feeling of unease hanging over me. I had a suspicion it was the beginning of a not so beautiful relationship. I was right.

5

Settling In

    Brunner cuddled his rat as he knocked on the door to my sanctuary (I didn't care *what* Brunner said, it still looked like a rodent) There was no answer, so he pushed it open and we entered. The room was neat as a pin. There was the same three bunk set-up as in Brunner's room, two of which had neatly made covers, the third—a top bunk, naturally—was empty and he motioned for me to throw my stuff there, so I did. Brunner shook my hand again and wished me luck with El Pachuco, then abruptly turned and left as I started to inquire as to what El Pachuco might consist of. I hoped he would be more hospitable than the slightly scary and possibly deranged Alfie had been.

    I was beginning to feel just a bit of frustration with this whole deal. Plus, I was getting just a bit tired of having buckets of insanity poured over me and then being dismissed without a thought. First Piazza had just turned and wandered away. Then that parody of a court had sized me up, changed my name, and kicked me out before I could say "Sigmund Freud." And now Brunner had apparently decided he was done with me as well and had just turned and slipped away, still cuddling his vermin.

    What kind of asylum had I gotten myself into? Was this weirdness act being staged for my benefit? If so, they were good. Then I remembered what Piazza had said about the twitchy, clammy major, and how he wouldn't leave his office and how he never came to the barracks, and another thought wandered through me.

    Maybe this was no act.

Based on what I had seen so far there was a better than even chance that these people were really the way they presented themselves. Besides, the whole thing was pretty elaborate for a screw-with-the-new-guy show. Well, I would just have to wait and see, wouldn't I? Right now my immediate problem was to get my gear stored and to await the arrival of the much anticipated El Pachuco and whoever else occupied the second bunk in this room. I noted that whoever it was the ad hoc welcoming committee had failed to mention him.

I didn't have long to wait for the entrance of El Pachuco. Within just a few minutes the door opened and in walked a short, handsome Hispanic guy, about 22 or 23 years old. He wore tight black pants and a red and green shirt. His thick black hair was swept backwards and he wore very pointy black Mexican boots with silver caps on the toes. Before I could say anything, he said, "You must be Marshal Dillon."

Well, that just sucked. I didn't even have the chance to try to overcome the Marshal nonsense by using my real name. People I had never met knew the stupid Marshal thing already. I nodded and he puffed out his chest and continued in a strong Mexican accent, "I'm Carlos Santiago. They call me El Pachuco. That's my bunk," he said, pointing, "that's my locker and that's my stereo. Don't touch my shit, man." He walked over to his locker without another word and opened it. I started to speak, "Look, I'm…." He cut me off in mid sentence.

"You speak Spanish, Marshal?"

"No," I said. "I always wanted to learn, but…"

"Then don't talk to me at all until you *do* learn," he swung his locker open and on the inside of the door was a huge hand printed sign that said "VIVA LA RAZA," with a drawing of a clenched fist on a green and red background.

Oh, great. As if the Brothers at Lejuene hadn't been bad enough about this stuff, I have to get stuck in a room with a Mexican radical who wouldn't even speak to you unless it was in his language.

My patience with being dismissed like an eight year old was wearing thin, so I took up the challenge.

"What's that all about?" I asked, pointing at the poster.

He looked a me with mild hostility, "That's about power to my race, the Spanish speaking people," he replied, then turned and pretended to busy himself I his locker. He spoke again, his voice muffled, "Maybe some day we'll get back what you have stolen from us."

"Stolen? Who stole what from you?"

"You did."

"I did? What did I steal?"

"You stole our land, man, after that so-called 'War of Independence'."

"What the hell are you talking about?"

"The Mexican American War, *puta*. You took Texas, New Mexico, Arizona, and California from us. You weren't fighting for independence. You fought to steal from us."

I didn't know what *puta* meant, but I was willing to bet good money it wasn't 'my friend'. Okay, enough was enough, "Get this, El Puke-o…"

"Pachuco, *puta*."

"Whatever. I didn't steal *shit* from you or from anybody else. And those that did are long dead. If your countrymen couldn't hold on to what was theirs at the time, well, guess what? That's not my problem because I didn't have anything to do with it."

We were both standing now, facing each other from across the room. "No," he said, "but your thieving government did."

"Yeah, well, maybe so. But that's they way it was in those days. Whoever had the biggest army was right. And if Santa Anna had had a bigger or better army your border would be somewhere along the Ohio River right now and *we* wouldn't be hearing any apologies from *you*."

People hate it when logic gets in the way of emotional conviction. This introduction to my new roommate was going poorly. We stood and glared at each other when a voice spoke from behind me.

"Don't mind Carlos, Marshall. He's touchy about certain issues, and has problems with people sometimes, most of which he creates himself. But he's harmless." I turned around. There standing in the open door was the toothpick chewer Termite and the high school jock looking guy they had called Cow. It was Cow who had spoken, and they were both smiling at Carlos. Cow walked over to me, "Tim Cowart," he said, extending his hand, "they call me Cow, short for my last name and has nothing to do with size, grooming or personal habits." Termite walked up and shook hands also, "Rick Dumas. Like the author, except we pronounce it DOOMAS, not

DOOMAH. They call me Termite. I don't have the slightest idea why," he said around a well-chewed toothpick. He still wore the raincoat, and as he spoke he spit the chewed toothpick into a small garbage can beside the door and, pulling a whole box of them from his pocket, he popped another into his mouth and began to chew it with gusto.

They began a pleasant conversation, the first non-threatening, relatively normal one I'd had in days. They asked where I was from, about my family, what I liked and didn't like, how long I had been in the Corps, and basic get to know you questions like those. Carlos grumbled something under his breath in Spanish, and then in English growled something about showing us just how harmless he was. He turned and busied himself putting a record on his stereo and turned the volume up. It was genuine Mariachi stuff, the kind they come around and annoy you with in a Mexican restaurant while you're trying to eat.

I can appreciate cultural differences, but this stuff just didn't make it. To make matters worse, the record quality was terrible, like someone had recorded it with third rate equipment in his mother's garage. It sounded like a lot of screeching interspersed with the occasional high-pitched trill of a tongue, a tinny guitar banging away in the background. It didn't take me very long to officially hate it. I know now that El Pachuco didn't like it that much himself. There is a lot of beautiful Hispanic music and I found out later that he had some of it in his locker. He could have played it, but he chose this particular class of music just to irritate us gringos. It worked, too, with Cow and Termite asking me if I had eaten yet between irritated glances at El Pachuco and his stereo. Which he casually ignored. When I said I hadn't, they invited me to go to the mess hall with them for evening chow and we left Carlos on his bed, jerking his foot to the questionable beat of his music.

After we had eaten an acceptable meal in the tiny mess hall (it was staffed by all Navy personnel, cooks and all, which explains why the food was edible) the two took me on a short tour of the base. I say a short tour because it was a small base, being just a few hundred yards square and surrounded by a high cyclone fence. Part of the compound consisted of the two neat rows of civilian housing that I had noticed earlier, the infamous Brownbagger's Row. Another part was the little strip center that housed the PX, a snack bar known in Navy parlance as the gedunk, a dinky theater and a two-lane bowling alley. In contrast, the back gate, with another guard booth staffed by a bored looking guy I hadn't seen before, led to the antenna field which, as they explained to me, was five *miles* around. It was pie shaped, bordered by a paved road known as Perimeter Road, and held a number of wire array antennas that were essentially a jump station for communications with our Sixth Fleet in the Mediterranean Sea. They also listened in to the Russians in the never ending Cold War game of cat and mouse. These were the antennas the strange major had spoken of. In a few years satellite technology would replace everything there—including us—but we couldn't know that then.

And most interesting to me—just outside the back gate (or Post 2, the front gate being Post 1) were the kennels. They sat apart in a small fenced compound of their own, and from about sixty yards away I could see several guys with dogs, German Shepherds, at their sides going through some kind of drill. On the far side of the small kennel compound I could see a dog attacking a man in a thick brown suit of some kind. As I watched the handler called the dog off and it returned to his side. My tour guides told me that these were sentry dogs and their handlers, the Marines that the Caddy For Jesus had called Dog Men. The antenna field was guarded at night by these sentry dogs. Their handlers and they went out at dusk every night and returned at dawn every morning. I was fascinated, and asked Cow and Termite just how one got to become a Dog Man.

"First," Termite said, "you have to request it through the Major."

"That should be easy enough," I said.

"Yeah," said Termite, "if you can catch the Major when he's in near-Earth orbit. In case you didn't notice he's pretty far out there. And we like it like that. He leaves us alone. No inspections. No surprises." "But even if you do manage to catch the Major on one of his Earth-bound days," Cow continued, "just putting in a request isn't enough. The Dog Men have to request *you*. See, they're kind of like a closed club. If there's an opening they pretty much get to choose who goes—and who doesn't. It wouldn't happen right away even if the Major approves your request. You've got a long way to go. You're too new, and they don't know if you're cool or not yet."

"What do you mean, 'cool'?" I asked. I thought I was cool anyway. Who doesn't? They looked at each other and I saw Cow give the tiniest shake of his head. "You'll find out," Termite said, and left it at that.

We headed back to the barracks because the two of them had to get ready for watch. As we departed, they to their room and me to the ethnic hell to which I had been condemned by committee, Cow said, "There's gonna be some of the Dog Men rotating back to the world in the next couple of months. Keep it in mind. Not everybody wants it because those dogs are the meanest sonsofbitches you ever saw in your life, and they like to eat handlers. But if you're interested, it's something to think about. My request is in. So's Termite's."

And think about it I did. That night, as I lay in my room listening to music that sounded like four cats being shaken in a bag, I thought a lot about it. And between wishing I could smash El Pachuco's stereo or find some reliable earplugs, or maybe give California back somehow so he would just *stop*, I could see the distant images of those Marines and their dogs and I wondered about the Dog Men and what I could do to become one.

Like most things in my life to that point, though, I would find out not through personal drive or endeavor, but through the circumstances of accident, fortune and misfortune, and just plain dumb luck.

6

Dark Dreams and Bayonets

The next morning I was assigned to a watch. I found out, much to my delight, that this consisted of being on duty for two days, four hours on and eight hours off, then being off duty for two days. This meant that every other weekend was a three-day weekend. There would be plenty of time off that I could use to explore Morocco and as much of the rest of North Africa as I could jam in with my new friends. I had vague fantasies of exploring these exotic climes, facing the fury of desert sandstorms and braving the fierce desert sun, all with my friends at my side. I read too much. There was only one small problem.

I didn't seem to have any friends.

Besides Cow and Termite, most of the rest of the place seemed pretty cool to my presence. They made no effort whatsoever to be friendly or even remotely sociable apart from saying "Howdy, Marshal," whenever they would cross my path and, me being me, I made no effort either apart from saying, "Howdy," in reply. It's another verbal habit I still have, by the way, many years later. I still say 'howdy' at times when I find myself in a casual or awkward situation. It's an effective, noncommittal greeting that manages to put you on neutral ground in whatever situation.

Anyway, I was pretty much left to my own devices for the first several days I was there. They weren't *unfriendly*, exactly. There just weren't any warm and fuzzy moments, and for some reason, they seemed somewhat wary of me. Being the type that likes being left alone, that suited me just fine.

The watch I was assigned to was easy enough. We would be issued a .45

at the beginning of each shift and take our turns manning any one of the small base's three guard posts. Post One was the main gate entry, the one I had passed through the day before. You had to be really squared away to work it. It required dress blues and the type of professional attitude that had successfully eluded me in my time in the Corps. I found early on that the type of Marine Post One needed required a great deal more effort than I cared to exert. I managed to keep myself off of this post, much to my relief. I ended up spending my first week at Bouk on Post Two, which was the back gate that led onto the antenna field. That was a little more to my liking, because all you had to do was wave the Navy folks through on their way to the big, secret communications building that sat in the middle of the antenna field, then back through when they had finished their watch. There were no logs to keep, and no paperwork to be done. Easy enough, and it suited me just fine—until I discovered Post Three.

    Post Three was a loafer's dream. Located immediately behind the big communications building, (which I discovered was referred to as "Oz" by the Marines) smack in the middle of the antenna field, it was a guard booth in a tower. It sat about sixty feet off the ground and could be secured by closing and locking a small grate behind you once you had crawled up to it on a long metal ladder. Nobody could sneak up on you to see if you were doing your duty, which made it ideal for me since my dedication to putting one hundred percent effort into my duty was lacking. This post was manned during daylight hours to watch the field. At nightfall the Dog Men took over. I would get up there with a rifle and a pair of binoculars to make sure saboteurs didn't damage or destroy any of the intricate looking antennas nestled in the field. I would also smuggle a paperback book up there and thoroughly enjoy my four hours on post. Most of the rest of the guys hated it because it was boring and limited their contact with other people. Limited contact with most of the rest of the human race was not a problem for me, so after I had sampled the post once I eagerly volunteered for it at every opportunity since I had developed a high level of skill when it came to loafing. I was never alone in Post Three. I passed the time up there in the select company of Kurt Vonnegut, Shakespeare, John Steinbeck, Edgar Rice Burroughs, and every DC and Marvel comic book I could get my hands on. I've never been a snob when it comes to the forms of entertainment I choose.

Anyway, this perfect posting went on for a couple of weeks and the strange denizens of the place continued to ignore me, and I them. Then there was a sudden and unexpected change.

I had finished a late watch one night on Two and had just returned to the barracks. El Pachuco wasn't in the room, and the owner of the third bunk in our room, a guy I still hadn't met because he had been back in the world on leave, was still gone. The room was uncharacteristically quiet. I poured myself a large glass of water for the night and had just settled in to enjoy the peace when there was a sudden crash somewhere on the other side of the barracks. Several voices were raised in alarm. By now I was getting used to the weirdness of the place and aside from the odd brush with the thuggish Alfie I was settling in nicely. I just turned on the small lamp at the head of my bunk and opened the book I was reading at the time, determined to ignore those idiots and enjoy my solitude while I could. Then, there was another crash and a shriek, and I could hear the voices take on another tone. One of frightened desperation.

Curious now I slid over the edge of the bunk, pulled on some pants and, carrying my glass of water, went into the hall. The noises were coming from the other side of the barracks and I made my cautious way there. About ten of the guys were huddled outside of Brunner's room, Cow, Termite, and the weird Crow among them. Crow was standing in the door, speaking in a low tone of voice to someone inside. I tapped Termite on the shoulder and he turned suddenly to face me. I can't describe the look on his face as his eyes caught mine, but some writers use the word 'haunted'. I wish the look could be described in those simple terms but it can't. Taking a quick step back, I quickly regained the composure that I had almost lost when we had locked eyes. I jerked my head in the direction of the room, "What's going on?" I whispered.

"Henley," he said, and started to turn away. I reached out and touched him on the shoulder. He turned back to me, his eyes losing much of the awful look they had held only seconds before. "Henley," he continued, "reenlisted for this place. After the 'Nam. He thought it would get rid of the dreams. It didn't. He was with the Ninth and he caught the shit. Bad. I was there with him, not in the same company, but the Ninth. So was Freaky Deac. We're OK, mostly, but he ain't. And, right now, he's asleep and he's got Brunner down on the floor with a bayonet to his throat because he thinks Brunner's an NVA and he won't wake up. And if we can't get him awake without freaking him, Mama Brunner's gonna be one sad lady tomorrow."

"Can't we rush him, or something?" I asked, and he looked at me like the fool I was.

"If we do, Brunner's dead in the first second, and probably two or three of us in the second. His platoon was overrun at night by NVA, and he fought hand to hand the whole night *with a bayonet*, and was one of six still alive when the choppers inserted the next day. My young friend....this is a very bad boy. Any *other* suggestions?"

I had none, this being so far out my range of experience that I couldn't even relate anything to it. From the doorway, I could hear Crow, who had seemed so bizarre to me, now talking in a low, rational, intelligent voice to Henley, "It's okay, man, its us, not them. We'll help if you let us." I edged toward the door and could hear Henley. He said, in a whisper, like he didn't want to be overheard, "Oh, man, oh, man, they're everywhere. Oh, shit, they're every fucking where. Crow? Stay down man. Take 'em *out*."

Crow continued talking to Henley, who was somewhere out of sight in the darkened room, "Henley, wake up, man. Wake up Henley, please wake up before it's too late and you make one *giant* motherfucker of a mistake." I stepped up and stopped beside the door and peeked inside. For the first time I could see Henley. He was sitting astride Brunner's chest, his shoulders hunched. I could see the light from a streetlight outside the window reflecting a pale, deadly sliver of the bayonet's razor edge. The point of the bayonet was touching Brunner's throat and a small trickle of blood was oozing down the side of his neck. Brunner, if he was still alive, wasn't moving.

Henley looked up toward the door and his eyes were *glowing* in the darkness of the room, something I'd never seen before. He whispered something else I didn't understand, then shifted his position on Brunner slightly, and I knew he was about to kill him. He pulled his right elbow up slightly for a killing thrust, and without thinking I took three quick steps into the room and threw my glass of water into his face.

Now, I have no idea how I knew that this was the thing to do. I only knew that, if I didn't try this, Brunner would meet his maker like *now*. If you throw water in a sleeping person's face, he generally wakes up, right? I hoped. And it worked. Henley gasped and quickly sat up straight, blinking rapidly. I jumped back, thinking at first he was going to come after me. It would have been an exercise in seeing who could have run faster, him when he's angry or me when I'm terrified because I wasn't going to stick around to reason with him. But it didn't happen.

He wiped the water from his face with his free hand, then looked at it in amazement. Somebody found the light switch, and the room was suddenly flooded with light. Henley looked at us one at a time, then at the bayonet in his hand. It seemed to dawn on him what had been going on when he looked at Brunner, who was just lying there staring up at him with absolutely no expression on his face. There was a small cut on his neck that bled freely but he didn't move to cover it or anything until Crow gently took the bayonet from Henley and handed it to me. He, Termite and Freaky Deac helped Henley up, and Cow and Rock helped Brunner to his feet. They checked the cut on his neck and it proved to be pretty superficial.

Brunner stood for a moment, and when Henley started to say, in a horrified voice, "Man, Timmy, I'm so sorry….," Brunner cut him off.

In that soft, aristocratic southern accent of his, he said gently, "Henley….under the circumstances, would you mind if I said you are one crazy sonofabitch?" Somebody brought him a towel and he pressed it against the cut on his neck. He pulled it away and looked at the blood on it. He said, in the same level tone, "Now, if you'll excuse me, I'll tend to this. Henley, we can talk about this later. By the light of day, preferably. And I'm sure you'll understand if I sleep in another room tonight. Goodnight," he turned to leave then turned back and looked at me, "and, thank you, Marshal, for riding to my rescue."

I nodded, not sure of what to say. I had gotten lucky and my little surprise had worked, that's all, and I was damn glad it did. It was luck, pure luck but, as I discovered then and still believe now, at the right time even luck counts. I sort of drifted out of the room shortly after he did, while everyone's attention was on the shocked Henley. Just as I got to the door Henley noticed me leaving and said, in a slightly quavering voice, "Marshal?" I stopped and looked back at him. He looked small and harmless and scared sitting there on the edge of that bed. A few minutes before he had looked frighteningly like what he had been trained to be and in reality was.

A stone killer.

The present incarnation of Henley started to continue with whatever he had to say to me as I turned back to him, then, instead of speaking, he looked me in the eyes and just nodded. That said it all, so I just nodded back and left the room. I wasn't being silently noble. I honestly didn't know what to say. I shut the door behind me, leaving Crow and Freaky Deac and one or two others talking softly to Henley.

In the real world, you would have expected someone to report Henley for the attack. People generally tell Somebody In Authority about a homicidal maniac waiting to happen, but nobody did because that's just not how we did things in those days.

In the days that followed everybody watched out for Henley. All knives and bayonets were taken out of his room and a light was left on while he slept. Brunner kept the cut on his neck covered and it slowly began to heal and all seemed well, but several weeks later, after he woke up in the night screaming, Henley turned himself in to the Company Gunny, Gunnery Sergeant Favor. It seemed that Henley was more afraid for the safety of the guys he cared for than we were afraid of him. We all had to give statements to some anal-retentive squid officer from Naval Intelligence Service who proved to be a real pain in the ass and treated us all like we were suspects in a crime. I wondered if he and the self-important cherub of a second lieutenant back in Philly were related somehow because they acted just alike. Maybe its something they teach in officer school, Asshole 101. Anyway, no criminal charges were pressed, but Henley was relieved of duty and ordered to return to the world for psychiatric evaluation.

It was for the best and we all knew that, but it was a sad day nevertheless as we watched Henley board that gray bus. A short ritual preceded his boarding.

He went from man to man as we stood in a small group at the pick-up point, shaking hands and smiling. When he got to me, though, the smile slipped fro his face. He put his arm around my shoulder and led me away from where everyone was standing.

"Thank you, Marshal," he said.

I was slightly embarrassed, "Hey, man, that's not necessary."

"Yeah, yeah it is. I would have killed Timmy that night. There's no doubt in my mind. And maybe somebody else. I'm glad I didn't. I'm glad for you being there. Tell me something, though."

"What's that?"

"How did you know that it would work?"

I flushed, slightly uneasy. I hadn't really brought it up to any of the other guys. Some things are just best left as they are. "I didn't," I told him, "I just did it without thinking. It could have made you kill Brunner."

"Yeah, well, it didn't," he looked away, "and I would have for sure if you hadn't done it. That's how heroes are made, Marshal. They act without thinking"

"I'm no hero, Henley. I was gonna scream like a little girl and run like a rabbit if you'd have come at me."

He laughed, "That's the second way heroes are made. They know when to fight and when to haul ass. Anyway, take care. You'll go far, if you just keep on the way you are." He shook my and gave my face a slap, then we turned and walked back toward the gathered Marines.

"Thanks, man," I said, a bit taken aback by the sudden sincerity after all the time that had passed since that night, "keep in touch."

He stepped on to the bus and we all stood there yelling at him to keep in touch, calling him names, and saying goodbye. The doors of the gray bus hissed shut and it rumbled away, taking Henley with it and out of our lives forever.

We heard from him several weeks later. He had been discharged on disability and thought it was quite a joke that Uncle Sam continued to pay him for doing nothing. They weren't even making him go to the shrink anymore, he said. Thanks, Uncle Sam, he said.

I didn't know if the nightmares had stopped for him, but I hoped so.

7

Acceptance

In the days after the Henley incident I noticed a perceptible warming in the ambient temperature of the attitudes displayed toward me by most of the crazies inhabiting this strange place. The odd Crow would wobble up to me with that Charlie Chaplin waddle, thrust his face into mine and say in his booming bass, "Well, howdy, Marshal," then waddle away like a spastic penguin. I tried to imitate that waddle when no one was looking, by the way, and was surprised at the degree of physical coordination being that stupid requires. Cow and Termite became even friendlier and we actually became friends, spending more and more time together. The Afro wearing Freaky Deac, whose real name I learned was Davenport, became more talkative and even friendly in his overall manner towards me. After Henley Night, the Deacon walked up to me and shook my hand without saying a word, then again went into the Black Power thing called the dap, which involved touching his fist with mine several times in different ways. As I said before, in those days this greeting was reserved strictly for the Brothers, none of the Caucasian Persuasion allowed, so I knew he was saluting me in a sincere, personal way. I kept my mouth shut and followed his lead on it and this time managed to pull it off with some dignity. When it was over he nodded to me like he had in Henley's room that night and drifted away. Most of the rest of the crew stopped treating me like I had leprosy, even my radical roommate, El Pachuco. This, however, had another catalyst.

    I was headed out the door for the late shift on Two, leaving my ethnocentric roommate on his bunk listening to those awful records. He seemed to have an infinite supply of these although I think he only had about three. They were just so bad it seemed like a lot more. Although the tone of our relationship was still not what you could call friendly, it had cooled to the point of mutual tolerance instead of mutual hostility. He was still ignoring me because I didn't speak the Mother Tongue and that suited me fine.

Anyway, on this particular night I got almost all the way to the Corporal of the Guard to check out my pistol when I realized I had left my cigarettes in my room, so I did a quick about face to retrieve them. I shot back up the stairs, dashed down the hall and opened the door to my room. And there was El Pachuco with the stereo going, as usual. What was not usual, however, was the music that flowed from the stereo. The voice of Karen Carpenter flowed from the speakers and the silky *Rainy Days and Mondays* filled the room. I stopped in surprise. El Pachuco sprang from the bed and dashed to his stereo, quickly taking the needle from the record. He acted like I had caught him with my sister or something. We stood and stared at each other across the room, and it was I that broke the strained silence in the subtle, diplomatic way of which I was capable. Being tactful was important at this time, I felt.

"You phony bastard!" I exclaimed, "You've been stuffing that other crap down my throat, and here you are listening to the *Carpenters*, for chrissakes! You fake! You just do that to make me crazy, don't you?"

At first El Pachuco did a fine imitation of a politician who had been caught with his hand in his secretary's pants. He blustered, wriggled and squirmed, "No, man. I just found that record in the hallway and wanted to see what it sounded like."

"You freakin' liar! All this time you've been a closet Karen Carpenter fan! El Pachuco, my ass. El Fake-o is more like it. The Carpenters, for Chrissakes. What's next, Peggy Lee? Dean Martin?"

This was fun. I had him squirming like an eel now.

"I don't know what you're talking about."

"Well, El Fake-o, let's just see if the other guys can figure it out."

"You wouldn't."

"I would. Like the town fucking crier, complete with ringing bell." I knew, see, that Carlos was fiercely proud of his macho image. He would rather have had his knees nailed to the floor that let the other guys know he was a secret

Carpenters fan. I also knew he would give up just about anything to keep our little secret.

"Okay, okay," he was defeated. In one short, accidental stroke I had won our little cold war. It was great. "What do you want?"

"What do I want? Oh, you mean to keep this just between us, the two caballeros?"

"Yeah, okay man, what do you want?"

"That's easy, Karen, er, Carlos. One: You stop playing that shit you play just to annoy me."

"I play that because it is the music of my people."

"Bullshit. You play that just to piss me off. I bet you don't even like that garbage. Who could?"

He looked as though he were going to bluster until I rang an imaginary bell and said, "Hear ye, hear ye!" He knew the guys would be merciless over such an offense as this. They would pull him apart like an overcooked chicken. Figuratively speaking, of course.

"Alright, alright, agreed. What else, *caberon*?"

"Two: If you're gonna call me names, from now on call me names in English. It's something I'm used to. That's it."

"That's it?"

"Yep. Unless there's some other concession you've been dying to make."

I like winning. There's something immensely satisfying about getting your way. In this case, though, I sort of met him just short of halfway, with my chunk the bigger of the halves.

We reached what I considered to be a fine compromise. I agreed that he could keep up his front of being completely ethnocentric and play that awful stuff if too many gringos invaded the sanctuary of our room, and he agreed never to serenade me to sleep with it again if I wouldn't eat cheese on him like a big fat rat and ruin his radical reputation. It was an agreement we kept until he rotated back to the world a year later, and it worked just fine for me. I was able to buy my own music and actually play it in our room with him there, and if he started to get radical on me I would hold my hands up to my mouth like paws and do my rat-eating-cheese imitation. He would desist, grumbling to himself in Spanish. Like I said, a fine compromise.

It was during this time that some of the Dog Men were soon due to rotate back to the world. One of them I didn't know had been attacked by his own dog and had to fly back to the States for surgery to repair damaged nerves and tendons in his hand. It made me hesitate for a second, but I was still fascinated by the idea of this unique assignment. So I, along with Cow, put my written request in with the Major, myself for the first time. For Cow it was a second request. While Cow and I were walking to the company office to do this we ran into one of the guys from the Seabee detachment that was assigned to Bouk. Cow had introduced him to me earlier as Sunshine. The whole time I was there I never heard him called anything else. I don't even know if he had another name. Sunshine was leaving our company office with a saw and a tool belt, and when he saw us he quickly put his finger to his lips in a *sshhh* gesture.

The Seabees are the Navy construction unit and are unlike the rest of the Navy, who we referred to as squids, swab jockies, deck apes and other flattering names. They returned the compliment by calling us jarheads and juggies. We got along great with the Seabees, though. After all, they were a combat construction unit who wore our utility uniforms and held much the same attitudes towards rules and regulations as we did. That is, they followed them just enough to stay out of jail. They had no respect for anyone, especially anyone in authority, and thought they were the best, just like we did. On the pocket of their Marine style utilities in place of the anchor, globe, and eagle that is the symbol of the Marines, was their logo, part of which consisted of a slightly insane looking little bee that we thought was great. There was a detachment of a couple of dozen of them at Bouk of which Sunshine was one.

Anyway, we were curious when Sunshine put his finger to his lips and motioned us off to the side, so we followed him a few feet off into the sand. He chuckled and said, "Howdy, Marshal, Cow….you guys will never guess what I just did for your Major." He looked back and forth at us like he expected us to guess and when we just looked at him blankly, he went on, "He had me put a peephole in his door! Yeah," he went on after we expressed our surprise, "a real trap door that he can open from the inside and see who's out there. Kind of spooky, huh? I think your fearless leader's losin' it, guys."

Well, *that* was no secret. We all knew that the Major had wigged. He still had well over a year to go before rotating because for some reason officers got a two year assignment here instead of an eighteen month assignment like us. We figured he would get a bit weirder, but even we were surprised about the peephole thing, so we went to see for ourselves. Sure enough, when we handed our written requests for assignment to dogs to Mouse, the company clerk, he walked over to the Major's door and tapped on it twice. There was a shuffling noise from inside his office, and then the trap door opened. We could see the just the twitchy part of the Major's face, then the clerk slipped the papers through the hole and the little door snapped shut. I couldn't see any lights on in the background, either. In a whispered tone I asked Mouse, a neat little guy with a tiny Errol Flynn mustache, "Just what the hell *that* was all about?"

Just as he started to say something the little door snapped open just for a second, then slowly closed again. It was kind of eerie, really and we all stood there, staring at it for several seconds, then slipped outside with the Mouse after he jerked his head toward the door. Mouse leaned against the side of the Quonset hut, looked around conspiratorially and said, grinning, "You know how the Major was supposed get a new exec? Ain't gonna happen. The last guy scheduled to come broke his leg. Then, they slotted another one. This guy caught meningitis. Cool, huh? Fucking meningitis. The Major was hoping to get an exec in here to do the hands on shit with the company so he can take a leave. He's got over a month coming and believe me, the motherfucker needs it. And now Mother Corps has to find yet another replacement for that exec slot and it'll take time to get one processed. I thought the Major was gonna stroke out when they told him yesterday. Could be as long as sixty days. Since Piazza rotated it's just him and the Gunny, so the Major decided to stay in his office and not come out. Wild, huh?"

Bad news for the Major, good news for us. Because it meant that we would be existing in an officer free zone for several more weeks. We would only have to avoid running afoul of Gunnery Sergeant Favor in the meantime. Cow and I felt it was our duty to spread this news among our comrades and we proceeded to do so in a most efficient manner. There wasn't a dry eye in the house upon hearing the news, and party after party sprang up throughout the land. It was then I discovered why they had kept their distance from me after I first arrived.

That evening I was off duty and lazing comfortably in my room. I had no money to go to town, so I was entertaining myself with the usual book and some music. Carlos and I were listening to *Santana Abraxas* on his stereo. We had found, under our new treaty, that he could now listen to anything he wanted under the guise of it being my music, so this was working well for all concerned, radical Latino *and* blackmailing gringo.

There was knock on our door and Crow entered, accompanied by one of the other Dog Men I had seen around but hadn't had much to do with, a guy named Schmidt. Crow waddled over to me and stared for a second. I gently eased the book I was reading to my chest and watched him warily, like you do whenever a demented person is near you. He smiled and spoke, "Howdy, Marshal!" he said in his usual greeting, "Me and the boys was wonderin' ifn you'd like to mosey on down to the bunkhouse with us fer a git together."

"Crow, you lunatic," I said reasonably, "I'm from Indiana, not the set of *Rawhide*. We don't talk like that in Indiana."

"Yep," he said, completely ignoring my feeble attempt at a protest. He spit on the floor and I looked down at it appalled as he continued with, "Well, git along, little doggie! We got ropin' to do! C'mon."

Well, this was different. Although they had been warmer towards me after the Henley thing, nobody besides Cow and Termite had actually asked to keep company with me. It was a social invitation I felt shouldn't be refused so I said, "Sure," and stood, trying to ignore the irritating way Crow had of keeping his face within inches of mine. They abruptly left the room and I followed. With me in tow they left the barracks and headed toward the back gate. We walked past Post Two, which was manned by the little guy I had met in Philly, Shorty. I hadn't had much contact with him since I had been there because we were on opposite watches. I spoke briefly but didn't stop to chat because I realized then where they were leading me.

To the kennels.

I was thrilled but had enough sense to keep my mouth shut and not babble questions like a giddy schoolgirl. As we approached, several dogs began to bark from their wire cages. A voice from somewhere yelled, "Knock it OFF," and they instantly shut up. The exterior gate was closed and a big red sign with "LOOSE DOG!" written on it in bold white letters hung there at eye level. Schmidt turned to me, "If you ever come up here by yourself and this sign is on the gate—stay the fuck out. Understand?"

I remembered what I had heard about the mauled handler who had been shipped back to the world, and thought of all the other stories about the vicious dogs that prowled the night in the antenna field. "Oh, yeah," I said, "I understand."

He opened the gate. I hesitated before I entered and looked nervously around, "What about the loose dog?" I asked.

"It's alright," Crow said. I followed them into the compound. I could see a couple of dozen of the wire dog runs and in them were some of the meanest looking damn dogs I had ever seen, all of them German Shepherds. But Crow and Schmidt apparently hadn't brought me up here for a tour. They herded me towards a small cinder block building that sat at the near end on the dog runs. It was painted USMC green and the windows, I noticed, were painted black and were closed. We entered the building, which was about the size of my room. On the walls hung what I assumed was dog gear, leashes and muzzles and harnesses and such, and around the room sat about eight guys. On a shelf in the corner, slightly illuminated by a small black light, a jury-rigged eight-track player was belting out Black Sabbath.

Crow closed the door behind me and somebody switched on a light. In the room were Cow, Termite with the inevitable toothpick in the corner of his mouth, Rock, the clerk Mouse, the Seabee Sunshine, a huge guy named Bear that I knew was one of the Dog Men but who I hadn't met before, and Brunner, who was cradling the repulsive J.R. And of course, Freaky Deac, who raised his right fist in a Black Power salute to me. They gave me the "Howdy, Marshal," thing that I was getting heartily sick of.

They invited me to sit and pulled a tattered chair out of a corner for me. Wondering, I sat.

Schmidt cleared his throat and spoke, "Marshal, we all decided to bring you up here today to thank you for what you did for Henley—not to mention Brunner."

"Yeah."

"Cool."

"Way to go, cowboy."

"Right on."

It was the first time since the incident that anyone had actually spoken to me specifically of it. I hadn't spoken to of it to anyone but Henley himself about it on the day he left. A bit embarrassed by the sudden attention I said, "Look, guys, don't mention it. I…"

Crow interrupted, "We also would like to know if you'd care to join us in a little—refreshment." Thinking that a cooler of beer or something like that was about to make its appearance I said, "Yeah, great."

From nowhere a strange device appeared and was plopped down into the center of the ragged circle we sat in. It stood at least three feet tall and was beautifully and intricately designed. On the top was a brass bowl looking thing about the size of a teacup. The bottom flared out into a round bulb shape and from it emerged six patterned tubes. It looked for all the world like a designer octopus. I was looking at my first Moroccan water pipe, or, as Lewis Carroll called it in his demented *Alice* stories, a hookah. I could see them watching me closely as they produced a cigar box and began to load the top of the pipe with a lumpy greenish powder. While this was going on, the huge guy Bear slipped out for a moment, then reappeared, saying, "Wolfgang's out."

As they finished the loading of the pipe Rock told me, "Don't go outside, Marshal. Wolfgang's loose and he will eat your ass." It was safe to assume that Wolfgang was one of those dogs out there and I had no intention of leaving, although the preparations with the pipe were making me nervous.

I had never been around much in the way of banned substances. In fact, it was only after I had joined the Marine Corps that I had ever laid eyes on it. Indiana farm boys could still be naive in those days, and I was. I had been booted from that electrician school and had gone to grunt land before I ever saw or smelled smokable contraband. A group of guys were standing in a circle at the end of the squad bay one evening and being new and curious I sauntered over to see what was up. As I stepped up to the circle one of them suddenly stuck a bright pink joint into my face, thinking I was there for a hit. I jumped back like he had thrust a snake at me. They thought this was great fun and were laughing at me as I retreated, red faced, to my bunk. That had been the extent of my experience with the illicit stuff that was so much a part of the culture in those days.

Until now, obviously.

Mouse spoke, "You smoke, Marshal?"

I decided to try to bluff my way out of this so I replied, as cool as I could, "Naw. I've tried it and it just doesn't do anything for me except make me cough." I had heard some of the smokers at Lejuene hacking their lungs up, so I knew this was one of the effects.

"Oh, well," Schmidt said, "you see, that's the purpose of the water pipe. There's chilled water in the bottom of the pipe. When you suck the smoke through these here tubes it goes through the water. That mellows it. Takes the harshness right out. You won't have to worry about coughing. Much."

"That's alright," I continued with my bluff, "you guys go right ahead. I'll pass for now. It just doesn't do anything for me." The last part was a little feeble, because they were looking at me oddly. Not threatening exactly, just examining, measuring.

Then Brunner spoke up, and it hit me what this was all about, "You wouldn't be a CID narc, would you Marshall?" So there it was. That explained why everyone had kept their distance, even after the Henley thing, and the cryptic 'cool' remark of Termite's the first day I was on board.

At Lejeune a guy suspected of being a narc, the term for inside agent or informer, was doused with lighter fluid in the middle of the night and woke up on fire, screaming in a bunk that had become an inferno. They never caught who did it, either. I remembered this very clearly because his screams woke me from where I was sleeping just six bunks down. I know now that this group of guys would never have done something like that but at that time— I just wasn't so sure. I felt my little bluff crumbling to ashes and I decided on a different tack.

"No way," I said cheerfully, "I've smoked before. Light it up." I was counting on the stuff *really* not affecting me. Yeah, right. What I didn't know was that, in that water pipe bowl, was not your routine weed, marijuana or whatever you wanted to call it. In that very bowl rested the very best hashish produced anywhere in the world. It's as common in Morocco as beer is in Germany and just as easy to get. They all smiled and put flame to the top of the bowl while several of them puffed on the end of the long tubes. After the thing was fired up, they offered me one of the mouthpieces. I took it and puffed heartily, the vision of that flaming screamer flickering in my head. They were right—I managed to get a good lungfull of smoke without coughing. I passed the tube to somebody on my right ad was immediately corrected.

"The bowl always gets passed to the left, Marshal." More ritual.

I nodded, watching them for a clue as what to do. Following their lead I held the smoke in for a moment before exhaling. This went on for several minutes, and as they got more stoned, the conversation became more animated and friendly, not to mention funny. I kept toking and passing the thing, "I swear this stuff just doesn't affect me," I said, so they kept putting it back in my hand saying that if it didn't affect me, there was no harm in being sociable and smoking with them, was there? I found myself becoming very agreeable, then downright friendly.

Suddenly it seemed like everything was funny. I asked Crow, "Hey, Crow. How come you're called Crow because you don't look like a bird, unless it was a stork."

"That's Cro," said Schmitt, "C-R-O. Not Crow. It's short for Cro Magnon Man. Look at this fucker's profile and tell if it doesn't fit."

He was right. Cro looked like one of those progressive silhouette things that shows the evolution of man from ape to now. Now that I thought about it I fell from my chair laughing. They helped me back up and I asked Brunner what Piazza had meant that first day by finding me a bunk *inside* the barracks this time.

Brunner laughed, "There was this little goonie pain in the ass chaplain's assistant who came to Bouk to set up a chapel and reform the heathen. That would be us. He treated us like we were island cannibals of some type."

"Holy shit!" I exclaimed, "the Caddy for Jesus!"

"The what?"

"The Caddy for Jesus. He wanted me to be a Chaplain's assistant with him. Nearly got me, too. I got away."

"Hallelujah!"

"Praise Jesus!"

"Sing it, Brother!"

"Amen!"

I took another hit from the pipe and passed it, "For Christ's sake," said Freaky Deac, "wipe the pipe when you pass it. No sloppy pipes passed here. Speaking of heathens." He sighed and shook his head, "White people."

Brunner went on, "Anyway, Pizza Man told me to get him outfitted with a bunk and shit. I don't know why every time a new guy gets here I have to be the one…" He started to drift off track until the others hollered at him and he picked up where he left off.

"Anyway, we didn't want the little fucker around because we knew he'd freak and dime us if he saw us partaking of mother nature, so we set up a place in the ammo storage bunker for him. He was all happy because he thought he was getting special treatment. He was." He looked the other members of our circle, "Should I go on?"

"Oh, do tell," cried Cro.

"We, ah, slipped a hit of acid that Sunshine's sister sent him into a coke and got him to drink it before bed. That night we slipped up to the bunker and Cro started talking down the exaust pipe like he was God."

I sat and stared.

"It was cool, because he started talking back. We were rolling. Then all of a sudden he comes running out of the door and off into the antenna field yelling, "I'm coming Jesus! I'm coming!"

"What!"

"Naked."

"What!"

"With a hard on."

"No way!"

"Yep," said Freaky Deac, "Took us two hours to catch the naked little fucker and drag him back."

"It was definitely an experience," Termite joined in, "He kept hollering about the how much he loved the Lord. And his dick stayed hard the whole time."

"It was gross," said Freaky Deac, "Fuckin' white people."

This went on until nearly dark, and I got more and more stoned as I sat there. Bear finally went outside and put his dog up. They explained to me on the way back to the barracks that nobody, but nobody would ever open the gate to the kennels and enter whenever that 'LOOSE DOG' sign is up, and when they decide to party in the kennel house, they let one of the dogs loose inside the compound. They were then as safe as you can get from interference from meddling officers or NCO's. I thought that was brilliant and said so. Several times, I think. We walked back to the barracks together. I stopped several times to marvel at the magnificent Moroccan sunset and I'm real sure I used the word 'wow' a lot on the short trip to my room. They helped me find my room, agreeing with me that the smoke hadn't affected me at all. After pouring me into my bunk they left, laughing all the way.

I eventually giggled myself to sleep and I remember thinking, as I finally drifted off, *see, I told 'em that stuff wouldn't affect me.*

8

Dog Man Days and Dog Man Ways

In the few days following my acceptance ritual I gradually became more at ease, worrying less and smoking with the heads more. They seemed to have adopted me after a fashion. The Henley incident was the catalyst behind all this sudden brotherhood, but I didn't bring the incident up again after the party in the kennel house and neither did anyone else. It was just accepted that it had happened, the thanks had been said, and the issue dropped. Some things are best left alone.

Then several things occurred nearly simultaneously that changed my lowly station almost overnight.

My roommate, the charming El Pachuco, was selected to replace the guy whose dog had maimed his hand, thus becoming the newest Dog Man. He was thrilled, and walked around with his chest puffed out even more, if that was possible.

"You're gonna hurt yourself," I said, pointing at his chest.

"Marshal, even you can't piss me off today."

I congratulated him on the assignment to dogs but actually I felt a bit grumpy, and my congratulatory handshake was executed with ill grace. I was grumpy because I had put in a request for dogs, but fair was fair. He had been there longer and was in fact senior to me in rank (although nobody at Bouk seemed to regard the USMC rank structure with any degree of respect, unless the rank happened to be sergeant or over and you had to recognize it for self-preservation reasons). The assignment to dogs appealed to the overwhelming code of machismo that Carlos lived by, so he was happy when he heard of his transfer. He was to report and begin training the day after he got the word.

Then, Henley woke up screaming and turned himself into Gunny Favor, and was shortly thereafter shipped back to the world. The huge, hairy guy called Bear also went back on orders for his regular rotation. That opened two more positions on dogs. I expected to be quite far down on the list and figured I would have to wait my turn, especially after my disappointment when Carlos was selected. But a funny thing happened.

After that guy got his hand maimed in a vicious attack by his own dog, several of the applicants for a dog job withdrew their requests. Can't imagine why. During one of our now regular smoke-a-thons the little company clerk, Mouse, told me that Cow, with whom I had grown close, and myself were the only ones still asking to take that insane assignment. Mouse was our reliable inside source of information and our inside help to get things done. With *Jesus Christ Superstar* pounding in the room, we asked him to prod the Major, or the Gunny, or whoever needed prodding to get us an assignment transfer. He assured us that the very next time the Major peeped out of his little trap door, he would remind him that dogs were two slots short. He then passed the pipe to the left, and promptly passed out.

Apparently he prodded someone, because the very next day Cow and I were both told to report to Sgt. Schmidt, the Kennel Master, for assignment. I was somewhat astonished that Mouse remembered to prod anything because the last time I had seen him the night before he had been passed out on the floor with his mouth hanging open and some of the guys in the room had been taking turns trying to make hoop shots in it with paper wads, so I thought he did well remembering, all things considered. Anyway, with my heart in my throat, Cow and I walked out of the compound, past Post Two, and on to the kennel compound for the first time as participants

Schmidt was waiting at the gate for us. He shook our hands, "Hi, Guys. Welcome to dogs. I'm the Kennel Master, and while you're up here I'll be responsible for your care and feeding. That will include your training as a Dog Man. My job is to run these kennels, and what I say here goes. Period. I coordinate all training and make sure you take care of your dog, because he will damn sure take care of you," he waved a hand at the antenna field, "out there."

I had known that Schmidt was the Kennel Master because of his regular appearances at our smoke-outs, but since he was an authority figure of sorts I had steered clear of him. No just because he was someone in a position of authority, but because of my track record with those people. I didn't want to piss him of before I had a chance to get to be a dog man. So I had kept our acquaintance casual and was glad now that I had made every effort to be friendly with him for all the right reasons instead of being my usual cocky self.

He began our first official tour, walking us down the two rows of kennels, "These are called 'runs' We have fifteen dogs up here and each has his own run. Which is good because they would tear each other apart if you tried to house them together. They do not work and play well with others. Even you, so if you want to remain scar-free pay close attention to what you're about to learn."

The three sets of runs sat at right angles to each other, forming an open ended box, and consisted of individual pens made of heavy gauge cyclone fencing that were covered by a common roof. There were fifteen runs, and each held a large, unfriendly dog. As we walked by each run, the resident dog it contained would run up to the gate barking and snarling viciously. The type of bark, combined with the look on each dog's face left absolutely no doubt in my mind as to their intent, and I was glad to see that each run gate was secured with a piece of short, heavy chain and a padlock that had a key already in it. Schmidt introduced each dog by name as we passed his run. Each had a different, odd sort of name, "This is Hasso, that's Benno, Mutley—watch that sonofabitch because he is a sneaky mofo." The dog, a large black and tan shepherd, had a shifty, sneaky look on his face and kind of reminded me of Meyers, "The one that looks like a gray wolf is Brutus, fat boy there is Big Rolf, the coyote ugly little fucker is Little Rolf. This is Sergeant Major Nero, our oldest dog. That's Argo, he's about the smartest dog up here. That's King, and this," we stopped in front of a run. In it sat a huge blond colored shepherd. Unlike the others he didn't bark or growl at us. He just sat there and looked at us through his yellow eyes with a malevolent intelligence that made me want to step back despite the heavy run fencing between us, "is Blackie. Blackie is psycho. He likes to fight and likes to eat handlers. He ate his last handler but good. One of you lucky campers will draw him, the other will draw Argo. Those are the two that are open now."

I noted that Blackie wasn't black at all, not even close. He was a light blond or palomino color. I strongly suspected that his name was more derivative of his personality that any physical feature. It was not a reassuring thought.

The introduction continued, "That jet black one is Wodan, that's Wolfgang, that sleek little fucker is King Kelly. That's Marko, and that's Shilo. Note this: each of these dogs has a distinct, and in some cases, dangerous, personality. All will bite a careless handler. A few will seriously injure one if they can, like Blackie, especially Blackie. Mutley, too. King, and Hasso are handler eaters if their handlers get careless. So….don't."

He went on, "If you want to know which ones are the special cases check their rank. We have a rank system. If the dog gets a bite in the line of duty he gets promoted. Nero is a Sergeant Major, That's E-9, so he's had at least eight bites. Argo's a sergeant. Four bites. They start off as E-1's just like we do. Now, when they bite a handler they get demoted. Blackie is a private. So is Mutley. Do I need to spell this out for you?"

"No, Sarge," we both said simultaneously. We were very clear on what he meant. We took a break and headed into the kennel house where I had gotten so blasted that night. Schmidt closed the door and told us to have a seat. He drew up an old chair and turned it around and sat facing us, leaning on its rickety back.

"First rule. What happens up here stays up here. There are no exceptions. You are about to join a very, very exclusive club. A requirement for membership is that you keep Dog Man business as Dog Man business. Got that?"

We nodded.

"Good. Now, that being said, Dillon, I have something to tell you. You would have been the next up no matter how many people had requests in. Henley asked me for that. I was going to honor that request. Turns out it wasn't necessary to pull any strings because you and Cow were the only candidates."

Henley. I'll be damned, I thought.

"Now, back to the issue of the dogs. You'll both go through a week of leash handling drills. By that I mean you'll snap a leash to the fence and learn all the motions of dog control. You'll learn the commands for sit, down, stay, heel, and stuff like that., and you'll do it until you're sick of it but you won't touch a dog until I decide you've learned what you need to know. You'll also learn how to bust his ass if you don't get immediate obedience. And," he paused and looked at Cow, "you'll learn how to handle him if—when—he goes for you."

"I've decided you get Blackie, Cow. And you get Argo, Dillon."

I glanced at Cow and he sat calmly, the only sign of apprehension was a slight pallor around his mouth.

"I decided to give Blackie to you," he said to Cow, "because you're substantially bigger than Marshal Dillon here. Argo weighs about eighty four pounds. Blackie checks in at about one-o-two. No offense, Dillon, but Cow's got you in size."

That was for sure. I weighed about one-forty five. Cow was about two-ten. "None taken," I said.

"You'll need all the ass you got if Blackie goes for you. That's a strong animal.

"Understood," said Cow.

"Understand this...all of these dogs will turn if the opportunity presents itself, and that includes Argo. If he's sick or pissed or if there's a bitch dog running in the antenna field and he wants to follow and you won't let him you can get bit. So just because he's not Blackie, that doesn't mean you're out of the woods."

My roommate, Carlos, had no corner on the macho market, he was just more obvious about it than the rest of us. It still applied to me and Cow, as well as the rest of the Marine Corps. And I suspect it still applies to most young men of that age. No matter what the chances were of being bitten or mauled by the dogs, we couldn't just stand up and say, hey, fuck this. To do so would be worse than any pain the dogs could inflict on us. It would bring the unbearable kind of pain that comes with the disdain of your peers or worse, a suspicion on the part of your fellow Marines that you might be that most awful of things.

A coward.

Some things are, and will remain, universal and the egos of young men are one of those things. We wouldn't—couldn't back out now. The Gods of Macho would not allow it.

So we accepted what we were issued. I would get my Argo and Cow would get the redoubtable Blackie.

You may think I'm being overly dramatic about this dog, but I'm not. To this day, over twenty-five years later, Blackie is still quite simply the most wicked dog I have ever met, rest his dark soul. And he's one of the only dogs I've ever seen that actually had yellow eyes. Much later in my tour of duty I would see first hand just how incredibly vicious he really was.

So we drew our gear, which consisted of a leash, choke chain, heavy collar and belt carrier for it all, and began our training. We learned that there were three classifications of working dogs in the military at that time. One was a patrol dog, which was trained in a similar manner with police dogs. These dogs could work closely with people other than their handlers, or work crowd control without devouring small children. They would attack only on command.

Then there were scout dogs. These dogs were used to locate whatever enemy you happened to be looking for at the time, using their keen noses and hearing and could be used for article searches, that is, to locate mines or booby traps. They had only a minimum of aggression training and could also work closely with people.

And last, but certainly not least, were the sentry dogs. These dogs were essentially war dogs. Highly trained in aggression to a hair trigger edge, they would bite anybody anytime and anyplace with or without command, even, on occasion, their handlers. These were our dogs, although ours were cross-trained as scouts, also. This was necessary to locate any potential saboteurs in the antenna field who might come in under cover of darkness to damage the antennas. Which happened. Thus the rank structure for the dogs.

Anyway, our training began. We learned the different leash techniques involved in drill, grooming, daily training—and self-defense. Starting that day we would be the only ones who would feed our dogs so that they began to bond with us. We fed our dogs cautiously, and learned to clean the runs of the dog's waste. This process is a joy, and is done daily by whichever dog man squad happens to be watch on at the time. Unless, of course, you happen to be the new guy. Then you do it all the time, at least until you start patrolling with the other guys when it again becomes a shared assignment.

So Cow and I became intimately acquainted with the art of picking up dog shit. It involves a shovel, a bucket, and most importantly, a hose with a pressure nozzle. Because you actually have to go into the runs to clean them. All of them. Surprisingly, I learned that the dogs would not attack that hose.

You always shouted the command, "Get in your house!" before you entered the run, then locked the lock behind you so that you were locked in with the dog. So that if he gets you, he can't get out to get anybody else. Comforting, eh? The first few times I did it I had paranoid visions of myself being mauled and lying there bleeding while waiting for someone to come along to subdue the dog that was standing over me snarling. Anyway, the dog would see the hose and run for his house, which was located at the far end of the run. You always kept your eyes on the dog, and the hose between you and him. If he started to come out on you, you sprayed him with the hose, and he would back off, snarling, into his house. When you finished scooping, scraping, and hosing you backed out of the run, the magically protective hose still between you and the dog. Then you locked the run, and repeated the procedure with the next one, until all fifteen had been done. Like I said, a joy.

The day came when Schmidt walked up to me, tossed me a new leash and said, "Take him out." I had been talking to Argo daily, when I fed him and in odd times in between. He seemed pretty relaxed toward me at this point, and when he saw me approaching with a leash and choke chain in my hand, he began to wag his tail and prance in circles. He hadn't been out of his run for days now, since Henley left, and seemed content with the idea of a change of handlers. Still, I was cautious when I opened the run and slipped inside. I gave him the command, "Heel," which he immediately did, placing himself at my left side. I slipped the choker over his head, leaned forward and shouted, "Dog coming out!" I waited a five-second span, then shouted again, "Dog coming out!" This was to prevent anyone who was careless enough to walk along to face of the runs without paying attention from getting a severe bite when your dog suddenly appeared beside him. It also warned other handlers of your impending appearance so that they could get their dogs well away from your gate. The dogs would fight savagely if they came in contact with one another, which I would discover later through first hand experience, much to my intense chagrin.

With the second shouted warning, Argo lunged forward, and I proudly walked him from his run for the first time.

Unlike my first meeting with Alfie, like Bogey once said to Louis in 'Casablanca'—it was the beginning of a beautiful relationship.

9

Shorty and the High Contact Incident

Shorty Callahan, the little guy I had met in Philly, was an extraordinary person. In a place full of as strange an assortment of oddballs, freaks and just plain weirdos that anyone could ever hope to accidentally collect in one small setting, Shorty managed to stand out as exceptionally gifted in the weird department. When I first met him in Philly he seemed relatively normal other than the fact of his admitted tendency to break things, but then I didn't get to know him well enough to realize that he could be—and often was—a walking disaster.

He lived up—or down—to his nickname because he was only about five—four. He was physically fit, toned and muscular, because he read Batman comics all the time and worked out like a crazy person to emulate his hero, the psychotic mythical character Batman. After getting to know him it would not have surprised me in the least to find him running around in a cape like a crazed, shrunken crime-fighter. But there was a big difference between the two that had nothing to do with size.

If it could be screwed up, Shorty could screw it up in fine style, and quick.

I didn't know this about Shorty when I first met him, of course. It took time and the witnessing of several small disasters, all of which contained Shorty at their swirling center. I began to get to know him a little better just after my new assignment to dogs. Shorty was assigned to Post Two in the afternoons, so each day after my training session I would pass him on my way back into the main compound, and he would greet me with the now inevitable, "Howdy, Marshal."

By then I had become so used to that stupid nickname and its usual manner of delivery that I would respond automatically with a simple "Howdy," and either pass on by or stop for a brief conversation. Shorty was witty and entertaining despite being a disaster magnet, so it was usually fun to stop for a chat with him. Often he would produce a small pipe, dig in his pants pocket for his stash, "Smoke-um peace-pipe, Marshal?" We would smoke dope right there on post because nobody would pass through post two but squids on their way to the big communications building in the center of the antenna field. We didn't wave it in their face of course, but they didn't stop to ask and we certainly didn't stop them to tell them that the two guys standing at the booth were smoking dope as they drove through the gate. They studiously avoided us and that was good.

The only person of that ilk we worried about was Chief Warrant Officer Fifer, USN.

CWO Fifer, USN, hated Marines with an unbridled passion. It was the topic of much uncharitable conversation among us. We theorized that his mother had undoubtedly been frightened by a Marine at some point, possibly when she had been a streetwalker in San Diego, and he carried that trauma with him. Or that his real father was a Marine, and he kept that a deep dark secret and hated Marines as a result the same way Hitler hated Jews because he was allegedly part Jewish. CWO Fifer, USN, as we always referred to him, would often make complaints against us to the base commander, a nice person named Lt. Commander Evans, who seemed at least as fond of us as Fifer detested us. Commander Evans would then pass the complaints on to our Commanding Officer, Major Moran, who was now commonly known among us as Major Malfunction, for increasingly obvious reasons. This had the effect of causing Major Malfunction to become even more withdrawn and twitchy, and the complaints were never acted upon. That had the further effect of making CWO Fifer, USN, even more hostile towards us. He couldn't do anything to us himself as since we weren't in his food chain and weren't insubordinate or disrespectful to him, to his face anyway. This was a source of considerable frustration for the Navy Warrant Officer.

We were kept apprised of the CWO Fifer, USN situation by our Seabee friend, Sunshine, who communicated with the regular Navy guys much more than we did, "Man, that fucker hates you guys. He told Chief Reichenbach that he wants flush you all down the shitter and he will bust you guys the first chance he gets." This pleased us greatly, knowing CWO Fifer, USN held us in such warm regard.

So, anyway, we had to keep an eye out for CWO Fifer, USN at all times, especially when we were smoking banned and illegal substances while on duty and at our posts. This was a practice that was frowned on by both the USMC and the USN, and getting caught doing so could possibly even jar Major Malfunction out of his lethargic state of hibernation long enough to make us suffer the wrath of the Uniform Code of Military Justice. CWO Fifer, USN would be immensely pleased if that happened.

One afternoon after training with Argo and cleaning runs, I was headed back to the barracks and there was Shorty on Post Two. He greeted me in the usual Gunsmoke idiom, then asked, "Wanna smoke a bowl?"

I looked around and the area seemed quiet enough and traffic to Oz was limited, so I said, "Sure." Shorty produced his pipe and a large leather bag of Moroccan hashish. He loaded the pipe, then put the bag on a shelf in the guard booth behind him, and we fired it up. After a few pleasant tokes I began to relax and get the buzz that stuff brings with it and that I had rapidly become accustomed to.

I had just taken a huge lungful of smoke and had turned, holding it in, when CWO Fifer USN, turned the corner about thirty feet away in a gray Navy truck, obviously on his way out of Post Two to Oz. And he was headed right for us like a great white shark. Shorty was standing there with the hash pipe in his right hand. He didn't see Fifer coming, so all I could do was turn back toward him and say, in a loud stage whisper accompanied by a cloud of smoke, "Shorty! Fifer!" Then I turned back toward CWO Fifer USN and whipped up a sharp snappy salute, hoping to distract him just for a second so Shorty could get rid of the pipe. But it was way, way too late. Fifer was already at the booth.

Most people would have fallen apart like a cheap suitcase at that point, and I felt my stitching begin to unravel somewhat, but Shorty didn't. He quickly cupped the pipe in his saluting hand and whipped up a crisp USMC salute with the pipe held against his palm and up his wrist. CWO Fifer USN glared like usual at us, then begrudgingly returned our salutes as he began to pass the guard booth.

It was then that Shorty remembered the bag of hash on the chest level shelf in the booth behind him. It would be easily visible to CWO Fifer USN as he drew abreast of the booth. Shorty's face paled, but there was only one thing to do. I watched in mounting horror as Shorty began to lean at the waist to the left, keeping his upper body between Fifer and an unobstructed view of our one-way ticket to Portsmouth Naval Penitentiary. With his hand still touching his brow in the salute position he leaned way to his left as Fifer passed.

I was ready to collapse into a quivering bag of jello-like nerve endings, but CWO Fifer USN didn't stop. He just returned Shorty's salute in that sloppy fashion squids have, looked at Shorty like Shorty had a large antler growing from the middle of his forehead as he leaned himself to a nearly 45 degree angle. CWO Fifer USN then drove on through the gate and into the antenna field in the direction of Oz.

Shorty and I watched as CWO Fifer USN faded into the figurative sunset. I felt drained and relieved at the same time.

Shorty hitched up his gun belt in an exaggerated imitation of the old movie cowboys, spit on the road, then said, "And don't come back if you know what's good for you! Right, Marshal?"

I was still more or less speechless because terror tends to do that to me, and just nodded my head. But, because I had to be cool and not let Shorty know I had just about wet myself, I said the only thing that would come to me at the moment. Staring at the rear bumper of CWO Fifer USN's truck I said in a feeble squeak, "Yep. Git along little doggie," and made a shoo fly gesture with my hands. Shorty and I both burst into the laughter of the safe, and I went back to the barracks amazed at his quick thinking, not to mention his physical coordination.

It wasn't the last time we would have a brush with CWO Fifer, USN.

In the meantime though, life went on—as did our partying. I was still in training and hadn't been able to walk post at night with Argo, so I was basically on a day shift mode for now, which was great for partying and the accompanying irresponsible behavior. I had always been skilled at irresponsible behavior and with the discovery that I liked smoking banned substances, I was honing my skills to a razor edge.

I found there were two types of guys stationed at Bouk. There were the smokers, and then there were the drinkers. I finally met my second roommate, a little guy named Jerry Davis, who had been on thirty days leave. He was a juicer extraordinaire and had earned the dubious if obvious nickname of Jerry the Juicer, because he was shit-faced most of the time. But he was harmlessly benevolent and silly when he drank so at the most we just had to pour him into bed or pick him up from the bathroom floor where he would decide to nap when he was good and smashed. There were a few others like that, but by far the smokers were the largest part of the population. And it showed. It was Jerry who had shown up drunk for the Chaplain's impromptu Sunday service that the Caddy for Jesus had told me about.

We would gather in a room at night and fire up the stereo along with the water pipe and, with Led Zeppelin, Deep Purple or the Moody Blues pounding the walls, we would fill the room and ourselves with smoke. It was on one of these evenings that Shorty, The Master Of Disaster, nearly got us all put away.

One of us, I think it was Termite, got his hands on a Cheech and Chong album, *Big Bambu*. Inside this album was a huge rolling paper about the size of a piece of legal pad paper. A real, giant rolling paper with glue on one end and everything. It looked like it could hold an astonishing amount of weed, and in the interest of empirical science we decided to see just how much that could be. We often traded old clothes and boots to the local Moroccan villagers—who we referred to as Bush Moes—for plain old marijuana when we tired of the hash, and they seemed to have an unending supply and would give us piles of the stuff for a pair of trousers and boots. So, one evening, much to our delight, we manufactured a joint about the size of a prize winning cucumber, and with lighters ablaze, proceeded to test it out.

Now, we didn't just throw caution to the winds when we did things like this because we had to watch for Gunny Favor. Gunny wasn't a real stickler for the rules, but we knew better than to put it in his face. He Old Corps enough to resent something like that and we knew it, so we were careful around him. He had a woman in town and left the base each evening around six. One of us would go into the hall to the telephone and call the main post, Post One, to see if he had signed out yet. If he had, the gloves came off, the volume on the stereo went up, and the weed and hash came out.

This night as we stared in amazement and reverence at the giant joint, Cro said, "Somebody go call Post One and see if the Gunny's gone yet."

Shorty, already stoned as always, spoke up, "I gotta go to the can. I'll do it while I'm out there."

We sat around and waited for Shorty to return, rubbing our hands together in anticipation of once again getting stuck to the wall. When he walked back into the room, Cow cocked an eyebrow at him and said, "Well?"

"Well what?" Shorty replied with his usual sharpness.

"Is the Gunny off base or not?" Termite asked.

"Oh, yeah. Yeah, he's gone." Shorty said with conviction, and all began to abuse that substance with enthusiasm.

A joint the size of this one produces a great deal of smoke, especially when there are six guys enthusiastically puffing away on it, and soon the room was filled with a dense cloud of highly intoxicating smoke. As the music pored from the speakers, we got mellow.

Suddenly there was pounding on the door. Startled, we all sat up, except for Shorty, who was in a stupor. Termite reached over and turned the music down. "Who is it?" he demanded.

"Gunny Favor," came the somewhat forceful reply.

In unison, we all turned our heads and looked at Shorty. "Shorty!" Cro whispered, nudging him with his foot to get his attention, "I thought you called Post One!"

"I did! I called and he was gone."

We relaxed a little then, thinking it must be Schmidt or The Deacon or one of the other guys, miffed at not being invited and just trying to scare us by imitating the Gunny's nasal voice.

"WHO is it?" Cow called, determined to get to the bottom of the issue so we could get back to the business of destroying our brains.

"Gunnery Sergeant Favor, United States Marine Corps! Open this goddammed door. Now!"

Oh, shit. It was the Gunny, really no shit. We were oh so screwed and we knew it. The room was so full of smoke that it looked like London in an old werewolf movie, but there was no place to go or even to hide. No escape. None. We were trapped. And doomed.

We all looked at Shorty again and he looked around helplessly. "I thought

I called," he said with a weak little grin. Cow and Termite both reached for his throat at the same time, then I spoke up.

"Guys. There's nothing else to do. We open the door." I walked over, flipped the latch, and opened the door. There, standing in the waves of smoke that came rolling out like the California surf, was the very, very angry Gunnery Sergeant Favor. I had devoted a large part my brief career to pissing off People In Authority, but seldom had I seen any of them mad enough to be in tears. Even I, master of attitude, rarely reached the lofty goal of making supervisors cry. Gunny Favor stood there, his chest heaving as though he were hyperventilating, and his eyes were a bright red. Tears were actually starting to trickle down his face and his fists were clinched tightly at his sides. If you don't think a black man can have a red face, you've never seen anything like this.

Oh, boy, I thought. And it really was not my fault this time.

Gunny Favor exploded, "You stupid sonsofbitches! What the FUCK is the matter with you? HUH? You gonna smoke this shit and let so much smoke out that I got a high contact just walking through the hall!" He said, "high contact" and not contact high, unconsciously adding another phrase to our ever growing lexicon. "Let me tell you motherfuckers something. If I ever catch you being this stupid again, I will have your sorry, sorry asses in Portsmouth. Do you fucking idiots read me?" One by one he made eye contact with each of us in the room, stopping in front of us one at a time. We were all standing at attention now, and replied, "Yes, Sir," in turn. Most humbly, I might add.

"I know you smoke this shit. Jesus fucking Christ, I'm not stupid. But if you ever, EVER, wave it in my face like this again I'll see to it you suffer more than you ever dreamed possible." This went on for quite some time, and let me tell you, nobody on this planet can chew ass like a Marine Corps Gunnery Sergeant. It is an art that they have mastered, and mastered well. When he finally stalked away, still mumbling to himself as I had often seen people unfortunate enough to be in charge of me doing, we all looked at each other in disbelief.

He had us cold. And didn't bust us.

He wasn't pissed that we smoked. He was pissed that we were stupid and disrespectful towards him enough to be careless about it. It was lesson learned, and we never again filled a room with that much smoke. And thereafter, when we did party a little more extensively that usual, we made damn sure that he had signed off base.

As he left we all sighed with relief and relaxed, then Shorty said, "Whew! That was close!"

We all turned our attention back to him. "Shorty....!"

"What? *What*?"

10

Dog Coming Out!

The next day I ran Argo through the obstacle course. The obstacle course was yet another self-contained compound with different objects set in a large circle that the dogs, upon the command of the trainer, would navigate. They would climb ladders, crawl over, under and through a variety of other things, all while running at the Dog Man's side. It was fun for both handler and dog, and was a good method to see if the handler really did have control over a notoriously flaky dog. There was no leash used in the O course, so you had no method of control other than verbal commands. If he turned on you during an O course run, well, you had a problem. You had better figure out a way to get control because it was just you and him. Nobody could help you.

Within a few months I was to witness that very thing, and it was a gut-clenching experience.

Argo and I had been spending the last several days on aggression training, and I was beginning to feel comfortable with his response to my commands and to me. Aggression training consisted of physically attacking a protective suited aggressor and the dogs loved it. It, too, took place in the confines of the obstacle course compound but it was a leashed drill, so the handler had physical control most of the time. Except when the dog was on the actual attack. They would charge the suited aggressor viciously, hitting whichever part of the suit that stuck out first. We generally thrust out an arm for them to take, and they would usually accept this offer. They would then do their best to tear it from your body until given the command "Out!" by their handler. Most of the time they would come out. Sometimes they wouldn't, and had to be "choked off" of the sleeve, which is exactly what it sounds like. The handler reached under the dog's throat, grabbed a handful of esophagus, and squeezed for all he was worth. When the dog couldn't breathe any more he let go of the suit and the handler dragged him away. It sounds cruel, but the dogs seemed to think it was the price to pay for a good time because almost all of them had to be choked off from time to time. It was also good practice for the handler in case he had to choke an overly aggressive dog off of a real person.

I was really nervous—well, okay, scared—the first time I was suited up in the aggressor role. But it became a thrill after I got used to it and I would miss no opportunity to suit up. I was fascinated with the way each dog displayed his personality on the hit. Some, like King Kelly and Hasso, were fast, chompy, hyper biters who would come up the sleeve toward your face if you let them. Mutley, whose real name was Baron but, because he was so dangerously treacherous, had been nicknamed after a sneaky cartoon dog of that time, would come around the offered sleeve every time and try to hit you in the body to knock you off your feet so he could get at your face. Or he would go for your groin. He was mean sonofabitch, long and lean, and he walked like a panther, with his shoulder blades working up and down and his head and eyes shifting from side to side. He and his handler, my new found friendly enemy, Alfredo Morales, were an excellent match.

And then there was the ubiquitous, ever vicious, Blackie.

Blackie would hit you like a thunderbolt. Nothing sneaky there. Just straightforward I'm-gonna-take-you-out linebacker style hitting. He would bunch somehow on impact with the sleeve then, still at full speed, would uncoil his powerful body and use his shoulders and chest to try to twist you down. He knocked me off my feet three times and each time I managed to twist and fall face down so I could cover my face until Cow got him off. Once he actually pulled hair out of my head before he came out. Thankfully, he usually came out on command. Then he would just stand there and stare at me with those eerie yellow eyes like he was thinking, "There, you bastard," before trotting back to the heel at Cow's side. When it was Blackie's turn to hit, everybody stopped to watch and we would walk away afterwards shaking our heads and saying, "DAMN!"

One day after training we put the "Loose Dog" sign up, then settled down to smoke and talk. The subject of Blackie and his savage attitude came up, and I, being an insatiable reader of Burroughs, Tolkien, and Howard, as well as being slightly stoned, said, "If he had been born a human he would have been a warrior king."

Alfie Morales looked at me, took a hit off of the bowl, wiped it dry, and passed it to the left, as was the unwritten rule of smoker's etiquette, and said with his usual sneer, "If he had been born a human, Marshal, he would have been locked up as a psychopath."

Which was most likely true, so I let the issue drop.

Another part of my training involved actual tactical searches in the antenna field during the day. One of the guys would go hide in the huge field, and Argo and I would have to find him. Argo would scent the wind, then when he got a scent of the intruder his head would go up sharply and he would swing into the wind, facing the direction of the target. I would then crouch down behind him and say, in a whisper, "Whatcha got, bud? Whatcha got?" If it were human, he would become very excited. I would then look between his ears, using them as a sort of sight to see where we were going, and then I would say in an excited whisper, "Find him, Argo!" He would begin to pull madly, scenting all the while, until we found the bad guy. If we lost the scent or if the wind shifted, I was taught how to reacquire it by using a method called 'quartering' the wind. I was also taught how to approach and overcome an armed bad guy without getting my ass shot off, which I felt was important. And how not to use a flashlight at night unless you absolutely had to because it lets every bad guy in the world know exactly where you are so they can come and kill you. And I learned to bust my dog's ass if he barked at night for the same reason.

Anyway, after several days of aggression and tactical training, then several more days of the O course, Schmidt called me over and asked, "So, how do you think you're doing?"

"Fine," I replied, and we were. Argo was responding well to me. He was an agile intelligent dog, and had no problems with navigating the O course. And because of his intelligence, he knew what was expected of him tactically, and trained me as much as Schmidt and the other Dog Men. That made things easy on both of us, and actually made me look good.

Schmidt nodded his head, "I have to agree with you. You go out tonight with Alfie and Cro. Second Boonies." The dog night patrols were divided into two shifts. Sunset to midnight was the first shift, known as First Boonies. Midnight to dawn was the second, known as Second Boonies. My indoctrination into a real patrol situation would come in the dead of night.

I nodded my head and looked at Argo, who was looking back at me with that intelligent "So-what now?" look that I would get to know very well.

Schmidt continued, "Groom him up, then put him away so he can get some rest. You go get some, too. You're gonna need it. Be here at 2330, dressed and armed."

Moroccan sunsets are the most beautiful in the world, at least in my experience. At this point, twenty-five plus years and many other countries later, I have never seen more consistently beautiful sunsets than I saw right there, and that day was no exception. After grooming and feeding Argo, I walked back towards the barracks, marveling at the multi-colored sunset that was taking place over the Atlantic, four miles to my west. I stood on the balcony of the barracks and watched as the red, orange, and deep purple of the sunset gradually faded into a deep moonless night as the sun swung away to light up the east coast of the world on the other side of the ocean. I was just too keyed up to sleep, although Cro eventually passed by and convinced me to try.

I lay on my bunk and stared at the ceiling. Carlos was on first boonies and Jerry the Juicer was the Corporal of the Guard, so I had the place to myself, and it was quiet and peaceful. The time until I had my very first boonie shift dragged like it had a dead mastodon attached to it with anchor chains. I hoped I would do all right if we jumped a bad guy, or if Argo turned on me, or if Martians landed in the antenna field or whatever. Having an active imagination can be a positive thing, but at times like these I wished it weren't quite so damned lively. But the time did pass, and I was up and dressed in the green coveralls of the Dog Men, got my .45 and ammo from the Corporal of the Guard, and was at the kennels at 2330, sharp.

Cro and Alfie were already there and had coffee made in the kennel house. My relationship with Alfie hadn't improved, but the edge had been taken from it somewhat and I didn't have to be totally cautious around him all the time. They were sharing a bowl when I walked in but when they offered me a hit I declined. I didn't say so, of course, but I was afraid I would shoot my foot off, or worse, shoot my dog by accident if we hit on something, or fall down in a quivering heap if the action started. Alfie started to dog me because, like always, he was merciless when he perceived any weakness, but Cro tactfully intervened by clowning and I was spared most of Alfie's barbs.

Outside the dogs began to bark, announcing the return of First Boonies, Carlos with Hasso, a guy named Bill Denver (known as John Denver, naturally) with Brutus, and Cow, on his first boonies with Blackie. After they had put their dogs away for the night they joined us for a smoke. I noticed that Alfie and Carlos seemed very cool toward one another, almost to the point of open hostility. Carlos greeted each of us, ignoring Alfie who was sneering in his direction, then he and John Denver left. Cow stayed to talk to me, and he was pumped, "You're gonna love this, man!" The two of us walked out of the kennel house together, and he went on, "This is great. You're out there in the dark and it's so quiet. Check those stars." I looked up. The sky was blanketed with the clearest stars I had ever seen. The entire sky, from horizon to horizon, seemed to be layered with a glittering diamond dust that looked so close it made me want to reach up to take a handful for luck.

"Feel okay?" Cow asked.

"Truthfully? A little nervous, I suppose. I just don't want to screw up."

"You won't. You got your shit together for stuff like this, man. And Argo's a good dog. He'll see you through."

I nodded, appreciating the words, "How's Blackie?"

Cow sighed, and I could feel him looking at me in the night, "Truthfully? Scary. He's gonna get me sooner or later you know. I can feel him waiting."

"No, man, you can..." I started to give him the same kind of words he had just given me, but he cut me off.

"It's okay. I can deal with it. It's gonna happen, and when it does I'm gonna bust his ass. I think he knows that, too. That's why it hasn't happened yet. Just don't tell any of the other guys I said I was scared, okay?"

"No problem, man. I just...."

Just then Cro and Alfie came out of the kennel house. There was a slight red glow behind them as the door was shut. They used red light in the kennel house at night so their eyes would adjust to the dark before they hit the field, like pilots in their ready rooms. They called for me softly. Cow shook my hand and said, "Go get 'em, Marshal."

"Alright, Marshal, saddle up. Let's go catch some bad guys," said Cro.

I went to Argo's run, and he was spinning in anticipation. At my command he ran back to his house so I could let myself into the run. He returned and eagerly came to my left side in the heel position without a command. I put the thick leather duty collar on him and snapped the heavy leash to it. Three runs down I heard Cro shout, "Dog coming out," then repeat it after five seconds, and he and Rolf were out and ready. Across the courtyard I heard Alfie do the same, and he and the treacherous Mutley were out and ready.

I yelled, "Dog coming out!" waited, then did it again and suddenly I was out, with Argo pulling me toward the rear gate that led to the antenna field. We got our spacing as I had learned during training, then the three dog teams quietly slipped out into the darkness of Second Boonies.

It had begun.

11

The White Lady and the Turd Lake Monster

That was the night I learned all about two legendary creatures that supposedly haunted the Moroccan night, the White Lady and the Turd Lake Monster.

Of course, as we entered the antenna field, I had no idea that my education that night would include chapter and verse on those two questionable legends, but along with Cro and Alfie showing me the ropes of dog patrol, I was also indoctrinated with the local lore concerning the ghosts and monsters that supposedly wandered the antenna field nightly. It was an obligatory lets-spook-the-new-guy ritual and I recognized it as such and stayed quiet to let my two hosts have their fun.

The antenna field, as I had mentioned before, was five miles around. It was divided into three sections, like a giant pie, and each dog team patrolled and was responsible for a section. Patrolling was done individually and not together, at least in theory and by regulation, but being what we were, the regulations and Standard Operating Procedures were casually ignored. That night they started me on the side nearest the kennels and walked me and Argo all over the entire field, assuming the roles of tour guides and making sure I didn't get lost in the dark.

I was nervous at first, my heart pounding in my chest. My eyes were wide as I tried to adjust them to the darkness. Overhead those magnificent stars glittered with the intensity that can happen when there is nearly no light pollution to dim their shine, affording just enough light to navigate by. We walked slowly, with Cro and Alfie taking turns instructing and advising me. They showed me the antenna arrays we guarded and identified the trouble spots, antennas that were located close to the boundary of Perimeter Road, or that were close to heavy brush. Bad guys would sometimes cross Perimeter Road and, using the brush and the night for cover, do as much damage as they could before slipping back across the road. Once they were across they were safe. We could not pursue. Argo alerted twice during the tour and my adrenaline surged, much to Alfie's amusement, because both times it was either the scrawny, semi-wild cattle that ranged freely over the field or one of the many sheep that scrambled about, mixing their small flocks with the cattle. I would soon learn the difference in the way Argo alerted when it was a beast and the intensity of his alert when it was a man. It really didn't take that long, either.

After about an hour of walking they took me to a huge concrete cubicle that thrust itsef out of the sand. We took our first break there. "What the hell is this?" I whispered.

"It's an old French bunker from the war," Cro replied, his voice a deep bass even in a whisper.

"Yeah," said Alfie. Remarkably, he managed to keep a sneering tone even when he whispered. "There are three of them, one in each section. So, when somebody tells you to meet them at bunker one, two, or three, you'll know where to go."

As Cro and Alfie lit a bowl and settled back for a buzz, I walked around the object, curious. It was about twenty feet square, and about three feet of it stuck up above the surface of the desert. The walls were eighteen inches of concrete and there was a firing slit on three sides, and a low door down three steps on the fourth. We tied our dogs to a rusting machine gun mount still attached to each firing slit, and I took a look inside. The bunker was about six feet from floor to ceiling, and was partially filled with sand. There was a romance about finding a deserted machine gun bunker in the desert, and youthful imagination took off at mach two. We finally settled down and smoked, our backs against the bunker and our eyes fixed to the canopy of diamond pointed stars overhead.

That's when Alfie told me about the White Lady.

"Hey, Marshal, anybody tell you about the White Lady?"

"The who?"

"The White Lady. She's here."

"What? Where? What the hell are you talking about?"

"Back during the French occupation of Morocco there was this rebel Berber chief who hated the fucking French. He was smart, this one, and *mucho hombre*. He would ambush their patrols, disrupt their supply lines. Just raise hell in general with those *pendechos*."

"What's this got to do with a lady?"

"I'm getting to that. Anyway, they couldn't catch this warrior chief. He made fools of them over and over again. So they got frustrated and they took his wife and family hostage. His wife was a beautiful Berber woman. They sent word to him that if he gave up, they would let her go."

I had no idea Alfie could tell such a tale. I didn't think he had it in him. I didn't believe a word of it, mind you, but I was enjoying the telling so I just kept my mouth shut and let him tell the story.

"Anyway, they swore he would be treated honorably, like a soldier and a chief if he surrendered. He loved his woman very much, as a man should, so he came in under a flag of truce. They were supposed to meet right here, in this very field.

They killed him, Marshal, because they had no honor. And when the woman demanded to see husband they showed her his head. She went berserk! She snatched the sword from the officer in charge of the whole thing and cut him down, then she ran screaming at the others. They shot her dead."

Alfie swallowed, "She comes back from time to time now, Marshal," he nodded out into the antenna field, "sometimes you can hear her scream out here, and you can see that white dress she was wearing when they killed her floating away. It moves fast."

I shivered slightly at the eerie tale but I was careful not to let them see me. I knew Alfie could be brutal if you fell into one of his traps so despite the charm of the story in it's around the campfire sort of way I was wary, "Okay, Alfie. I believe you." I looked at the two of them, seated now on top of the bunker and staring out into the field. They weren't smiling. Cro tapped the ashes out of the pipe and slipped it into the pocket of his coveralls, then stood. I could feel him looking at me, a vague dark shape silhouetted by those stars.

"He's serious, Marshal. I've seen her. She didn't scream that night, but

I saw that white dress. Right over there next to the Helix tower. I tried to get Rolf to go over there, but he wouldn't go. So I went the other way. Never saw it again. They say you only see her once."

We were silent for a while. I had been confident at the start of the story that it was bullshit and was just intended to scare me on my first night on boonies but now, listening their intensity, I didn't know if they were pulling my leg—and doing a damn fine job of it—or not. I sort of suspected that Cro had smoked a bit too much fun stuff the night he saw that white dress, but I decided not to bring that into it. To play it safe I just grunted in acknowledgement and didn't say anything more about it. We got our dogs and continued on.

The next stop as well as the next spooky story was at the two-acre sized sewage retention pond respectfully christened by the ever-observant Marines at Bouk as Turd Lake. This time it was Cro who assumed the role of story teller and he started the story with "Now this ain't no shit….," so I knew it was just that, and I relaxed and let him tell the tale of the Turd Lake Monster.

It seems that a Dog Man and his dog had been ambushed by a bad guy one night. They fought, and the Marine and his dog had badly wounded the bad guy, then he and his dog chased the guy in this direction after he broke loose and ran. The bad guy stumbled into this pond and drowned. They never did find his body. But somehow a combination of the chemicals, germs and various mass animating cooties in the pond brought him back to life and he now emerges from Turd Lake on the darkest of nights, dripping with slime and moss, and prowls this part of the field, looking for the Marine who had killed him.

"Who," Cro assured me, "looks just like you." It was a typical, if creative scare-the-new-guy type of thing and was as transparent as crystal but they were having fun with it and I let them. Then, with a timing that could never be planned, some huge gas bubble or some unidentifiable something was released from the bottom of the pond and burst with a loud splash on the surface about thirty feet from where we stood. I nearly left my skin. That kind of sudden, unexpected noise after hearing all about the White Lady and the Turd Lake Monster in the dead of night can cause a man to downright embarrass himself, I'm here to tell you. And I did, crouching and grabbing at my holstered pistol with cowboy speed. Cro and Alfie laughed so hard they had to separate and sit down so they wouldn't lose control of their dogs. They pointed at me and he-hawed. Grumbling, I put the pistol away, humiliated.

Well, I'd done it now. I knew what this would bring tomorrow because the hope that they would keep their big mouths shut about my quickdraw reaction was too far fetched to even entertain. And I was right.

It was bad enough that I had the Marshal Dillon thing attached to me, as unremoveable and as indelible as a jailhouse tattoo, now I had a genuine Wyatt Earp, Matt Dillon every-cowboy-movie-you-ever-saw quickdraw episode to add to it. Those two bastards wasted no opportunity to spread the word. For weeks afterwards the "Howdy, Marshal," greeting was accompanied by a lightning quickdraw of a finger. I knew there was no chance whatsoever that I could get them to stop it and to try to get them to ease up on that stuff would only make it much worse so I didn't even try. I had some vague, pathetic hope that it would eventually die a natural death. It finally did, but the Marshal thing stayed with me like a bad reputation.

Anyway, the remainder of my first night on boonies night was spent touring the rest of the antenna field. Finally the stars began to fade, and we watched as the truck carrying whoever would be in Post 3, the tower, emerged from the compound and creep toward the COM building, Oz. As the gray light of the coming day took over, we walked back to the kennel house to put up our dogs for the day. We had really walked them, and they quickly moved into their runs to lie down. The three of us then went into the kennel house and lit up a final bowl. I drifted back to the barracks after that, hazy and relaxed. When I went to sleep that morning I dreamed vividly of a beautiful White Lady, eternally enraged, drifting over the sand of the antenna field seeking revenge on those with no honor.

It was a great story, but I put it aside and had forgotten it, really, until several months later when something happened to remind me very vividly of her and her story. Since I'm on the subject and it has no other bearing on the tale, I'll tell it now.

It was over the Christmas season in 1972, and we were running light in manpower so some of the guys could go home for the holidays. I was never into the Holiday Cheer sort of thing, so I volunteered to take some extra boonies so some more of the guys could go. During this time only two Dog Men were assigned each night, and one night John Denver and myself had second boonies.

We had gone directly to the old bunker after getting our dogs from the kennels. By now we had cleaned out the bunker and equipped it with candles so we could hang out there when we felt like getting stoned and bullshitting instead of doing our jobs, and that's how we felt this particular night. 'Twas the season, after all. After getting to the bunker, John Denver tied Brutus to a machine gun mount on one side, and I tied Argo to a mount on the opposite side. We then proceeded to light candles, smoke dope, and stimulate our intellects by reading comic books by candlelight to pass some of the night. It was a chilly, partly cloudy and somewhat windy full moon night. The clouds would cover the moon and it would be as dark as the bottom of a coal mine, then the clouds would part, and the field would be bathed in a brilliant silver light almost bright enough to read by. Denver and I had settled comfortably into the dereliction of our duty when, from somewhere immediately outside the bunker, came the most piercing scream I have ever heard. It was long and shrill and lasted all of five or six seconds. It made the hair on my arms stand up and shot an immediate shiver down what was left of my quickly melting backbone. Denver and I looked at each other, eyes wide, then right back down at our comic books. From the rusted machine gun mounts outside one of the dogs voiced a tiny whine. It was Denver who spoke first as he casually turned the page of his Spiderman comic, "Well, Marshal. Think we ought to go see just what the hell that was?"

I turned a page of the comic I was reading and sighed in resignation, "Wouldn't be my first choice but, yeah. Yeah, we should."

Reluctantly we put down our toys and emerged from the bunker, our .45's gripped in our hands. What we saw then was not encouraging. Both of our dogs were huddled against the side of the bunker, staring off towards the north. We untied them and told them, "Find him!" Those dogs didn't want to find anybody. They sat there slightly cowed, staring. This was spooky indeed, because it never occurred to us that our dogs could be scared of anything. We actually had to pull them away from the bunker. It was then that the moon came out from the clouds again, and we could see some sheep that were all bunched up together about a hundred yards away, looking in the same direction the dogs had been. We started that way, and could see cattle now, standing in the same type of bunch, all looking at some unknown thing.

Then, suddenly we saw it. A flash of white to our front, moving quickly away from us. We stopped in our tracks and right then the moon went back behind the clouds, plunging the area into darkness again, then we were plowing into the darkness in the direction of the fleeing whiteness, running after it full tilt, trying to see in the blackness and trying to catch whatever it was.

But, by the time we got to where whatever it was had been, it was gone.

The dogs began to act their normal selves, and we nervously laughed the incident off, convincing ourselves that we had seen and heard one of the strange nightbirds that dwell in the desert. We didn't try to diagnose the dog's behavior, or that of the cattle and sheep, because we didn't really want to know, or to look at it too closely. And for one simple reason. We had to be out there every dark night.

To this day I really don't know what we saw and heard that night. I'm not, and never have been, a believer in the supernatural but that morning I dreamed again of the White Lady and woke in the afternoon almost wanting to believe in her and her eternal quest for vengeance. I never saw her—or whatever that was—again. Cro's words came back to me about only seeing her once. I sometimes found myself hoping that the night I saw her—or whatever—was the last night of her quest and that she could finally find some peace.

I never did see the Turd Lake Monster, though. Probably just as well.

12

A Cold Blast from the Past

It was very shortly after my initial boonies baptism that we received some news that made us very uncomfortable indeed.

A new executive officer was on his way to Bouk. Our frolics in the Officer Free Zone would most likely come to an end soon, especially if this guy was a real Marine.

Mouse told us that the orders had come through and that the new company executive officer would be reporting in a week. There would be a welcoming ceremony, then Major Malfunction would be on his way home for a few weeks with what was left of his sanity intact. The amount of stitching still holding his marbles in a neat little bag was questionable, but be that as it may, we would have a new officer to contend with soon.

There was much speculation among us about the makeup of the new second in command. Would he be laid back, and just let the place run, like Major Malfunction? Of course, our Major Malfunction was one squeak away from a white coat and heavy medication, but that didn't count as far as we were concerned. The man left us alone, and with his impending departure looming and the possibility of some real Marine expecting proper discipline from us, he suddenly achieved a status similar to sainthood in our eyes. Would the new exec be a hard charger who would want to do USMC things like (gasp) inspections? That meant shining shoes, making beds, and doing all the military things that were just out of the question at the moment. During our smoke-a-thons there was much moaning over this possibility. And would he want to make us do the much hallowed, and heretofore ignored, USMC ritual of exercising regularly?

When this was brought up there was much more moaning. One of the things that the United States Marine Corps was truly good at besides shooting, saluting, hunting down and killing the enemies of this country, and marching, was PT. That's physical training. That means running three miles, doing push-ups, sit-ups, pull-ups, and anything else that had an 'up' in it anywhere, as long as it involves pain, and makes you sweat. This is a ritual back in the world that Marines went through everyday. Nobody had done it once since I had been here as far as I knew, not in the organized sense anyway. And nobody wanted to. With Major Malfunction safely locked away in his self-imposed asylum we never had to consider following the most basic regulations, much less one like this. The very thought of it was downright depressing.

We pestered Mouse to find out as much about the incoming XO as he could, and with his usual attention to detail and his connections with other clerks in other places, he dug about and reported to us. What he found just increased our apprehension.

He couldn't find out the name, but he found out that the new XO was a Second Lieutenant. An XO spot is generally reserved for First Lieutenants but with potential XOs for Bouk dropping like flies the Corps took what they could get. This was a mixed blessing. Second Lieutenants are often hard chargers who obey the rules, shine their shoes, and expect everybody else to do the same. They can be a pain in the ass as a result.

They are also relatively inexperienced and are therefore often stupid when it comes to dealing with experienced shit-head slackers like us.

We wanted a pushover, the way the much-revered Major Malfunction had been. In our ignorance we decided that a Second Lieutenant, no matter how gung-ho at first, could be properly trained given the right amount of patience and skill. We would have him housebroken in no time. So we relaxed and awaited the arrival of our new XO with only a small amount of trepidation.

The day finally came when the new XO arrived. Cow, Termite, Cro, and Freaky Deac, along with my humble self, all missed the arrival because we had all been huddled up in Cow's room staring out the window at the deliciously voluptuous and highly illegal shape of CWO Fifer USN's seventeen-year-old daughter. She had been bouncing around between the gedunk and the Navy Exchange for about an hour now. She had blonde hair and huge, bright blue eyes. A marvelously stacked young body swiveled and throbbed like German machinery beneath a creamy come-take-me-if-you-can face. We watched and commented from Cow's window, which happened to provide a very clear view of the shopping strip across the street.

"My, oh my," Termite said, chewing even more vigorously on the third toothpick in less than ten minutes.

"Yes, indeed," I agreed.

"Portsmouth," said Cro pointedly.

"Yes, *indeed*." I agreed with emphasis. The Marine Corps would frown mightily upon any dalliance with the innocent seventeen year old daughter of a Navy Warrant Officer. Even though she was obviously about as innocent as a female wolverine.

"That's the only good thing about white people," Freaky Deac said.

"What's that?" I asked.

"White women," he replied, not taking his eyes off her bouncing form.

"Yeah," I agreed, "I like 'em, too." Everyone nodded.

Termite sighed, "It's got to be jelly 'cause jam don't shake like that."

"That's trouble on the hoof for somebody," Cro said.

"There is no fucking way that mutant Fifer produced something like that," said Termite, "I wonder who the mailman was?"

On the heels of that observation Mouse burst into the room, "Hey, you guys! The new exec's here. Come check him out."

We were a lot more interested in what we had been checking out across the street but we reluctantly tore ourselves away and slouched out the door, headed for the back balcony where we could get a view of the company office and perhaps a view of the new speed bump in our lives.

"He's in with the Major right now. I think he kind of freaked when the Major peeked out his little door at him," grinned Mouse.

"We'll wait," said Cro, sitting down cross legged and pulling a bowl from somewhere.

It turned out we didn't have that long. Right at that moment the door to the Quonset hut that served as the company office opened and our new Second Lieutenant walked out with Gunnery Sergeant Favor at his elbow. They were headed for the barracks.

I've only felt like fainting twice in my life. Once was at my first wedding when I married my first future ex-wife, which was still some years in the future. And the other was when I could clearly see our new XO.

There was a sudden roaring in my ears, as though I were standing in front of a large box fan with it blowing in my face. "Hey, Dillon," said Cow, "you don't look so good."

"Oh, fuck."

"Yeah, man," said Freaky Deac, "you pale, even for a paleface. That's a nasty color for somebody to be. Yech."

"Oh, fuck."

"Man, what is wrong with you?"

What was wrong with me was the fact that I could now clearly see our new XO, and he may have been new to the rest of the group but he wasn't new to me at all.

It was Meyers.

"Oh, FUCK!"

Cow actually reached over and got me by the shoulders, "Okay, share. Give it up. What is your problem?"

"It's him." I stepped back into the doorway and peeked around the corner at the oncoming figure, one that I had hoped never to see headed in my direction again.

"It's who?"

"The Possum King, the sergeant I told you about from Lejeune. The one who hates me."

"It's *who*?" said Cow.

"Meyers, dammit. I told you all about him."

"Sergeant? I thought the XO was supposed to be a Lieutenant," said Cro.

"He is, man. He told me before I left Lejeune that he was getting a commission. I didn't believe him. Oh, fuck me. I am so screwed," I moaned.

"Oh, come on, Marshal," said Termite, "it can't be that bad."

"Oh, yes it can. He fuckin' *hates* me. He thought I was going to Iceland or some shit and when I found out I was coming here I really rubbed his nose in it. He wanted to kick my ass. And that was on top of the fact of the possum that shit on his new car seat. Oh, *man!*"

"The *what*?"

"I'll tell you about it later. Right now I don't know what to do."

"Well, brother man, you better think of something quick cause here he comes. And here I go," Freaky Deac disappeared into the barracks, which I thought was an excellent idea. I started to follow suit but it was too late. Gunny Favor had looked up and seen the small group on the balcony.

"Company formation!" he hollered, "Let's go! Fall in, people. Let's meet the new XO."

Shouts of "Formation!" echoed through the barracks. I was doomed. I had no choice but to fall in to my place in formation. I pulled my hat as low as I could get it without looking like something from Li'l Abner and started toward the basketball court where we held our infrequent formations.

It was not to be.

"Dillon!"

I froze in my tracks. I knew that voice all too well.

"Well, well, well. Lookie here." Slowly I turned around. Meyers looked every inch the Nazi still, even in civilian clothes. That same sneaky, vicious look was on his face as he grinned at me like a hungry wolf snarling. Behind his eyes was that same indefinable something I had recognized at Lejeune. "You forgot how to salute an officer, dipshit?"

I snapped up a sharp salute and didn't say a word. He nodded in return—Marines don't salute out of uniform—and I cut my salute. As the others ran past us on their way to the formation they saluted and he ignored them, drilling me with those death's head eyes. "You know, there is a God after all. You know what, Dillon?"

In the Marine Corps one does not become insubordinate to an officer no matter how much of a prick he may be. It can cost you greatly. At Lejeune I didn't care about anything because I really had nothing to lose, nothing that really mattered anyway, so I taunted Meyers for all I was worth. Things had now changed. First off, now he was an officer. Second, for the first time I had something to lose. If I got stupid I would lose Argo. I would lose my friends. I would lose, period. Because nothing at this end of the galaxy would have pleased Meyers any more than to see me shipped out of this place under guard. He had won, and I had lost. It was that simple and as clear as crystal to me. It was now up to me to keep that degree of loss under control.

"What, sir?" was all I could say.

The others had fallen into formation and were standing at attention, the Gunny barking orders for them to dress it up. I could feel their eyes on Meyers and me as I stood locked at attention, Meyers hovering tightly before me like great blond Nazi bloodsucking fly.

"Sir," he sighed, "that has a nice ring to it coming from you. When I found out that I had drawn this assignment I actually prayed, *prayed*, that I would get you in my command. And now look. I think God likes me," he smiled waiting for me to say something that could get me slammed.

I didn't say anything, but when he made the comment about God liking him I thought, *I doubt it*. I would have said so at Lejeune. But not now. He seemed disappointed and snapped, "Fall in, goddammit!"

I did a quick about face and ran to my position in the formation, aware of being very much the center of attention.

He stepped in front of the Company Gunny who saluted him and told him that we were all present or accounted for, then quickly turned and walked to the rear of the formation. To our left front we could see the company office. Major Malfunction had not made an appearance, but we saw the curtains move just a bit. He was watching from his cave.

"Now hear this, people," Meyers stood with his hands on his hips, drill instructor style. "I am Second Lieutenant Meyers. I am your new Executive Officer. As of right this second I am taking hands on control of this company. I will get to know each and every one of you. Two weeks from now I will become your acting Commanding Officer because Major Moran will be taking a well deserved two month leave. Know this: I know about you people. There are too many salty motherfuckers in this company. I have been briefed by command about you all, and I'm here to tell you all this. I am going to break this company's back. Know this also: You are Marines. You will look, act, and perform your duties as Marines."

Behind me, Termite moved the toothpick from its hiding place under his tongue long enough to whisper, "Oh, fuck. Here we go again."

"Before we go any further I have a message for Private Dillon and Lance Corporal Lawrence." That was Cro but I had so seldom heard his real name used that I hadn't known who he meant at first. "I was asked to give this to them by Major Moran just before he left, but I've decided to read it in formation."

He pulled a folded piece of paper from his shirt pocket, "Dear Major Moran," he read, "You don't know me, but my name is Kathy Henley. My brother was William Henley, who served in your command. He asked me, should anything happen to him, to write you and tell you how much he enjoyed serving with you. He also asked to send greetings to all the guys there, particularly someone named Marshal Dillon and Cro. Two weeks ago my brother shot himself. He couldn't deal with the dreams any more. I thought you should know. Regards, Kathy Henley."

I was stunned, and so was everybody else. Henley? How could he have done this? We thought he was getting better. And now this bastard Meyers had announced it like he was reading a personnel roster.

"Another one who couldn't hack it," he said, stuffing the now wadded paper into his trousers pocket. I felt a wave of rage wash over me at his callous attitude, and I felt it wash over the company like a breeze through a field of wheat. But again, I was impotent. I could do nothing, nor could anyone else.

"Be warned," continued Captain Bligh, "Prepare to shape up. Company Gunnery Sergeant! Dismiss the company and meet me in my office."

"Aye aye, sir!" replied Gunny Favor. He returned to his place at the front of the formation, "Company, dismissed!"

We fell out, stunned and enraged at Meyers. We were going to be at his mercy. Major Malfunction had turned him loose on us. I had a very, very bad feeling that this would get ugly and the rest of the guys were feeling the same. I had experience with the guy so his actions didn't surprise me, but the way he had delivered the news about Henley was a barometer that would give the rest of the guys a good feel for the storm he would bring with him.

We slowly walked back to the barracks where we spent the afternoon in misery. We didn't even smoke for fear Meyers would show up unexpectedly. We couldn't go to town because we all had boonies or watch that night, so we just sat around depressed, and they listened to my tales of what a miserable prick Meyers really was. The mood was grim. A bleak grayness had spread among us. Henley was dead. After surviving a year of intense combat in Vietnam he was dead by his own hand in Milwaukee. It just didn't seem right to us then, and it still doesn't even all these years later. We sat and talked, subdued by our grief.

Several of us had just sort of gravitated to my room, which had somehow become an unofficial meeting point, after formation. Cow, Cro, Termite, Shorty and Freaky Deac gathered there, bitter and angry that the news of Henley's death had been hurled on us like a bucket of dirty water by someone like Meyers. I wasn't above taking the opportunity to take a swat at the Nazi, "See? That's what I'm trying to tell you guys. This guy is a world class penis."

I needn't have bothered trashing Meyers. Nothing I could have ever said or done would have convinced the people at Bouk about his character as well as he himself had just done. I realized this as I listened to them talk, so instead of adding any more fuel to the fire I just shut up, sat back, and listened. A few more of the guys, Rock, Animal, Timmy Brunner, and Schmidt found their way to my room and soon there was a standing room only Meyers-bashing going on. It was great. Even Alfie showed up and stood off by himself, staring down at the floor in a sad way I hadn't seen from him before.

"Man," said Freaky Deac, "That was low life, just bustin' up with it like that. What was Major Malfunction thinking, letting that little fuck just come and trash Henley's memory that way?"

"I don't think Malfunction meant for him do it like that, Freak," said Cro.

"I don't see that happening, either. He probably meant for him to tell Cro and Dillon in private after formation." Termite spit his well-chewed toothpick on my floor and popped another into his mouth. I just looked at the shredded sliver of wood and didn't say anything. It just didn't seem important at that time.

"No," said Cow, "I think our new XO was trying to impress us with how hard he is."

"Well," replied Freaky Deac, "I don't think he's hard. I think he's a prick, pure and simple."

Alfie was standing to my right and a bit behind me just inside the door, slightly away from the group. I was the only one who heard him when he muttered, "The pure and simple is rarely pure and never simple."

I turned, surprised. He was still staring down at the floor seemingly unaware of being overheard. "Quoting Oscar Wilde, Alfie?" I asked. His head snapped up and he glared at me, "Fuck you, faggot."

He straightened, still glaring, then turned and stormed from the room, slamming the door behind him. The abrupt hostility of his departure got the attention of a few of the guys. Cow asked, "What the fuck was that about?"

I stared at the door. I didn't know what to say, so I just said, "Just Alfie being Alfie, I suppose."

And with Alfie *being* Alfie that was quite enough of an explanation. The incident was quickly ignored as the conversation once again turned to trashing Meyers.

"I know this guy," I told them, "and he's gonna get worse. Much worse."

"Well aren't you just a ray of fucking sunshine?" asked Termite.

"Trust me. It's gonna get worse."

*

We found out later, by the way, that Henley had stuck a .45 into his mouth and had blown the back of his head off when the dreams became just too much. The government shrinks had decided he didn't really need therapy anymore.

Thanks, Uncle Sam.

13

Pogo Makes a Move

I had told the guys it would get worse with Meyers and get worse it did.

Two weeks after Meyers arrived, Major Malfunction left on his long awaited vacation. He would be gone two months, leaving Meyers as our acting Commanding Officer. I knew right away that Meyers would become a Frankenstein monster, powerful and out of control.

I was right.

Meyers began to institute all those hallowed traditions of service in the Marine Corps. As we feared the inspections not only started but grew more and more frequent. Meyers began to gradually flex more muscle and became quite the topic of conversation among us.

"Man," said Freaky Deac in his usual succinct way, "this motherfucker gives *motherfuckers* a bad name."

Cro, who Meyers had just written up for having hair that was longer that regulation put it a different way, "This guy is interfering with my lifestyle." Cro shaved his head completely in protest, which I thought a bit extreme. It had just grown back in from his having shaved it the last time.

"He's been interfering with mine for a while," I told him.

Shorty, ever the innocent, didn't seem bothered by Meyers, "I dunno. He's not that bad. I mean, if we were back in the world we'd be standing inspections and doing P.T. It's not so different. We're still in the Marine Corps."

"Shorty," said Cow, "shut the fuck up." Nobody wanted hear applied logic when it came to Meyers.

We were right in the midst of Meyers bashing, a new tradition I had grown quite fond of, when my door flew open and Brunner ran in.

"Apache's coming!" he shouted, "tomorrow morning, 0700!"

He turned and fled, and all the guys jumped to their feet and started for the door. "Wait, wait!" I shouted and everybody stopped, turning back to me, "What the hell is he talking about? Who is Apache?" I was alarmed at the sudden, excited flurry of panicked movement. Sudden energetic motion wasn't the norm here and besides that, just a few moments before the room had been filled with morbid and bitter contemplation. Now it looked like a submarine when general quarters are called. I figured Apache must be a big deal, whoever or whatever he is.

I was right. He was.

"Apache is the dope dog from NTC, Marshal," the Freaky Deac explained on his way out, "We got his handler out of some shit in Kenitra a while back. Some guys from Sidi were gonna stomp his ass for being the dope dog handler. We intervened because we just figure it's his job and he has to do it like the rest of us and he's a Dog Man no matter what it is his dog does. Anyway, after we saved his ass he promised he'd call if Apache ever was scheduled to hit us. The man called in his debt tonight. Cool. Get rid of your stash. Your friend," he looked at me, "didn't waste any time after Malfunction left to slam us, did he?"

"He's not *my* friend. I think he ate all his friends."

They all started to make for the door again, but I had an idea that I thought might work well. To this day I have no idea where it came from. "Hey, Cro, you still got that hot plate?"

"Yeah. Why? This is no time to be cooking...."

"Trust me. Go get it," He wanted to argue that there was no time for games but I convinced him to help me for just ten minutes and he reluctantly agreed "This better be good or there's gonna be a showdown, cowboy," he warned.

While everybody emptied their rooms of hash and herb we boiled water. When it was at a good rolling boil we added a handful of well ground hashish, and when it dissolved it turned the water a nice shade of almost military green. We then took the pot of hash water and with *Jesus Christ Superstar* once again providing the background music, we initiated a bizarre christening, splashing it everywhere with great ceremony. Cro, now enthusiastic because he recognized the potential of the whole thing, assumed the role of psycho priest, carrying his ironwood staff and wearing his jelaba, and soon we had a small group of followers shouting, "Amen!" and "Hallelujah!" each time we christened a toilet, or the recreation room pool table, or the concrete stairs. Termite found a water gun somewhere and filled it with the stuff, then proceeded to spray everything in sight.

The end result was remarkable.

Apache arrived the next day, along with his handler, as well as the Colonel, and some very anal-retentive looking officers and senior NCOs. We noticed that they had brought an empty van with them, most likely to cart away all the offenders they expected to catch with their sneak attack. We were called to formation, and Meyers proceeded to read us the riot act with the battalion Commander, a Colonel whose name I have thankfully long since forgotten, standing to one side beaming his approval.

Meyers waxed wroth about the evils of drugs, and assured us that whoever was using the evil weed would this day pay the price. He knew, he said, that it was only a small percentage of us, but those bad seeds must be rooted out, dug up and removed before they contaminated the rest of us. I actually had to bite the inside of my cheek to keep from smiling. If they only knew. I noticed that Gunny Favor stood at attention, letting no expression cross his face. Meyers did a fine act for the Colonel's benefit and we stood and listened.

Apache was then called forth, and he and his handler, a tall thin Brother, went to work. If you've ever seen a real drug dog work you know just how efficient and effective they can be. They can find almost any amount of drugs secreted almost anywhere, and they alert their handler by pawing vigorously at anything they scent drugs in. Or on. Apache was no exception. He was good at his business. Unfortunately for him, and for Meyers' little surprise bust, everything in that barracks smelled like hashish. Except, of course, our rooms. Apache alerted on the stairs. He alerted on the toilets. He alerted on the sidewalk. He alerted on the grass where we had dumped the last of the hash water.

At first the anal retentive officers really focused on Apache, cheering him on as they watched because they thought they would lead at least a few sobbing miscreants away to jail, where the evil dopers could regret their actions accordingly. Some people live to punish others, finding a degree of self-satisfaction in inflicting punishment that they would find in no other aspect of their lives. We had a flock of those types standing before us now. They would stop at nothing to see someone, anyone, go to jail after this day's work.

For a while after that whenever I would begin to feel a bit guilty for being so rebellious at authority just because it was authority I would think back on that afternoon. Then I would feel all better.

One group of senior NCOs even got a shovel and began to dig the lawn up where we had dumped the hash water that had been left over after our barracks baptism. They no doubt assumed we were stupid enough to bury something anywhere near the barracks. Actually it was buried about a thousand yards away in the antenna field. Good luck to them if they wanted to look for it there. It took them about twenty minutes before they finally figured out there was nothing where they were busily digging. They had a nice deep hole dug by then, too. When the group of Anals, as they became known to us, realized that Apache wasn't hittin' on shit, as we said in those days, they became disgruntled, then angry.

Eventually they called Apache off and, disgusted, they all got in their little Navy vehicles and left, the disappointingly empty van bringing up the rear. The darting looks sent in the general direction of Meyers were not lost on us. It was obvious to us that he had set this whole thing up, selling Battalion on the idea. We were careful not to cheer or smile and wave as they departed because we could see, even from our formation, the little pulse thumping in the side of Meyers' head. He had been cheerleading Apache on, hoping to see one of us—most likely me—busted so soon after taking over for Major Malfunction.

Freaky Deac put it well while Apache was working, "Look at that motherfucker. All he needs are pom-poms and a little skirt. Cheerleading little prick."

Termite had another question as he watched the Anals leave, "Hey, Marshal, you're the brain. Answer this. When a bunch of assholes are together, is that a flock of assholes? A gaggle of assholes? A herd of assholes? What's the proper term?"

"I think that would be a knot of assholes, actually," I replied.

He stuck another toothpick in his mouth, "Oh. Just wondering."

Angrily, Meyers told the company Gunny to dismiss us. He stormed away, angry because nobody went to jail. It was a very satisfying thing to see.

After the failed raid we were pretty full of ourselves, and I found myself to be the hero of the hour again because of my idea concerning the hash water. The guys felt we had won a great victory. I wasn't so sure we had won anything and I tried to voice a cautious warning because I knew Meyers. I was shouted down in the exultation of the moment, so I relaxed, and we all got stoned and joked about Meyers, the abortive attempt to bust us, and the look on the Anal's faces when they knew they'd been had. Gradually, though, the conversation began to turn to other things, as stoned conversations will.

"Hey, Marshal," Termite said, "what are you gonna do after you get out of this green motherfucker?"

"Know what? I don't have a clue. Something with no authority figures involved, I can tell you that. You?"

"Man, I'm gonna get me a Harley and do whatever I please, go wherever I want to go. I refuse to have ambition."

"Sounds like a fine ambition, not to have ambition. How 'bout you, Cow?"

"Finish school. Teach maybe. I don't know." He shrugged. "What about you Deac? What are you gonna do when you get out?"

"Well, my white brethren," he said, taking a hit from the pipe and passing it to his left after wiping the stem, "I may not get out."

"What?"

"I may just stay in this green machine."

I was appalled, "You're kidding, right?"

"Nope. I'm not for sure yet, though. But you never know. Beats workin' on the docks back home, or workin' in a fucking grocery store or some such shit. You never know—maybe someday I can dance all over dickheads like Meyers. What about you, Shorty?"

"I'm going back to school. I'm good at math, so I'm thinking of going into engineering."

"Engineering?" Cow looked at him like he had just grown another head, "Remind me not to cross any bridges *you* build." He looked at Brunner,

"What about you, Timmy?"

"I am going back to L.A.," he lowered his yellow glasses and looked at me, "that's Lower Alabama to all you Yankee farm boys. And I'm going to take advantage of the generous nature of my rather wealthy parents. I intend to spend as much of my inheritance as possible without working a lick. I'm like that, you know." He hit the pipe and passed it, a satisfied look on his face. He was obviously comfortable with being a leech.

"I got a question for you, Marshal," said Cro, drifting into another subject, "How come Meyers hates you so much?"

"Oh, lots of reasons. I wouldn't kiss his ass for one thing. He requires regular sessions of ass worship and I'm not giving it up. But mostly he hates me because of the possum."

"Possum? What possum? Okay, you said something about a possum before. What the fuck are you talking about?"

I took my hit from the pipe and passed it to my left, "Well, it's like this…"

And I told them the story of Sgt. Meyers, me, and a possum.

Meyers and I had quite the history of animosity between the two of us. He did his best to make me miserable, and I did what I could to return the favor. I had to be careful, of course, because he was a sergeant and I was a lowly private. Therefore I had to do what I could to make him unhappy in a more subtle way. He knew this. And that's why Meyers suspected that I had been the one to put a live possum (they were everywhere at Lejeune) in his civilian car, where it immediately and copiously defecated on his front seat. I have been a fan of possums ever since and I don't like nasty little critters.

Actually, it hadn't been me who put it there. It had been an unlikely coalition of people who disdained Meyers every bit as much as I for his total inflexibility on anything involving the Corps rules and regulations, his skill at making people miserable, and the joy he got from fucking people over. A ridge running ass-scratcher named Spencer, who was from somewhere in the Kentucky mountains and was known around the company as Huckleberry, had actually caught the beast. It was a natural for him. A Latino kid from Los Angeles whose name I can't remember had picked the lock on Meyer's car door, while a black guy from Harlem, one Tyrone (T-Bone) Jefferson stood watch.

They gathered around me in a small conspiratorial knot as I lay on my bunk, sulking as usual after losing yet another run-in with Meyers. "Yo, Dillon," T-Bone whispered glancing about conspiratorially. "We got this, like, *thing*, you dig? And we want to know if you want to par-tici-pate."

Wary but curious I glanced at the three of them. "Participate?" I asked. "Participate in what?"

"Well, you see," he said. "It's like this. We want to give The Man a little token of our 'preci-a-tion. Show brother Dillon what we got, Huckleberry."

Spencer, who had been holding a laundry bag which I had at first foolishly thought actually held laundry, reached into the bag and pulled out the biggest possum I had ever seen and it was not a happy camper. Possums, I had always been told, are supposed to play dead when they're in situations like this one, with a large redneck holding them up by the tail. Well, here was one who didn't know that.

It was pissed. It thrashed and snarled, spitting and hissing like an angry cat. I was impressed and immediately saw merit in their plan and I didn't even know what it was. I just knew it was designed to somehow introduce Meyers to that thrashing and unhappy possum. Spencer stood grinning, holding his prize like he had given birth to it instead of having caught it somewhere in the surrounding wooded areas.

"Ok, that's great, Huck. Nice rat. Now, what do you plan on doing with this thing?"

Spencer put the angry possum back in the laundry bag and carefully pulled the rope that puckered the top tightly closed.

"We're going to give it to Sgt. Meyers. We heard he ain't been gitten' no possum. That's why he's always pissed off." All three were all grinning maniacally.

"Guys, I don't think Meyers is interested in Wild Kingdom. I don't think he'll want your possum."

"That's why we decided to leave it for him in his new ride. Sort of anon-nee-mus," T-Bone explained.

"So," the Latino kid whose name I can't remember asked, "you in?"

I wouldn't have missed this for an honorable discharge.

"Damn right I'm in, but I have one question. How come you decided to use a possum?" I asked.

Spencer looked at me like I was stupid, "Couldn't find a skunk," he replied matter-of-factly.

"Of course," I said as I heaved myself off of my bunk and strolled out of the squad bay with the confederates, "I should have known."

So, I'd been an enthusiastic and approving audience while the other members of the Sgt. Meyers Fan Club had dropped the squirming, enraged beast into his car. We all four then retreated back to the upstairs squad bay and watched from a window until Meyers opened his car door. By then the possum had worked itself into a fine rage and immediately went after a startled and dancing Meyers before making it's escape. We howled in laughter, stopping only when Meyers recovered his dignity and began glaring about, searching for the source of the mirth which he immediately figured belonged to whoever had placed the huge, angry, defecating possum in his new car. We had no idea the possum would crap on his seat, by the way, or that it was capable of such an impressively massive deposit. That was a bonus, as was the fact that the enormous pile of possum crap was an interesting, upholstery staining deep shade of purple. Must be the berries they eat or something. As we watched, Meyers headed for our barracks. I turned to the Latino kid whose name I can't remember. "Can I use your Bible?"

Meyers, of course, came looking for me with blood in his eye.

"You little fuck," he said, trembling with rage, "I ought to drag you down there and smear your nose in it like a fucking puppy."

I was sprawled on my bunk reading, the picture of innocence. "What, Sarge?" I asked, laying the Bible I borrowed for the occasion on my chest. I looked up at him, eyes wide with the look of the innocent lamb.

"You know what, you little bastard," he fumed.

"No, I truly don't, Sarge, but you seem really disturbed about something. Would you care to pray with me? I find that prayer gets me through times of tribulation." I put as pious a look on my face as I could muster and reached for his hand.

Looking back I can say that I felt a mixture of emotions at that moment. Pride was one, because it takes real skill to make someone's face really turn purple with rage. I mean, you hear about it all the time, but never actually see it. The other emotion was fear, because I thought for a second he was going to leap on me and pound me to a quivering pulp.

Luckily for me he managed to stifle the obvious impulse to beat me to death and stood there shaking with rage. A small, strangled noise came out of him and he turned on his heel, stalking away in a fury. He, of course, knew that if he'd beat me into jelly he'd have a hard time explaining why. The conversation in the Company Commander's office would go something like this:

Captain: And just what were you doing when Sgt. Meyers started beating you, Private Dillon?

Me: I was lying on my bunk reading my Bible, Sir.

Captain: Did you do anything to provoke him, Private?

Me: I just offered to pray with him, Sir.

The obvious complications of beating some gentle soul about the face and neck who had offered to share a prayer with you had not been lost on Meyers.

Anyway, I was downright flattered when he accused me. And since he couldn't prove anything and nobody was talking, especially my three amigos, I just let him guess about my part in it. After that every shit detail to come down the line was graced with my presence.

"And that, boys and girls," I concluded, "is why the Possum King hates me. Or part of the reason, anyway. Boy, those things can really leave a pile of shit, too."

They just stared at me for a second. "Dillon," Freaky Deac looked at me with a level gaze and said slowly, "you are one throwed off motherfucker."

"The Possum King. Pogo! That's him! Pogo!" Cro chortled.

The others quickly concurred with Cro that Pogo was indeed just the name for Meyers.

I objected to the Pogo nickname because I thought Walt Kelly's wisely philosophical little possum didn't deserve being associated with the likes of Meyers, but again I was out voted and booed down. My hero status for coming up with the hash water idea was quickly forgotten when they wanted to put a derogatory name on Meyers, and since they couldn't think of any other possum name, Pogo it would be.

I couldn't share their joy in the christening because I knew deep down that they could name him all the funny names they wanted and it wouldn't change one crucial fact:

This possum was a rat. And a sneaky, dangerous one.

14

The Great Bullfight

We figured there would be dramatic changes with Pogo as our XO and we weren't disappointed. As I expected, Pogo started conducting a weekly inspection of our rooms, uniforms, haircuts and all the other things that the USMC considered pertinent to maintaining good order and discipline. We considered these things unnecessary intrusions into our lives and a huge pain in our collective ass. Also, Pogo had done nothing to endear himself with anyone at Bouk with his callous act at his first formation with us. I knew him, and I knew he was trying to show how hard he was. All he showed anybody was how much of a jerk he was. He lost any credibility he could have possibly have had in just a few minutes where as it would have taken me weeks to convince people what he really was.

Then, as if dealing with Pogo and his bullshit wasn't enough of a reminder that we really were in the military, a new sergeant arrived to fill Piazza's empty position.

He was a tall bald guy by the name of Sgt. Wilson, who bore an unfortunate resemblance to Barney Fife—if Barney had been bald and on steroids—and he was immediately tagged with that name. The very first time he was introduced to us by Meyers, Termite, in his usual position just behind me in formation, muttered another of his editorial comments, "Jesus Christ! I wonder if he brought Aunt Bee and Opey?" I snickered at the unexpected comparison, which, unfortunately, got the attention of Meyers. He then decided that it was necessary to Make An Example Of Me. Since he would miss no chance to humiliate me, hoping for a suicidal response, he naturally did this in front of everyone. This started with the customary USMC ass chewing, with me standing helplessly at attention. It was concluded with the equally customary warning that I had better straighten up or he would see to it I paid for my attitude, it was time for me to get with the program, he wasn't going to put up with my shit here like he did at Camp Lejeune, etc., etc.

I left formation with my ass and my dignity thoroughly mauled. I wondered if there was some way I could just tape record one of those USMC ass chewings, thus saving Meyers or some future supervisor the time and trouble of telling me the same stuff I had heard numerous times in the past. Whenever he felt strongly that I had been remiss in my duty and started with his particular form of that tirade, I could just hold up my hand and say, "Wait a minute, Lieutenant," produce that tape recorder, bring myself to attention, and play the ass chewing, thus saving him the effort. He could go have coffee, or abuse a small animal or torture a Girl Scout or something until the tape had played itself out. To me, it was a thought with some merit.

I found Termite, who was much amused that I had been nailed when it had been he that had initiated the whole thing. I was threatening him with death and he was laughing and pointing at me when Timmy Brunner came into the room cradling that disgusting little J.R.

"Hey, guys, guess what?" J.R. made that squiggling, Cousin It sound, and Timmy continued, "Barney wants the oncoming watch here at 0700 in the morning for PT."

This was terrible.

There was much commotion over this, but since Barney was a Sergeant he would have his way. It was evidently a fact of life that we had just better become accustomed to. We didn't want to push him too hard just after he first arrived at Bouk because he was an unknown quantity and we didn't know how far we could go without serious consequences, so there was nothing to do except show up for PT, run the traditional three miles, then get away from the maniac as soon as we could. This first little go round wouldn't affect me anyway because I had second boonies that night, and in the morning my watch would start a three day weekend. The guys coming on would have to play little reindeer games with the new sergeant. Like it or not, it looked like we were back in the Marine Corps.

That night I reported to the kennels at the usual time. It was Cow, Carlos, and myself going out. We all slipped out of the back gate, agreed we would check our posts, then meet in about three hours at our bunker clubhouse.

I had the middle section that night. It held nine antennas, and was brushy and slightly hilly, with numerous small gullies and dips scattered over the post. That particular post was also known for the occasional bad guy slipping into it and damaging and antenna or two, then slipping out. I generally stayed more keyed when I was working that area. The night was overcast with a thick layer of clouds and in the resulting blackness I couldn't see a thing beyond a few feet. I was learning to feel my way through Argo, detecting changes in the ground through the leash that connected us and making my adjustments accordingly. It was a skill I would develop to a high degree in the next year. I suspect that it is similar to the way blind people can feel the subtle changes in the physical position of their seeing-eye dogs and make their adjustments as necessary.

Argo and I had become close, working as one living being instead of two, each responding to the slightest nuance of the other. It was a formidable creature that prowled to Moroccan night, one with a human brain and the senses of a well-trained German Shepherd. Not to mention a .45.

That night I followed Argo through the brush and up and down the slight hills from antenna to antenna. We had been at it for a couple of hours, and I was just thinking about heading to the bunker for my rendezvous with Cow and Carlos when, suddenly, Argo stopped.

I could feel the tension in him and I crouched behind him in the nearly impenetrable blackness. I could barely see him, but I could tell he was alerting on something hot. He was too tight for it to be one of those cattle or a sheep. I tried to peer between his ears but, while I could barely see his ears, I could see nothing beyond a couple of feet ahead of us. I whispered, "Whatcha got? Whatcha got?" He strained ahead, and I thought oh, boy, rock and roll. "Find him, Argo!"

Argo lunged forward, pulling me with all his weight. My adrenaline was pumping, and all my senses were screaming for input. I reached down and partly drew my pistol, then hooked the sight on my holster and used that leverage to jack a round into the chamber, then reholstered and snapped the flap back over the .45.

Argo pulled me to a spot between the two antennas closest to Perimeter

Road. We started down a small slope and plunged through some waist high bushes. There was a sudden violent eruption underneath me. Something huge came from nowhere like the ground exploded beneath my feet and threw me into the air. I did a complete flip landed hard on my back, the wind gushing out of me with a woof, but I still had control of my leash which was laced over my left hand. My flashlight had flown out of my coverall breast pocket and hit me a stinging smack in the face when I was mid air, then flew off to parts unknown. I could hear heavy breathing and could dimly see a huge shape just in front of me, and I scrambled backwards crablike, dragging the struggling Argo with me, to get some distance between me and whatever the hell it was we had just run upon. Argo was pulling hard toward the heavy breathing shape, wanting to attack, but I yanked him along with me. I had scrambled back about six feet when my hand fell on my errant flashlight. I grabbed it and stood up, pulling Argo to my side. With a shaking hand I pointed the flashlight at my unknown assailant and pushed the button.

There in the beam was one angry little bull. I had run right on top of one of the little semi-wild cattle, in this case a bull, which had been sleeping deep in the brush between those two antennas.

He had come to his feet in a hurry, throwing me back and knocking the wind out of me, and nearly scaring me to death. He stood there, head lowered, and shook his curved horns back and forth. A low rumble came from him, and he glared at me standing there in the glow of the flashlight beam. Now, those little cattle were notoriously timid and would trot away when we came anywhere near them so in my wisdom I decided I would just stomp my foot and yell, thus frightening the little bull away. So I did. I stomped my foot and yelled, "Get out of here!" The reaction it produced wasn't the one I had expected.

He charged.

He was pissed off and unafraid, and he lowered those wicked horns and came right at me. I dived aside, then Argo was on him roaring. If you think a dog can't roar, think again. Argo was on the little bull's face, biting and ripping furiously. The bull was bellowing and swinging those horns from side to side, trying to hook Argo. The dust billowed up around them in a cloud, backlit by the flashlight's beam. It was a scene from a nightmare story. I saw what the bull was trying to do with those horns and I tried pulling Argo away, but he had a hold on the bull's face and wouldn't let go. In the heat of the fight he ignored my frantically shouted commands to come out. I watched in mounting fear as the bull tried his best to impale Argo, charging back and forth and twisting his head up and down and from side to side.

There was only one thing left to do. I wasn't going to let him hurt my dog, the dog that was in there fighting to protect me. I dropped the flashlight and joined Argo in the fight.

I leaped in screaming unintelligibly and kicked as hard as I could at the bull's head. My combat boots pounded into the side of his head time after time and it was like kicking a moving cinderblock. The bull bellowed in rage as my boot thudded into his head again and again. He managed to throw Argo off of his face, then lunged at me, but Argo was back on him in an instant, still biting. I was shouting incoherently and cursing and kicking, sharing the blind berserker rage that consumed Argo and the bull. Then suddenly the little bull had had enough. He broke contact and backed away. The three of us stood there, chests heaving, staring at each other, then the bull, with a final rumble, whirled and trotted off into the night with his tail held high.

I watched him leave, then stood for several seconds listening to him crash through the brush as he retreated. I wanted to make damn sure he was gone before I checked Argo. When I was certain the bull had left the battle for good, I picked up the flashlight and shakily examined Argo for injury. To my immense relief I found that the bull had not succeeded in hooking Argo with those wicked horns. He seemed none the worse for wear.

He was happy. He leaped all over me like he was saying, "We showed that sonofabitch, didn't we?" We had indeed, and for the rest of the night I was floating on the cushion of adrenaline the unexpected fight had produced. We had just whipped a bull in a hand-to-hand fight after all. I don't know many people who can say that.

I met Cow and Carlos at the bunker later. They had heard the bull bellowing in the distance but they thought it was coming from the other side of Perimeter Road, so they hadn't investigated. I told them the story of the fight, well pleased with myself and Argo. Then Carlos asked a question that he felt was pertinent to the whole situation.

"Hey, Marshal," he said, "how come you didn't shoot him?"

I stopped and thought for a moment, "You know, it didn't occur to me. I could have shot him, huh?"

"You think?" Cow asked sarcastically.

After all the fear and concern and during the entire course of the hot fight it hadn't once occurred to me to draw my pistol. I could have, and with plenty of justification, shot that bold little bull. I just didn't. I leaped into the fight like a drunken Viking and didn't give a thought to drawing my pistol. My instinct for self-preservation will simply not allow that sort of stupidity under most circumstances. I still can't explain it.

The next day during afternoon training my story made its rounds among the other Dog Men, with various responses. Cro and Cow were convinced that I just lost my head in the heat of battle and didn't think to draw my gun. Alfie had another opinion, "It's a bull story all right. Bull*shit* story."

I felt my anger flash, "What do you mean?" I knew perfectly well what he meant but I wanted him to say it.

"I'm saying you didn't fight no fucking bull. You probably chased down one of those sheep and put your dog on it, faggot."

"First off, don't call me a liar. Second, stop calling me a faggot."

"Hey, if the ballerina slipper fits, wear it, *maricon*" he sneered, "and if you lie, you lie."

This drew response from a very unlikely quarter.

Carlos stood up when Alfie called me a liar and said, "You're a fine one to talk. You wouldn't know the truth if it bit you."

There was a quick, angry exchange between the two in Spanish, then Alfie leaped to his feet and the two were chest to chest in a flash. We pulled them apart and Schmidt ordered them to stand down, so they did. Alfie backed away sneering and gathered his gear. We watched as he left the kennels, still swaggering.

Later that night I asked Carlos, as we laid in our room listening to Armed Forces Propaganda Radio, "What's the deal between you and Alfie? I know there's more to it than you defending my honor. And you two are both Latino. You'd think you'd get along."

Carlos thought for a moment, then said, "Alfie has no pride. He only cares about number one. He isn't proud of his race and he has no honor, and he pisses me off for that because we need to be proud. We have that right. We've got a long history to base it on and we're a proud people, and sometimes those are the only things we got. Alfie doesn't care about any of that. He's only proud of himself. He thinks I'm a cliche', and I think he's a cartoon, a freakin' Frito Bandito cartoon. Every time somebody looks at him they think we're all like that. We're not. He's a poor example of a proud race. And it pisses me off because he'll never change."

In the background Karen Carpenter sang a new song in her rich, beautiful style and we listened in silence for a few minutes. He was a rabid Karen Carpenter fan, and he knew now that little secret was safe with me.

Carlos was right about Alfie. Alfie was a thug. A sometimes likeable thug, but a thug nonetheless whose probable future would likely involve the phrase 'burden on society'. I was silently mulling over the irony of the only two Hispanics at Bouk hating each other, when Carlos spoke up again.

"You know what I'd really like, more than anything?"

"What's that?"

"I'd like her," nodding in the direction of the nearest speaker which was reproducing Karen Carpenter's voice, "to sing me to sleep. Just once. Just to sit right beside me and sing me to sleep. I wouldn't touch her, I'd just listen. Now that, my gringo friend, would be something worth living for." As ambitions go that one was fairly modest, but as I listened to that velvet voice I had to agree with him. The song faded away and I began to doze.

I dreamed that night of the proud little bull who still roamed the antenna field with strength and honor, a prince of the bush.

I'm glad I didn't think to shoot him.

15

Accidents Happen in the Best of Families

It was just after the Great Bullfight that two more of the old handlers from the other watch left on their normal rotation, creating two openings on dogs. Termite had put in a letter requesting the assignment, and we were pretty sure he would be chosen since Termite kept a low profile and Pogo hadn't focused on him just yet. But, as far as we knew, he was the only one who had volunteered for the slot, and now there were two openings. We went around for a day or so asking some of the more select guys if they would like to be a Dog Man, but didn't get much in the way of positive responses because nobody really wanted to work with our insane dogs. We needn't have bothered.

Major Malfunction selected Termite for the job all right. He also selected Shorty Callahan.

Unknown to us, Shorty had put in a letter about the time Pogo crawled onto base. He never told anybody, and Mouse had neglected to pass on that little tidbit to the proper destination. That being us. "Sorry guys," he said sheepishly, "I knew there was something I was supposed to tell you, but I forgot."

"Mouse—Shorty will die up there," Cow said.

"Those dogs haven't killed anybody yet," I said.

"Not the dogs. One of us will kill him." We all nodded wisely in agreement with this and passed the pipe.

"Being around Shorty is like being in the blast radius of a grenade. He fucks everybody up that even comes close to him," Termite said.

"Man, how could Major Malfunction pick Shorty?" This from Alfie, the eternal pessimist.

"Alfie," Mouse said, "he doesn't know Shorty. All he knows of Shorty is his service record, which is good, no disciplinary actions, and fairly good evals from back in the world. He looks at stuff like that. Major Malfunction may be nuts, but he still knows how to do his job. Sometimes."

"What do you think, Marshall?" Cow asked.

I liked Shorty. The fact that he was a walking disaster wasn't lost on me, but I've always been a sucker for cases just like his and, in fact, I seem to attract them to me like flies for some weird reason. I looked like I was thinking for a second, then spoke, "It really doesn't matter what any of us think. Major Malfunction has spoken. I just think we need to help him along and keep him out of Pogo's sights."

"Yeah. And stay out of his way," said Alfie. "Things go wrong when he's around. He doesn't even have to be involved for your shit to crumble." Thinking back to the Gunny Favor incident the guys nodded their heads but agreed with both of us. It was Major Malfunction's decision, not ours. I suspected Meyers' hand was in there somewhere, too. That would explain why the Dog Men themselves hadn't been consulted about who was chosen as had been tradition previously. Meyers didn't work like that.

Shorty was due to start training the following Monday. That night I had first boonies, from dusk till midnight, along with Cow and John Denver. Argo and I passed an uneventful evening in the field by laying on Perimeter Road and watching those brilliant stars glitter overhead. Well, I watched the stars while using Argo as a pillow. He relaxed and snoozed. I dozed off and on myself, secure in the knowledge that no one could get within a few hundred yards of us without Argo detecting them and letting me know. Midnight rolled around quickly, and we met the oncoming shift of Carlos, Alfie, and Cro at the kennels. Carlos and Alfie were ignoring each other in fine style. They had been told by Schmidt that another fight at the kennels would cost them. This was hallowed ground. All personal differences were to be left outside the gate.

I noted that Carlos seemed more subdued than usual and I asked him about it. "Man, I don't feel good. I got a cold or something. If I didn't have boonies I'd be in bed."

"Tell you what. I'll stand your watch."

"No, man. You just got off. You got to be tired."

"I spent most of the watch laying on my ass on perimeter road with Argo. I'm fine. Go back to bed, dude. I want to stay out, anyway."

He finally agreed, and we both ignored Alfie when we heard him mutter, "Pussy."

Carlos was grateful though, and really didn't give a rat's ass just what Alfie thought. We traded pistols so he could turn mine in to the Corporal of the Guard. It didn't matter which warm body was out there, but each pistol was signed for and had to be turned in at the end of the shift, so mine had to be logged back in now. I would turn Carlos' in when Second Boonies ended at dawn.

Argo was excited to be going back out but around three in the morning both of us were a little tired. We found Alfie and Mutley near one of the helix towers and Alfie and I decided to slip back into the kennels for some coffee.

We put our dogs into their runs and made coffee in the kennel house. We were just having our first cup and being reasonably civil wit each other when the dogs started barking. Alfie cut off the red light and eased open the blacked out window, "Hey, Marshal. Shorty's at the gate, man."

"Shorty? What the hell does he want?"

"I don't know, but he's got that squid with him, the big one they call Slick."

I looked out and sure enough, there they stood, the diminutive Shorty nearly lost in the shadow of the huge sailor. Alfie and I walked to the gate, returning Shorty's greeting.

"Hey, guys," he said, as we opened the gate to let the two of them in, "you know Slick."

That was stretching things a bit since we had seen him around, but we didn't really know him. We greeted him anyway and watched him as he looked around nervously. We walked the two of them back toward the kennel house, and the closer we got to the runs, the more nervous Slick was getting, and we were watching him very closely, "Shorty, what are you doing up here at this time of morning?" I asked.

"Slick's tripping hard. His sister sends him blotter acid on the back of the postage stamps she puts on his letters. Pretty good, huh? She doesn't use spit to wet the stamps, she uses an eyedropper and puts liquid acid on 'em. That way Slick just cuts the stamp out, chews it up, and bingo! In thirty minutes he's cruisin'. This time his sister put a *lot* on the stamp. Anyway, he needed to walk a little to come down. We didn't want him to run into CWO Fifer USN or Pogo. He'd go meltdown if he did. We were talking to Timmy at Post Two and I saw you guys come in. I thought this might be a safe place for a while."

"So, you're babysitting, is that right?" Alfie asked.

"Yeah," Shorty said, "I guess so."

"That's one ugly baby," Alfie replied, with his usual charity.

Shorty looked pretty stoned himself as we settled back into the red lighted kennel house, and he produced a pipe, stuffed it full and fired it up. Slick, the tripping, already paranoid squid kept looking around nervously. He was spooky around us most of the time anyway, and he was scared to death of the dogs, so he sat in the red light, his eyes, with pupils the size of skillets, darting from me to Alfie. I looked at him for a minute, then asked a fateful question, "What's the matter, Slick?"

"Are those guns loaded?" he asked, pointing at Alfie's .45.

"Yeah, they're loaded. What'd you think, we could guard you squids with unloaded guns?" said Alfie, looking at him with the Alfie sneer. He looked over at me and said, "This guy's head's glowing in the dark."

"Oh, man, you guys be careful with those things," Slick said. The acid was obviously melting his brain into warm mush.

Shorty spoke up, "Slick, it's alright. Nothings going to happen." Shorty looked at Alfie, "Maybe you guys should unload your guns."

"I'm not…." Alfie began, but then Slick spoke up, "Yeah," he said, "that would be good."

Alfie looked at me and rolled his eyes, "Alright, Slick," he took his pistol from his holster, pushed the magazine release on the side and dropped the magazine. He then thumbed back the hammer, pointed the pistol at the floor and snapped the trigger on an empty chamber. "See, all empty."

At the snapping of the hammer falling Slick jerked like someone had suddenly slapped him. He stared at me while I drew my pistol and began to drop the magazine. Slick stammered, "Now, now be careful. People are killed with unloaded guns, you know."

I dropped the magazine, "Don't worry," I said as I thumbed back the hammer, "It's perfectly safe," I pointed the pistol at the floor, "see?" and pulled the trigger.

BAM!!! The .45 erupted, the explosion huge in the small room, and a huge ball of orange and green flame shot from the muzzle. Carlos! I had traded pistols with Carlos! He always carried a chambered round, I never did! In the orange muzzle flash I saw Slick spring to his feet. He made a shrill, strangled noise that sounded something like, "Waaaaaaa!" and bolted for the door. He shot through the door like a rocket, headed for the gate. Shorty latched onto the back of his belt, hoping to slow him down from his headlong flight, "Don't run, Slick! Don't run!" he shouted. But Slick wasn't listening, nor was he about to slow down. He obviously had decided in his acid soaked, melted-down brain, to put as much real estate between him and gun toting Marines as he possibly could. He had his head down and his shoulders bunched, and he was moving like a champion sprinter, with Shorty attached to his belt with both hands. Slick had the size and power of a fullback. Shorty was five-four. The last we saw of them was as they disappeared around Post Two. Shorty was still attached with his heels dug in, being pulled like a plow behind a runaway mule, a cloud of dust swirling in their wake. Slick never slowed down. I don't even think he knew Shorty was attached.

As we listened to Slick's high pitched noise disappear into the distance, Alfie sighed and looked at me, then at the pistol still in my hand, "Carlos' pistol, huh?"

I looked down at it, my heart pounding and my hand trembling, "Yeah. I forgot I switched with him."

We both looked back toward where Slick and his appendage, Shorty, had disappeared. We could see Timmy Brunner standing there watching them disappear as well. He looked over at us and shrugged, then went back into his guard booth.

Alfie sighed again, "See. All Shorty has to do is be around, and the world falls to shit."

As I holstered the now truly empty pistol I reflected that it would be difficult to argue that point right now. I then proceeded to go into one of my prayer-fests and thanked God, Jesus, Allah, Jehovah, Buddha, all of the saints I knew and any other religious symbols including once again those from Norse, Greek, and Roman mythology and anyone else that I could think of that I hadn't pointed that pistol at Slick in a childish attempt to frighten him.

The results of that kind of lack of judgement could have been disastrous.

Anyway, Slick never spoke to us again (despite profuse apologies offered by myself and Shorty) and would shy away from us like a skittish pony whenever we would come within thirty feet of him. Alfie took to sneaking up behind him whenever he saw him around the base and shouting, "BOOM!," which would cause him to jump, turn pale and leave the immediate area in a hurry, searching for a bathroom facility, no doubt.

Alfie. What a prick.

I wonder if Slick ever got over that fear of sudden loud noises?

16

Li'l Pogo's Amazing Drug Bust and Road Show

As the days went by it almost seemed as though Meyers was easing up on us somewhat. The inspections became less frequent, and even Barney eased up a bit on the PT, but that was probably because he was beginning to fear us a tad as he began to become more aware of his environment. As it should be, we felt. Meyers, however, was unafraid and he had no real reason to ease up. Cro was suspicious, "It's quiet out there, Marshal. Too quiet," he would say in that ridiculous TV cowboy voice of his. Looking back, I realize we should have listened to him.

Termite and Shorty became full-fledged Dog Men, mostly without mishap. Termite drew Nero, the old Sergeant Major. Nero was old and fat now, and laid back. He would attack on command but generally didn't give much of a shit anymore, and we all related with his attitude, so he was well liked. Shorty, on the other hand, drew Benno. Benno was a weirdly disheveled little dog, with a coat like a Chia Pet, and one ear that stood up while the other flopped off to one side. They were a good match and seemed to get along just fine, Shorty and Benno, and did the job as well as could have been expected.

Disaster still seemed to stick to Shorty like fly paper, though. Shortly after his training period he had taken to wearing a shoulder holster on boonies and as a result he lost his pistol one night when it fell out of the stiff new holster. He didn't even miss it until he returned to the kennels at dawn because he had gotten himself stoned into orbit around some distant star.

"Uh, Shorty. Where's your gun, man?" asked Carlos. We all stopped what we were doing and gathered around. Shorty grabbed his holster with a blank look on his face, "Oh, shit," he said.

"Shorty," I said, "when Pogo finds out about this you are fucked." There was no way to hide it either. Those pistols were turned in and accounted for by serial number. This was disaster. He had no time to look for it. So with his head held low he went to the Corporal of the Guard to report the loss of his weapon, a cardinal sin in the United State Marine Corps. We all expected Shorty to face a court-martial for it because Meyers, being Meyers, would have no mercy.

That day Meyers had the entire company on skirmish line in the antenna field, looking for Shorty's pistol. Somebody finally found it, too, laying in the sand, locked, loaded, and deadly. Shoulder holsters became forbidden equipment after that. Surpising all of us, Meyers never did anything to Shorty for that either except what's called non-judicial punishment. Shorty was confined to base for thirty days and fined one week's pay. Believe me when I tell you that this is a very, very light punishment in the Marine Corps for losing a weapon.

I found this astonishing. Had it been me who lost his pistol, Meyers would have had me court-martialled for sure, after he had me flogged. Go figure.

"See, man," Alfie said, feeling vindicated, "Nothing ever happens to that little fucker."

Shorty also lost his dog one night, the leash slipping off of his hand. Benno, who had alerted on a hedgehog or sheep or something, lit out for parts unknown. Shorty ran around the antenna field at 2 AM yelling, "Loose dog! Loose dog! Here, Benno!," for about an hour. We brought our dogs close to our sides until Shorty found Benno, or Benno found Shorty, whichever. With those two you really couldn't swear which one had been lost or who had found who in the end.

We decided we needed to get away more, for the sake of our collective sanity and we set out to find a way to do just that. Termite found, God only knows where, a 1960 Ford Falcon that he bought for a song. After fixing everything he could fix on it, it was still a ragged piece of junk. I still remember Cow, Freaky Deac and I walking up on him as he labored over it with a hand held torch, repairing some minor structural crack. When we realized he was welding a hole in the gas tank and hadn't even bothered to empty out the last few gallons of gas we scattered like a covey of quail. From a safe distance we loudly conveyed our opinions of his extreme stupidity as well as his obvious lack of anything remotely resembling a survival instinct. He just raised the goggles and looked at us with that Termite grin, stuck another toothpick in his mouth, and went back to work. Freaky Deac shook his head, "He's gonna die. Fuckin' white people." We left, expecting any second to hear a hefty boom notifying us when Termite ceased to exist in a fiery ball of flame, but somehow he defied all logic and various laws of physics and finished the project without exploding. He and I and Cow then proceeded to take that car all over Morocco. It was a standard, with the shifter on the column and it had no second gear. Parts for Falcons were scarce in Morocco so we never found a replacement for the worn out transmission. As a result you had to wind it out in first until the engine strained, then shift it straight into third, where it would bog down until it got up enough RPM's to cruise. And cruise it did.

We took that car from Casablanca and Marrakech in the south, to Tangier in the north, and from the Atlantic in the west to the Algerian border to the east. It was an amazing little beast with tons of heart, and never left us stranded anywhere despite our constant abuse. We found an 8-track tape player somewhere (the only radio stations we could pick up were all AM in those days, and were all in Arabic anyway, which is somewhat limited entertainment-wise) but after we had installed it, we were appalled to find that tapes were rare in that neck of the woods. The only two we could get our hands on were the soundtrack from "*American Graffiti*," and Elton John's "*Don't Shoot Me I'm The Piano Player*." The Black Sabbath tape at the kennels was taboo and stayed where it was. But we cruised through the Atlas and Rif Mountains, and on to and across the edge of the Sahara with those two tapes playing over and over. I still know every word to that Elton John album, and every time I hear "*Daniel*" I think of sweating (no air conditioner) or freezing (no heater), and being stoned to the bone (no morals) in that car.

We no longer had to depend on the Navy liberty bus to get us back and forth to Kenitra, either. We would spend our off days in town whenever we could afford it, coming back to base when we had to report for duty. Or when we had to report for morning PT with Barney. One morning the three of us drank an entire bottle of peach brandy on the way in for PT because we figured, with the stupidity of youth, that it would be fun to run when we were shitfaced. We were wrong. Ever try running three miles with a bellyful of brandy? Don't. Trust me. It's miserable, and we got what we deserved because we suffered mightily.

Everything was cruising along just fine when Major Malfunction went on leave. As soon as he was gone Meyers, who then became the acting commanding officer, took the gloves off.

Suddenly our lives became hell. We had stand down inspections twice a week. We were written up for things we had gotten away with for so long that we took them for granted, or just plain forgot we were supposed to do. Like keeping our hair regulation length, or shining our boots. He even wrote up several of us Dog Men for not shining our boots before boonies. Not only that, he inspected the kennels and made us get rid of the eight-track player and the black light. We had been able to hide all illegal substances because the "Loose Dog" sign on the gate stopped him from just coming in on us. He was the only officer to ever invade the sanctity of the kennels.

We put the eight-track player and the black light back as soon as he left, by the way. Some things are sacred.

This went on for six weeks. He ran rampant and took a sadist's joy in making us as miserable as he could. One thing we were grateful for, though, is the fact that for some reason he never came into the barracks. We felt as though we had a bit of sanctuary from him and as a result we dropped our guard. It was an almost fatal lack of perception on our part because the little bastard set us up nicely.

He had begun to call impromptu company gatherings in the tiny theater to discuss regulations, or to go over evacuation plans for the civilians and the squids on the base should it become necessary. We had gotten used to these gatherings and treated them as a matter of routine. It was exactly what Meyers wanted.

One day the word came out to gather in the theater, so we put what we were doing aside and answered the call of our illustrious second in command, yawning, scratching and rolling our eyes on the short walk over. After the entire company, except for those actually on post, were gathered in the theater Pogo sprang his little surprise.

"Afternoon, gentlemen," he said from the podium on the small stage. "Today we're going to do something different. Today we're going to have an inspection."

Okay, yeah, yeah. That's different, we all thought. Boy, what a surprise. An inspection. Yippee.

"This time we're going to be more up close and personal. One three man room at a time you will accompany me and Gunny Favor to your barracks where we will inspect each man's wall locker and other personal spaces. Any marine found with contraband will be subjected to disciplinary action immediately." Despite himself he had a smug 'gotcha' look on his face as he said it.

That was different all right. We were fucked and we knew it.

"Set up like a bowlin' pin," Freaky Deac whispered.

"You know it," whispered Cro.

Pogo had outsmarted us.

He had just lulled us into a sense of false security, then had sprung his trap. Like Cro had prophesied, it was too quiet, partner. We hadn't circled the wagons and now we would all be scalped.

The first group left with Pogo and the Gunny. Barney stayed with us in the theater to make sure we didn't escape into the Moroccan wilds or something. The Gunny carried a cardboard box about half again as big as a shoebox to collect any contraband they found. Termite looked at the box and said, "They're gonna need a bigger box than that." We all nodded gloomily, knowing the truth to that statement and wondering what the inside of Portsmouth Naval Prison really looked like and if they would make us fly back to the world in shackles like on TV.

"Oh, god," moaned Cow, "I'm gonna be somebody's prison bitch."

"Yeah," said Freaky Deac, grinning, but just as worried as the rest of us, "You're gonna be Tyrone's bitch and he's gonna make you wear sun dresses."

"This is no time for jokes, Deac," admonished Termite who, thinking about the large amount of illegal substances he had stashed in his locker, was a bit pale.

"I ain't jokin," replied Freaky Deac, swallowing nervously. The smile faded from his face.

One group at a time we were led to our doom. I felt like I was going to my own funeral as my group was called forward and marched without ceremony to the barracks. My roommates, Carlos and Jerry, didn't smoke so they had no hash or weed, but Jerry the Juicer had a half gallon of Crown Royal in his locker, which is considered contraband because USMC regs say you can't have alcohol in the barracks. Hypocrites. Jerry watched his booze go in the box and his name was written down by the Gunny. Carlos was clean.

Then it was my turn. In my locker they found a small stash of hash and about an ounce of weed. Pogo, naturally, was ecstatic. "Well, well. Look at this. Get out of this one, Dillon." I couldn't and I knew it. So did Meyers. He began humming the Marine Corps Hymn as he finished the search of my wall-locker, "Catchy tune, isn't it, Dillon?" he said.

I just stood there miserably at parade rest and watched my life flash before my eyes. He also found a beautiful pipe I had bought just the week before during one of our runs to Marrakech. It was one of a kind, made from blue blown glass and exquisitely designed. I was quite fond of it, but he took it anyway, and I didn't think it was prudent to bring up the fact that I was attached to it right then. It all went into the box, which was now full, and my name went onto the ever-growing list along with the substances I had been caught with.

We were ordered to wait in our room until the conclusion of the shakedown, so we sat glumly, pondering our fate at the mysterious and inconsistent hands of Military Justice, and still wondering what the inside of Portsmouth Naval Penitentiary looked like. It took about two hours, two hours of anticipatory hell, then the Gunny went through the halls shouting for us to fall out into formation.

As we left the barracks we were greeted by an awesome sight. There at the foot of the stairs was a large box like the type that movers use, nearly large enough to ship a washing machine in. We found out later that Meyers had gotten it from CWO Fifer USN, with whom he had hit it off well. Naturally. Termite had been right about their choice of containers, though. They needed a much, much bigger box than the little thing they had optimistically produced when they had sprung their little trap.

Because this huge box was full. To the top. There was booze by the bottle, and several kilos of hashish. There were bags and boxes of weed. There were pipes and papers and other paraphernalia of every description. Sticking out from the top of the box like a mutant octopus cast ashore by the tide was the huge water pipe Cro and company had first used to corrupt my tender virtue. Meyers and Gunny Favor were standing there, Meyers with a very pleased smile but the Gunny appeared to be in shock, staring into the box and not saying a word. Mouse stood by looking miserable with a notebook in his hand.

We quietly fell into formation, cautiously watching the Gunny and Meyers. We were waiting for the axe to fall. We, most of us anyway, would be going to jail and soon.

And then, fate stepped in.

A gray Navy truck pulled up and Major Malfunction got out. He was back two weeks early. He saw the two standing beside the box and made a beeline for it. There was an exchange we couldn't hear because we were too far away. We could see Meyers greeting Major Malfunction and waving his hand toward the over flowing box of goodies. He had the very same expression on his face a cat has when it proudly brings you a dead mouse. The Major stood for a second, staring into the box, then said something to Meyers.

Meyers' face fell and he said something back. The Major then became animated, waving his hands and pointing to the box. The Gunny, whose eyes had never left the box, nodded slowly in complete agreement with whatever it was the Major was saying. The Major then turned and stalked to his office, no doubt to return to the solitude of self-imprisonment.

The Gunny came over and told us to fall out and return to our rooms and not come out until we were told to do so. We went, wondering the whole way.

That night Mouse put us up to speed.

After the Major got out of the truck and walked up to Meyers it went something like this:

Major: What are you doing, Lieutenant?

Meyers (pleased with himself): I just busted them, Major. I have enough evidence in that box to put almost all of them away.

Major: You do, huh?

Meyers: Yes, Sir, I do.
Major: Do you know what you have in that box, you fucking idiot?
Meyers (stunned): Sir?
Major: I said, do you know what you have in that box?
Meyers: Well, sir, there's hashish and mari-
Major: No, you fool. You've got my career in that box, and the Gunny's. (Gunny nods sadly, understanding a long time before idiot Lieutenant).
Meyers (now confused): Sir?
Major: Just what do you think will happen when you prance your happy ass to Battalion and say, 'Colonel, Colonel, look at this. I just caught almost every Marine at this high security top secret base that *I'm second in command of* with loads of drugs and booze. Ain't you proud?' We'll all three be finished, you short sighted fool!

Meyers (comprehension dawning and now starting to stare at the box like it contained snakes): Oh.
Major: Oh. Yeah. Oh. Get rid of this shit, Lieutenant. This never happened.
Meyers: Get rid of it sir?
Major: Are you fucking deaf?
Meyers: But... what do I do with it?
Major: I don't care. Burn it, bury it. Fucking *eat* it. I don't care. But get rid of it. I was told you were fucking up, Lieutenant. That's why I came back early. Just in time, it turns out, before you fucked us *both* up with your stupidity. Now. Gunny, put 'em in the barracks until we clean up this mess.
Gunny (relieved and avoiding looking at Pogo): Yes, SIR.

Meyers' ambush had been a success. The problem was that it had been *too* successful. If they had initiated action on all of us their careers would have been over. In the Marine Corps a commander is responsible for everything in his command. If 90% of your command is simultaneously busted with drugs, you got some 'splaining to do, Lucy. Oops.

Meyers had not only outsmarted us in setting up this bust, he had outsmarted himself. He would be disgraced and relieved of his command. His career, the Gunny's career, and the Major's career were sitting right there in that box with all our stuff and he knew it now. Not to mention our short careers.

Unbelievably, we were safe.

There was no way Meyers would or could turn over the names, or the evidence. And he never did. All that stuff just disappeared. Even Mouse never found out what they did with it, and they sure weren't talking.

Meyers never again tried to pull another sneak attack like that, and we were once again reasonably safe. It was never again mentioned by any of the command rank at Bouk. Major Malfunction was incommunicado anyway. Gunny Favor would just look at us and shake his head from time to time.

Meyers, however, looked at us with pure hatred.

17

Simple Solutions

It was shortly after Li'l Pogo's Amazing Drug Bust and Road Show, which the debacle came to be called, that we heard of a place that made us pick up our ears. There was a rumor circulating among the bases about a town high in the Rif Mountains called Ketahma, a veritable Shangri La, where the Moroccan hash we smoked as often as possible was made. It was supposed to an exotic resort town of sorts, where European and American hippies gathered, drawn by the lure of cheap hash and the exotic setting. It struck a chord with us, being the curious types. We had the Falcon, we had three days off every other weekend, and we really had nothing better to do, so we decided to find Ketahma. If it was a real place, that is. It sounded too good to be true. So we decided to try and find the place.

We checked all of the local maps we could find with no luck. We couldn't know then that the Moroccan government had stopped putting it on maps several years before because of the region's major cash crop, hashish. They didn't want tourists flocking to the place and staying until their money ran out and becoming a burden, not to mention an embarrassment, to their government. The local authorities had a rather severe way of dealing with people who become a social pain in the ass, and that included wandering stoner hippies looking for a Nirvana just like Ketahma in which to let their brains rot away. So the Moroccan government decided somewhere along the line that if they stopped showing people just where the place was it might ease that problem somewhat. You might wonder just why they didn't move in and eradicate the place if they knew about all of the hashish being made and smuggled from there. The answer is, naturally, simple economics. We would find out later that local government officials were paid quite handsomely to keep their hands off of the place, and they did. And with the fact that the town wasn't on maps anymore it managed to keep a relatively low profile, much to the satisfaction of all parties involved.

Then, of course, there was us.

Finding Ketahma became a weird little obsession. Every time we would take one of our two or three day Falcon cruises around the country we would ask the locals about Ketahma, which is how we became certain that the place wasn't just a myth, but everyone was vague as where we might actually find it. Some said it was in the Atlas Mountains, others said it was in the Rif Mountains. It was finally located on a map by a very unlikely party.

Shorty.

While Termite, Cow, and myself were out wandering the countryside looking for clues to the existence of the place like the guy from King Solomon's Mines, only instead of being on safari we were in a Falcon and stoned, Shorty scratched his head, cleared the fog from his toasted little brain, and did something that made us feel like imbeciles. He went to the local library in Kenitra, found an old atlas of Morocco, and located the elusive Ketahma.

"A library," I said, feeling like an idiot. We looked at each other in amazement. It had never occurred to us that there could be libraries in Morocco. But of course there were. We had unwittingly become fine examples of The Ugly American Syndrome, automatically assuming that things like libraries and other advanced repositories of knowledge must only exist in modern, western countries and never thinking to look here for what we needed. We conveniently forgot that the Arabic world had universities, modern medicine, advanced science, fantastic architecture, great art and literature and yes, libraries while Europeans were still wallowing in the corruption, filth, and disease of the dark ages and learning to count by figuring out the number of teeth they had left after the age of twelve. We felt more than a little sheepish when we returned from one of our explorative jaunts to find Shorty in possession of our Holy Grail, a map to Ketahma. And just bursting to tell us all about it.

After our initial embarrassment at having Shorty just plain out-think us we were overjoyed. It really did exist! It was right there on the map! "The map *I* found," reminded Shorty. Yep, there it was, nestled in the very center of the Rif Mountains, with one winding highway up and in, and one equally winding way back down and out. We decided that our next three-day weekend would be the date of our trip to the Promised Land. There was only one small catch.

"I want to go," said Shorty, "I found the place."

Now, this was serious. It wasn't that we didn't like Shorty because we did, of course. Shorty could be witty, funny, and sharp and was really and all-round nice person. It was just that he attracted disaster unlike anyone I had ever seen. There were two points in finding Ketahma. One was just because it was there and it sounded like it would be fun. Two was to buy some of the local product and bring it back to Bouk. And since we intended to be transporting copious quantities of illegal goods, having a disaster magnet along did not seem like a wise idea. I was not convinced, "I don't know, Shorty."

Termite tried to be diplomatic, "You know, Shorty, there's no sense in all four of us getting busted. You should maybe pass on this one."

Cow was just plain blunt, "Fuck that. You ain't going.

This spawned much debate among the three of us. Much against my better judgement I pointed out that he was in fact correct. While we had been blundering about the country in search of clues to the location of Ketahma, Shorty went to the library and checked out a book with the map in it. "Making us look like idiots," I added.

"Wait a minute, Marshall," said Cow, "you actually want Shorty to go? He's a shit magnet!" He leaned forward, "What about that night on boonies when he was playing quick draw and his supposedly unloaded gun went off and he almost shot you in the foot? Remember that?" Of course I remembered. I didn't sleep for two days after that. The incident was never reported and he got away with that one, too, although a lynching nearly followed. "If we bring him along we'll get busted sure, or drive off a cliff or something." Cow had a tendency to look at the down side of things.

"Yeah," said Termite, "we'll all die."

"Except him. He'll be the only survivor. Nothing ever happens to that little fuck, just to everybody around him." Cow glumly stared at the floor.

"Oh, we won't die," I said, not comfortable with the fact that I had somehow become the advocate for Shorty to come along, despite nearly being a victim of his total lack of focus, "we'll just keep an eye on him. He'll be okay."

"It's not him I'm worried about," Cow moaned, "I'm too young and handsome to die. And I don't want to spend the rest of my life in a cell with the Moroccan version of Bubba The Buttfucker, either. If he comes along we'll get into shit, I just know it."

"Yeah," said Termite, "we're doomed."

"We're not—would you guys quit it? Okay, let's do this… We'll take a vote. If you really don't want Shorty to go, we'll vote on it and the majority rules." This perked them up and I could see I was about to lose in a swift and dramatic fashion. I didn't want to be the one to tell Shorty that he wasn't wanted so I raised my hand to put the vote on temporary hold, "But," I said, "If you guys vote down taking Shorty, you have to tell him. I'm not."

"Well, that sucks," said Cow.

"Oh, man," said Termite.

"That's the way it is, guys," I knew I had them. Neither of them wanted to be the one to hurt Shorty's feelings. "I'm not gonna tell him he's not wanted."

They exchanged looks and I moved if for the kill, "Okay, so let's vote. I vote he can come," I raised my right hand in that can-I-go-to-the-bathroom gesture used by schoolchildren and senators, "all in favor?"

There was some hesitation and more looks were exchanged, then the two hands slowly, reluctantly, went up in agreement, "Motion carries, Shorty's in. There now," I said cheerfully, "don't you feel better knowing you did the right thing?"

"Fuck you, Marshal," said Cow. They stood gloomily.

"We're doomed," repeated Termite as they moodily drifted toward the door of my room.

"Yeah," Cow said, then repeated his earlier gloomy prophesy, "We're all gonna die. And, just to let you know," he said as he turned the doorknob, "I'll strangle his little ass if he screws up. I promise. And it will all be your fault."

"Look, guys, everything will be fine, you'll see. And nobody will have to strangle anybody, not even Shorty," I said to reassure them. And to reassure myself.

As the door closed behind them I could hear Termite say to Cow, "I wonder if the Moroccan Bubba The Buttfucker will make you wear sun dresses like Tyrone?"

"Shut up," said Cow, evidently worried that the fact that he looked a little like a young, blond haired, blue eyed version of Tarzan might make him a favorite among the sexually deprived denizens of whatever Moroccan prison he would end up in due to some errant folly committed by Shorty, "That's not funny."

"Everything will be fine," I said again as their ensuing argument faded down the hall, "Just fine." I plopped down on a bunk and thought of Shorty's penchant for bringing disaster upon those who dared to orbit too close to the gravity well of mishap he carried around with him, and said to myself, "I hope." I looked at the door for a moment and briefly considered finding Shorty. I would put my foot down and tell him he couldn't come. I would just have to be hard. I would......

I would do nothing because it wouldn't be right. And, besides, we had voted. Even though I had used extortion to assure the outcome, like the unions, we had voted. And now, Shorty was coming along with us to buy and smuggle hashish in a land of drug growers, dealers, crooked cops and soldiers, and even dealers who would turn you in and get the hashish returned to them by a thankful constabulary. They get your money and their dope back. And the cops get to keep whatever cash they find on you before sending you off to some horror of a prison. Or so we heard.

"We're doomed," I mumbled to myself.

Shorty was adamant, "Look, you guys. If I hadn't found that atlas you'd still be looking for the place. I've earned a spot. And I want to go. It'll be great!"

This spawned much debate among the three of us. Much against my better judgement I pointed out that he was in fact correct. While we had been blundering about the country in search of clues to the location of Ketahma, Shorty went to the library and checked out a book with the map in it. "Making us look like idiots," I added.

"Wait a minute, Marshall," said Cow, "you actually want Shorty to go? He's a shit magnet!" He leaned forward, "What about that night on boonies when he was playing quick draw and his supposedly unloaded gun went off and he almost shot you in the foot? Remember that?" Of course I remembered. I didn't sleep for two days after that. The incident was never reported and he got away with that one, too, although a lynching nearly followed. "If we bring him along we'll get busted sure, or drive off a cliff or something." Cow had a tendency to look at the down side of things.

"Yeah," said Termite, "we'll all die."

"Except him. He'll be the only survivor. Nothing ever happens to that little fuck, just to everybody around him." Cow glumly stared at the floor.

"Oh, we won't die," I said, not comfortable with the fact that I had somehow become the advocate for Shorty to come along, despite nearly being a victim of his total lack of focus, "we'll just keep an eye on him. He'll be okay."

"It's not him I'm worried about," Cow moaned, "I'm too young and handsome to die. And I don't want to spend the rest of my life in a cell with the Moroccan version of Bubba The Buttfucker, either. If he comes along we'll get into shit, I just know it."

"Yeah," said Termite, "we're doomed."

"We're not—would you guys quit it? Okay, let's do this... We'll take a vote. If you really don't want Shorty to go, we'll vote on it and the majority rules." This perked them up and I could see I was about to lose in a swift and dramatic fashion. I didn't want to be the one to tell Shorty that he wasn't wanted so I raised my hand to put the vote on temporary hold, "But," I said, "If you guys vote down taking Shorty, you have to tell him. I'm not."

"Well, that sucks," said Cow.

"Oh, man," said Termite.

"That's the way it is, guys," I knew I had them. Neither of them wanted to be the one to hurt Shorty's feelings. "I'm not gonna tell him he's not wanted."

They exchanged looks and I moved if for the kill, "Okay, so let's vote. I vote he can come," I raised my right hand in that can-I-go-to-the-bathroom gesture used by schoolchildren and senators, "all in favor?"

There was some hesitation and more looks were exchanged, then the two hands slowly, reluctantly, went up in agreement, "Motion carries, Shorty's in. There now," I said cheerfully, "don't you feel better knowing you did the right thing?"

"Fuck you, Marshal," said Cow. They stood gloomily.

"We're doomed," repeated Termite as they moodily drifted toward the door of my room.

"Yeah," Cow said, then repeated his earlier gloomy prophesy, "We're all gonna die. And, just to let you know," he said as he turned the doorknob, "I'll strangle his little ass if he screws up. I promise. And it will all be your fault."

"Look, guys, everything will be fine, you'll see. And nobody will have to strangle anybody, not even Shorty," I said to reassure them. And to reassure myself.

As the door closed behind them I could hear Termite say to Cow, "I wonder if the Moroccan Bubba The Buttfucker will make you wear sun dresses like Tyrone?"

"Shut up," said Cow, evidently worried that the fact that he looked a little like a young, blond haired, blue eyed version of Tarzan might make him a favorite among the sexually deprived denizens of whatever Moroccan prison he would end up in due to some errant folly committed by Shorty, "That's not funny."

"Everything will be fine," I said again as their ensuing argument faded down the hall, "Just fine." I plopped down on a bunk and thought of Shorty's penchant for bringing disaster upon those who dared to orbit too close to the gravity well of mishap he carried around with him, and said to myself, "I hope." I looked at the door for a moment and briefly considered finding Shorty. I would put my foot down and tell him he couldn't come. I would just have to be hard. I would......

I would do nothing because it wouldn't be right. And, besides, we had voted. Even though I had used extortion to assure the outcome, like the unions, we had voted. And now, Shorty was coming along with us to buy and smuggle hashish in a land of drug growers, dealers, crooked cops and soldiers, and even dealers who would turn you in and get the hashish returned to them by a thankful constabulary. They get your money and their dope back. And the cops get to keep whatever cash they find on you before sending you off to some horror of a prison. Or so we heard.

"We're doomed," I mumbled to myself.

18

The Flight of the Falcon

We went around and collected money from everyone the day before we left. About twenty of the guys donated to our venture because they were tired of the Bush Moe weed. When we finally pulled out of the main gate of Bouknadel we had money, time and, thanks to Shorty, a map to Ketahma. I secretly hoped the map was correct and wouldn't lead us to some border somewhere, never to be seen again. It was, after all, something Shorty had been involved in.

Cro once again became our psycho priest and blessed the expedition by smoking a bowl and tapping the ashes out on the hood of the Falcon in the weird ceremonial fashion he had. After that little ritual we were set and with Elton John playing over and over in that eight-track player we chugged our way east in the little Falcon to the Rif Mountains.

It was, in the words of Jerry Garcia and company, a long, strange trip. The country of Morocco is a beautiful land, a land of exotic and powerful images. During the first day of our trip to the Rif we were on a narrow highway that wound itself among some low, rolling hills. We hadn't seen a town for some time and just as the sun was about to set we came around a curve atop a series of low hills. There in the distance, nestled on a hillside, was a small town. It was all in white in the Arab style and partially surrounded by a high white wall that probably dated from the time of the great sultans. The setting sun was like a spotlight on the place and it seemed to be deliberately illuminated, as if proud of its shining isolation on that distant hillside. It was like a scene from an Arabian Nights story, slightly magic and mysterious, and it was not hard to picture the Berber horsemen that once held these hills galloping in and around the village in the last rays of a closing day. We stopped by the road and sat on the car and just looked at it as the sun slowly faded, the spire of the town Mosque the last of the town to be favored by its light. As the shadows crawled up the hill and the light slipped upward to the top of the spire, some trick of the wind, combined with the awesome silence of the place, brought to us the sound of the *muezzin* singing his final call of the day for the faithful to come to prayers. We sat in silence, watching and listening, not willing to move or speak for fear the spell would be broken, until the first stars began to twinkle over the hills and the little town finally faded from view, swallowed by the night as if covered by the protective hand of God.

When the first cool breeze of the night caused us to shiver, we climbed back into the Falcon and continued on, still slightly awed by the experience we had just shared. Nobody spoke for several minutes until Termite said, "Wow." We just nodded and sat quietly because there just wasn't anything else to say.

Termite, who would let no one else pilot his beloved Falcon, drove all night until about three in the morning, when we finally stopped to sleep for a while. When we woke the next morning about eight we discovered with the light of the new day that we had made it to the eastern edge of the hill country we had been driving through for most of the previous day. To our right were the dun brown hills from which we had emerged in the night. To the left was the edge of the Sahara. It stretched as far as the eye could see, grim and brown. A hot breeze was beginning to blow off of it, causing tiny dust devils to kick up out on the flat sand and the day was already beginning to heat up. To our southeast were the jagged sillhouettes of the Rif Mountains. It took us about four hours to reach them, driving in a blast furnace of heat. The Falcon had no such thing as air conditioning so we had to drive with the windows down until it became so hot it was like sitting in the wash from a jet engine. The heat was amazing, and we finally had to roll up the windows and suffer in the closed heat of the car, chugging water that we had the foresight and good sense to bring along in quantity.

Two hours after we reached the Rif the terrain began to change, the dusty, dun colored hills giving way to deep ravines and we climbed into a pine forested, beautiful place. The little Falcon chugged along gamely despite the incline the highway took and the fact that it had no second gear. Termite was a master of coaxing the little car up those grades despite that particular shortcoming.

We kept checking the map and, just when we felt we might have been getting close, we hit our first guard post.

We had just inched up an incline and the highway had briefly leveled out as it twisted between two forested peaks. As we made a curve in the road, there it was. A guard booth manned by Moroccan soldiers. Expandable steel spikes lay across the road to flatten the tires of anyone stupid enough to try and avoid the roadblock—which is a much more practical and final way to do a roadblock that the American version—and a soldier with a small submachine gun flagged us to a stop.

"Oh, shit," we all said in unison as the Falcon slowed to a halt.

"Everybody stay cool," said Termite. This was wasted advice on me since I had frozen neatly in place.

The machine gun toting soldier came up to the car and said something in Arabic, which none of us spoke. He didn't actually point the muzzle of the gun at any of us, but he kept it just below eye level, the muzzle still in our general direction. Termite smiled and handed him his passport, motioning for us to do the same and we quickly complied. The soldier took the passports, looked at us suspiciously, and disappeared in the direction of the guard booth. We sat, rigid with apprehension. When self-officious individuals take your passports in third world countries, a little apprehension is permitted.

About five minutes passed and the soldier returned, this time in the company of someone who had to be an officer. He was armed with a side arm on a white belt instead of a submachine gun and his uniform was cut better that the first soldier's. He had a smug, self-important look on his face and, in fact, his whole air was cocky and arrogant. Just like our Meyers. I wasn't the only one to make the connection, "Jesus Christ, it's Pogo," Cow observed.

"Where do they get these guys?" Termite wondered as the officious looking individual approached the Falcon, our passports in his hand.

"Here it comes," said Cow, glaring at Shorty as though he were at fault and had placed the roadblock there himself, "I fuckin' knew it."

"What?" asked Shorty.

The officer stopped and looked at the car critically, then stepped forward and leaned partly in, looking closely at our faces, comparing each with our passport photos. We smiled and tried to be cordial without overdoing it. Either that must have worked, or they were looking for someone else because without ceremony he tossed the passports into the front seat of the car between Termite and myself and waved us on. Two soldiers, the one who had stopped us and another, scampered to move the spikes as soon as the officer made a little waving motion. As soon as those spikes were slid back we slid onward. Gratefully, I might add.

"You know," I said, "I'll bet he makes those guys as miserable as Pogo makes us." Some things, like officers who enjoy being a prick, are evidently universal.

"Where do they get those guys?" Termite wondered again.

The highway continued to climb as we left the guard booth in our wake. As soon as we had put a couple of miles between us and the unsmiling officer, Shorty produced a pipe and proposed that we smoke to take the edge off. We soundly vetoed the idea in a quick, decisive manner, somewhat hurting Shorty's feelings by our lack of diplomacy.

"Are you fuckin' crazy?" Cow said, "Put that thing away!"

"Are you nuts?" I added simultaneously.

"If you light that, you'll be walking," Termite promised, "There's just too good of a chance of running into another one of those roadblocks, Shorty. Just wait. Okay?"

Grumbling something about us being paranoid little old ladies, Shorty replaced the pipe and leather drawstring bag of stash into the top of the cowboy boots he was wearing. He and Cow had just begun engaging in a spirited dispute over the merits of caution when suddenly Termite said again, in a little whispering voice, "Oh, shit."

We all glanced around, startled, thinking that another roadblock was approaching. We didn't see anything and when we looked at Termite again he was staring off to the right side of the car. To our left the mountain soared up, lost in the pine forest as it rose from the road. To our right the mountain dropped away into a deep valley. We still didn't see anything to cause alarm and because of that we were becoming alarmed, looking around in all directions and asking Termite, "What? WHAT?"

"I think we're here," he said, suddenly subdued.

"Where?" I asked, "What do you mean?, with Cow and Shorty echoing the same questions.

"Take a look down that valley, Marshal. What do you see?"

I peered at the valley, wondering just what the hell Termite was talking about. There was not a living soul in sight. The valley seemed peaceful enough. It was cleared of timber and covered by a deep green carpet of plants that reached far up onto the mountain on the other side of the valley nearly to the timberline. I couldn't see anything unusual about the view other than the plants seemed to be uniform in appearance and....the plants. It was the plants. Cow realized what it was that Termite had seen at the same time I did, and we said in unison what had become the catchphrase of the day, "Oh, shit." We all climbed from the car together with Shorty still saying "What? What?," and stood on the edge of the road, looking out and down into the valley.

"Just look, Shorty," Termite said softly.

Shorty stood with us and looked into the valley and when he finally saw what we saw he uttered, "Oh, shit."

The entire valley, from the road's edge to the timberline on the opposite mountain and as far as we could see in both directions up and down the high valley, was covered in marijuana plants. There, at our feet, were thousands, tens of thousands of acres of weed. That had to belong to somebody. We realized then that this was so much more than we had expected. This was a very big business indeed and that we, the four of us who thought we knew so much, were way, way in over our heads. Right before our eyes was more dope than most people will ever see in a lifetime. Several lifetimes. This was big, big business. And with that size and scope of this particular business comes the unpleasant fact that people who engage in said business do not fool around. None of us had really known what to expect if and when we found Ketahma, but this was beyond our wildest imaginings. We were awed by the sheer size of that high valley and what it contained. And we were also awed by the fact that now we had a whole new set of problems.

What were we going to do now?

We had started this trip out of a sense of adventure more than a need or desire to make some kind of big haul. After all, we could buy the stuff right in Kenitra. But we had become obsessed with the idea of finding Ketahma and we had made quite a production of it. We had gathered up money, been wished luck and had even had the Falcon blessed by our resident psycho shaman, Cro. So, this led to our current dilemma.

When we began to realize the size that the trade in this area just had to be after looking at that valley, we just weren't sure we wanted any part of it. Way, way too many things could go wrong. And when you deal with people that were as deeply involved as these people had to be in this particular trade and things go wrong the best you can hope for is to get away with a whole skin, unperforated and intact. A worst-case scenario just didn't bear thinking about. But backing out wasn't all that simple, either.

We had let everybody know we were off on this great adventure. There had been much hoopla and fanfare and we had walked around like roosters, our chests puffed out with bravado. We couldn't back out now. Once again we were bound by the rules of Macho and were helpless in their domain. If we backed away and left with our tails between our legs we would never live it down.

Our only option was to sail on and hope for a fair wind.

It was four very somber young men who climbed back into that Falcon. And right around the next curve was a sign we should have been eager to see, but which now caused knots of apprehension to form in my stomach.

It said, "Ketahma 5 km."

19

An Education in the Rif

We rolled into Ketahma with our apprehension barely hidden under the thin veneer of the bravado we put on for each other's benefit, as young men do. We weren't fooling anyone, especially each other, but it was better to pretend than to admit fear. Shorty didn't seem to notice the apprehension. He chirped and pointed, pleased as punch that we had finally made it to Ketahma. The rest of us weren't so sure we should be happy to be there. To our immense relief we discovered that it wasn't just some little dirtwater place with drug lord hit men lurking on every corner, but a bright, clean, charming little town with the air of an exclusive mountain resort. And, even though we hadn't seen another car since that grim little checkpoint back down the mountain, the place was crawling with what appeared to be Europeans and even some Americans. "So much for the keep-it-off-the-map-and-they-won't-find-it theory," I observed.

There were a couple of small hotels—which meant we'd have a bed to sleep in if we stayed the night—some nice cafes, and the inevitable medina, or souk, that sold everything from meat to silks and gold.

We were delighted, and quickly forgot the fears of just moments before. Termite found a place to park the Falcon and we wondered over to a neat little outdoor cafe', where we ordered roast beef sandwiches and Heineken beer and discussed our next step.

"Okay," I said, "We're here."

"Oh, brilliant Holmes, simply brilliant," mocked Termite, "We're here all right. The question is, now what?"

"Now what, what?" asked Shorty.

"So what do we do now, Shorty? Do we just walk up to some guy and say, 'Excuse me sir, would you happen to know where we can buy a large amount of very illegal stuff?'"

"Yeah, and without us ending up as fertilizer or with Cow as Bubba's bitch."

"I wish you guys would stop saying stuff like that," Cow glared at us, "that shit's not funny." So, of course, we didn't stop but instead began to give detailed descriptions of Cow's impending domestic situation. We were at a loss as to what we were going to do next pertaining to fulfilling our mission, so abusing Cow would do until we figured it out.

Once again it was Shorty who unexpectedly came up with the answer.

After we had finished our food and had started on a second beer, Shorty, bored with the logistics of our situation and not really being asked his opinion much anyway, wandered off to the medina to browse the stalls. We had gotten to the point where we realized that we didn't have a clue as to how to proceed from here, but we all agreed that however we did it, it must be done discreetly. Shorty then reappeared, a well dressed Moroccan teenager in tow.

We all clammed up as they approached to keep our unlawful mission safe from the stranger. They stopped at the table and Shorty said, "Guys, this is Ahmad. Ahmad, these are my friends, Termite, Cow, and Marshal Dillon."

Ahmad shook hands with each of us, his eyebrows arching at the odd names, and said in very clear, almost accentless English, "I'm very pleased to make your acquaintance." We were surprised at the well educated tone of his voice but not nearly as surprised as when Shorty followed up the introductions with, "Ahmad's gonna take us to his dad's place so we can buy our dope."

Cow leaned his head forward and softly began to bang his forehead on the table, quietly mumbling to himself. Termite, who had just taken a mouthful of Heineken, began to choke and sputter, the beer running down his chin. I just sat there with my mouth open. It was me who managed to speak first, "Ah, Shorty, do you…I mean…how did you….I mean….how did he…?"

"How did he know what we needed?" Shorty asked.

I nodded, pointing in that 'that's it' gesture. Termite stared, dripping, and

Cow, still mumbling something over and over about not wanting to meet Bubba, continued to softly bang his head on the table. Shorty replied, "I asked him. I ran into him in the medina and we started talking. His dad's one of the leading producers here and he says he'll be glad to take care of us. He likes Americans as long as they aren't hippies."

"But…" I started, them Ahmad spoke.

"I can assure you, my friends, it's quite safe, if that's what you're worried about. If you're here to buy, you may as well but from my father. He is very respectable and will give you the best deal in Ketahma."

Cow stopped banging his head and looked up. We all three looked at each other. There was about fifteen seconds of dead silence and then, as one, we shrugged. It was decided without a word of debate. This one was as good as any. They were all strangers and potentially tons of untrustworthy trouble. There would be no way to tell if one of them would rob us or worse. One was no safer than another based on the limited information we had to work with so it was decided. I clapped my hands sharply in the accepted fashion to summon the waiter and he came swiftly, carrying our check before him. We paid, tipped well—mostly out of guilt for the hand clapping thing since I still felt awkward and embarrassed to summon anyone in that manner, but it was not only accepted, it was proper and if you wanted service you used their methods. We climbed back into the Falcon to follow Ahmad (who drove a new Toyota by the way) to his father's house and whatever fate awaited us.

We didn't have to wait long to find out just what that was. The drive from Ketahma took about ten minutes. We drove down the curving highway in the opposite direction from which we came. Along the way that incredible valley stretched off to our left and we could see other, smaller valleys connecting to it, twisting off in other directions. All, it seemed, containing the same cash crop, and millions of dollars worth of it. Ma and Pa Kettle would have been proud. Ahmad turned off the main highway onto a smaller dirt road that, although not paved, was well maintained. Termite concentrated on guiding the Falcon down the road without ending upside down at the bottom of the valley. I watched the beautiful scenery between glances at Cow, who was working his big hands, clenching and unclenching them and glancing at Shorty's throat from time to time. Shorty saw the look in Cow's eyes and asked, "What?" The road twisted and turned back and forth as it dropped sharply into the valley and soon we were there.

A medium sized Swiss chalet style house stood on the mountainside surrounded by several outbuildings. Smoke issued from a chimney and the whole picture was like a scene from an exotic episode of the Waltons combined with The Sound Of Music. After everything else that had happened so far that day seeing Julie Andrews coming around the house dancing with Grandpa Walton and Gentle Ben doing the mambo in the background wouldn't have made me raise an eyebrow. As the cars pulled up a slim, middle aged man came from the house and embraced Ahmad. There was a brief conversation between the two of them during which I heard my name, or rather that of Marshal Dillon, mentioned, then the man turned his attention to us. He greeted us in a kind, friendly way, "I am Farouk. I welcome you as my guests. Please, come to my house for tea."

After shaking hands all around followed Farouk into a large kitchen type area that smelled strongly of cooking chicken. Three women or girls were busy preparing what appeared to be the evening meal, and two of them immediately lowered their heads and slipped out a rear door as we entered. The third was a plump, cheerful woman in kaftan and scarf, "This is my wife, Khadijah." He didn't mention the two who had slipped away as we entered. I figured that they were daughters and under no circumstance would we be allowed to meet them, or speak to them in any way. Farouk rattled off something to Khadijah in their tongue and she smiled a brilliant smile and gestured to an adjoining room. We entered a beautifully decorated den, full of plush carpets and the typical if expensive Middle Eastern art and wall hangings. A fireplace burned in one corner because the afternoon had grown into early evening and the first mountain chill was beginning to make itself felt in the valley shadows. It was a comfortable, well-decorated room and I felt warm and welcome.

Farouk seated us on thick carpets around a low, ornate table. Khadijah slipped back to the kitchen and presently reappeared with a large silver teapot and glasses for all of us. In Morocco tea is not served in cups but rather in medium sized water-style glasses, and is generally a tasty mint tea blend, sweetened with heaps of sugar, which this was. It was hot and delicious and to this day I'm still fond of mint tea.

We relaxed, sipping our tea, and Farouk engaged us in a witty conversation which was part general talk and part careful questioning as he felt us out.

"You are Americans? Where is your hair?"

"Our hair?" I asked, then it dawned on me, "Oh! We're military. We have to cut our hair."

"So you are not hippies. This is good. Too many of the hippies come here, then want something for nothing." He looked at us in a pointed way, and I caught the hint.

"We expect to pay for anything we get, Farouk. We would not insult your hospitality." That seemed to please him. He smiled and called to Khadijah who brought another silver pot of tea. It was warm and relaxing, but I saw that he was carefully feeling us out.

He often asked pointed questions without appearing to do so and I knew he was satisfying himself that we weren't up to no good as far as his business was concerned. He asked much about us and was pleased when he learned we were Marines because he had read much about the Marine Corps and was impressed with our history. My name, Marshal Dillon, amused him because reruns of Gunsmoke, dubbed over in Arabic, were very popular here. He also gave information about himself and his family. Ahmed, who had disappeared as we came into the house, was seventeen and attended an exclusive private school. In Switzerland. He mentioned that he had daughters but did not discuss them further, and we had the good sense not to ask. That can be a very sticky and downright dangerous subject in their culture.

As we talked, Khadijah brought a steaming bowl heaped with boiled chicken, and another with cous-cous, a sort of thick boiled corn meal. Finger bowls of water were placed beside each of us and we ate with our right hands in the Arab and Berber style, rinsing our fingers in the bowls of water. It would have been impolite to refuse the invitation so we ate, even though we had eaten just a short time before. Being impolite to an Arab—or in this case Berber—host is another risky venture in that neck of the woods. They take being hospitable very seriously and offend easily.

Farouk proved to be a charming host and when the meal was finished and Khadijah (who did not join us, as is their way but who appeared from the kitchen like a cheerful genie whenever we needed anything) had cleared the dishes he got down to business. He glanced at his watch, "Ah. We have time to see my workers and what I do here. I think you may find it interesting if you'd care to join me."

We agreed, surprised at such an invitation. "First," he said, "as with all things we shall start at the beginning."

He took us to a large barn type out building. Inside the building hung hundreds of pounds of mature marijuana plants, all in bundles and all upside down. As we gazed upon them in awe, Farouk explained, "It takes seven kilos of plant after it is cured, dried, and stripped from the stalk to make one kilo of hashish. That is why you see so much hung here. When it is first harvested it is hung upside down so that the resins will drain to the tips of the plant as it dries."

"We did the same thing back home with tobacco," I said.

"The principle," he said, "is the same." In one corner two men were stripping the dried leaves from the stalks and placing then onto a wagon of sorts. Farouk greeted them and they smiled broadly, waving. They appeared friendly and open, right down to the two AK-47 assault rifles with banana clips that leaned against the wall at their fingertips and the sharp look in their eyes. They were obviously not your average farmhands. We smiled and waved to them in greeting, the sight and meaning of the weapons not lost on us. Farouk then shooed us outside and escorted us to an adjoining building.

There we saw how the process works. In a large room were four women, all covered from head to toe in the usual kaftans and scarves, but wearing what appeared to be some type of breathing masks. Each held some sort of long flexible paddle. In the center of the room was a huge pile of the dried marijuana leaves and the women were busily beating the hell out of it. A cloud of greenish dust arose from it. Farouk pointed to the walls, "The walls are covered with sections of a heavy gauze or light burlap on which the dust settles. The dust is, of course, the resins from the plant, the actual cannabinol. After the pile of leaves is beaten until no more dust arises, the burlap is removed a section at a time, and the dust is carefully shaken from it and deposited in separate bins. The higher on the wall the section of burlap is, the lighter the resins that have attached themselves to it, and the higher the quality of hashish ultimately produced from it. I am pleased to say that I produce some of the finest in the world right here."

Then we were shown the next step. The resin dust is collected and mixed with alcohol to bind it, then its pressed into blocks about six by ten inches and about three quarters of an inch thick, each weighing two hundred and fifty grams, or a quarter kilo. It's then wrapped in a plastic wrap to keep it from drying and stored in his warehouse, waiting shipment. "Come," he said, "let me show you my storage facility."

It was the warehouse that brought me back to reality.

Farouk's warehouse was a separate large shed about the size of a two-car garage and it contained more illicit material than I had ever seen in my life and ever hope to see again. The entire shed was stacked, floor to ceiling, with one-kilo bundles of hashish. There must have been more than a ton of the stuff there. We stood in awe at the sight of all that dope. I think the only comment made for a moment was by Shorty, who said, "Wow."

If that wonder of the international drug trade had them awed, it nearly caused a panic attack in me. Termite exchanged glances with me and I knew he was thinking what I was thinking. This was huge. This much dope could get you killed without so much as an afterthought by almost anybody who did such things. I wanted very much to finish this and go home. And I swore to myself that I would never, ever again do anything as remotely foolish as blundering around a foreign country in search of something I knew to be illegal—highly illegal—and get myself into a mess like this. The thought of armed soldiers just a few miles away from where I was standing in a warehouse full of thousands of pounds of hashish was giving me a healthy case of the heebie jeebies, not to mention Farouk's employees, who looked like they knew exactly what to do with those AK's.

Farouk explained further, "I am waiting on a buyer from Amsterdam who comes in twice a year. You have come at a good time. I have plenty of the stuff, and to spare, and I can give you a good price." Of course, after seeing all that stuff and beginning to understand the sheer volume of what he did and the amount of money he must deal in, we were a little embarrassed to tell him that we had managed to scrape up a little over five hundred dollars from about twenty of our compatriots for this journey.

He laughed it off, "I understand that soldiers are not involved in high finance. I admire you for your courage in undertaking such a task." I wished he wouldn't use words like undertaking, but I kept what I thought was a thoughtful and dignified expression on my face and thanked him for his generous thoughts. He called to one of his workers who darted into the warehouse and he and another man returned momentarily carrying huge armloads of the quarter kilo bricks. "It is five kilos of my best," he said. He pulled a pocket knife out and carved off a piece from one of the bricks, smelled it, then passed it around for us to smell as though he were a wine steward at a restaurant passing the cork from a top shelf wine.

Our jaws dropped. Five kilos. Two point two pounds to a kilo. Over ten pounds of hash. Enough to last us forever. Enough to launch us into legend at Bouk. And enough to get us put away in some Moroccan prison for the rest of our lives, however brief that may be, if we were caught with it. Farouk saw the expression on my face and must have read my mind because he laughed again and asked that Termite bring the Falcon down to a small barn just outside the house. There, in the white glow of working lamps, his workers took off all of the door panels, front and back. They then heated each brick over a small kerosene stove, then bent them and carefully taped the bricks in an even layer on both doors, both sides. "This," he explained, "was so that when you get stopped at one of the checkpoints on the way down. And you will. They stop everyone who leaves this place. They will tap on the car doors looking for a difference in tone to indicate if there was anything there. The way we distribute it the sound would be the same all around. The bricks are soft when heated and mold nicely. You can even send it out in furniture."

"Er, Farouk, may I speak to you alone for a second?" I asked. Farouk and I walked a few yards from the others who stood staring at us, wondering what I was up to. What I was up to was simple, as they would see. Farouk called out to his men and a few minutes later they showed up carrying another load of the hash bricks that was identical to the first.

"What are you doing, Marshal?" asked Termite.

"Investing in my future," I replied.

"Hey, man," said Cow, "that's a lot of dope. If we get caught with this much...."

"It will make no difference if you get caught with five kilos or ten or thirty," Farouk interjected, "The results will be the same. What is the expression? You may as well be hanged for a sheep as for a goat. But, if you listen to me you won't get caught. Unless you make a serious mistake, of course."

So they also stored the five kilos of hash I had just spent every dime I had saved for almost a year on in the body of the Falcon. And, after about an hour they had finished and he demonstrated, starting at the front and tapping his way around the car. I have to say the man knew his business. There was no difference in tone anywhere. Finally he leaned back, satisfied. Termite, Cow, and even Shorty were kind of miffed that I hadn't let them in on what I had in mind, but I told them to get over it, so they did but only after some more questions.

"What are you gonna do with all that, Marshal?" Termite asked.

"Trust me, guys, it's an investment that may pay great dividends some day." They grumbled but let it go after that.

Farouk insisted we stay the night and we went back to his house. His wife showed us to our rooms and had already laid out soft cotton jelabas for us to sleep in. After a hot shower in a beautifully tiled and surprisingly modern American style bathroom I crawled between soft sheets covered with a beautiful down quilt and lay there, thinking of this bizarre day and the risks we would run tomorrow and wishing with all my heart I had never gotten myself involved in this insanity. Despite my show of bravado to the others, I was scared and hoping it was worth all this, and that the phrase 'investment in the future' wouldn't become my epitaph. I thought of Cow's threat to strangle Shorty and how, oddly enough, almost everything Shorty did this time around had worked out just fine. There would most likely be no Shorty annihilation this trip.

But, when I finally drifted into sleep and began to dream, I dreamed of none of that. I dreamed a peaceful dream of that isolated beautiful white town. It was shining on the brown hillside as the last fingers of sunshine brushed it with their light touch like the fingers of God brushing the eyes of a sleeping child.

20

Blind Luck and Fast Thinking

We left early the next morning after a Moroccan style breakfast of fruit, bread and cheese and more of the hot, delicious mint tea.

Farouk wished us luck and waved a cheerful goodbye to us as we chugged back up the mountain, the little Falcon laboring away in first gear. In a few minutes we gained the main highway and turned onto it, heading the opposite way from which we came in. Farouk had assured us that it was less treacherous and steep, and that the government checkpoint about thirty kilometers down the road was sometimes unmanned. We were on our toes nonetheless as we approached the guard booth, but, true to his word, it was empty. We coasted through gratefully and settled in for the trip home.

At Termite's suggestion Shorty produced his pipe and stash bag from his boot and we celebrated what was sure to be a safe trip now that we had cleared the checkpoint. We were laughing and shouting and smoking and generally having a grand old time when, as the Falcon came around another curve, there it was.

Like a nightmare, another military checkpoint straddled the highway like a vision from hell. Termite said, "Oh, fuck!" and began to slow the Falcon while we were still several hundred yards away. I turned around and snapped to Shorty who was sitting like he was in a trance with the pipe still in his hand, "Shorty!" I hissed, "Put that away! Hide it! Now!"

Shorty moved with the lightning speed he was capable of, putting the pipe and stash bag down into the top of his boot. I turned around as we rolled up to the guard post. Without moving my lips I whispered, "Shorty, is that thing put away?"

"All secure, Marshal," Shorty replied.

As the Falcon ground to a stop in front of the inevitable spikes two Moroccan soldiers approached, one on each side of the car. Both were armed with the same ugly little submachine guns we had seen at the first guard post. The one on the passenger side looked into the car, minutely scrutinizing the front seat, then the back. Then, with his companion watching us, he began a slow circuit of the Falcon and, to our horror, began to tap on the car with a knuckle. I remembered Farouk's advice as they plastered the inside of the body of the car with hashish, "Stay calm, whatever you do. If they see you get nervous they will become curious and that will be very bad for you, my adventurous young friends."

We sat trying not to panic as he tap-tapped his way up and down and all around the vehicle with his head cocked, listening intently. Evidently, he'd done this before. He eventually stopped beside his companion. They looked at each other and the tapper shook his head and shrugged slightly. The one who had posted himself on the driver's side then jabbered something, some form of instruction no doubt, to Termite in Arabic. Termite started to say something, raising his hands from the steering wheel to try to sign that he didn't understand.

That nearly ended our little expedition right there.

With a shout, both of them jumped back and pointed those damn machine guns at our faces, their fingers on the triggers. Something Termite had done had been interpreted as a threat although for the life of me I didn't know what it could have been. We froze in place and slowly raised our hands, glancing at the muzzles just a few feet from our eyes.

This was touchy. Any misunderstanding at this point would result in our immediate demise. The two testy, trigger-happy soldiers looked like they would be most willing to hose us if we twitched the wrong way. Despite the early morning chill that still permeated the air, I could feel sweat beginning to bead on my forehead. A bead ran down my back and I resisted the sudden urge to shiver. It was a classic standoff. Nobody, them or us, seemed to know just what to do to safely end it, either.

Someone once wrote that impending death focuses the mind wonderfully, and I'm here to tell you there is truth in that statement.

My mind was clicking like a computer, examining and discarding ways to end this without disaster, then I remembered the few words and phrases of French that the daughters of the wonderful Robair family, Beti and Dani, had taught me when I was visiting in my guise as a counterfeit Jew. I stammered out in halting French, asking if either of them spoke that tongue. One of them, the one who had done the tapping, nodded and replied in French as bad as mine that, yes, he spoke some French. What of it?

I then stammered out that we were American military from Kenitra on leave in their beautiful country and we were....

"*Militaire?*" he said, then broke into halting English, "You are American *militaire?*" Uh oh, I thought. This could be bad. I may have just made a huge mistake. The American military does not always enjoy warm and fuzzy welcomes from military folks in other countries. I hoped I hadn't made a deadly blunder but there was nothing to do now but go on with it and hope for the best.

Yes, I said, we were Marines.

His eyes lit up, "Anybody corporal?" he asked.

Termite, who was the only one of us to hold that exalted rank at the time, nodded slowly and said, "I'm a corporal." Very slowly he retrieved his wallet and produced his ID card that said very clearly 'corporal' in the spot marked 'rank'.

The Moroccan soldier cried, "Me Corporal, too!" Suddenly they were laughing and shaking our hands in greeting like we were long lost relatives. It went from life threatening to bizarrely friendly in ten seconds flat. I was a little stunned by the sudden turn around but I didn't question it. I was grateful not to be looking down the barrel of those ugly little machine guns anymore, and I shook hands and smiled at them like a used car salesman when it was my turn.

They invited us to come with them to their guard shack for tea and we, of course, accepted. The shack was about the size of our kennel house and sat back a little way from the road. We all trooped over there, leaving the Falcon in place right there in the highway. The two soldiers made tea and between their broken English and my deplorable French, we managed to have a reasonably civilized meeting. They told us that their job was to check the vehicles coming down from Ketahma for smugglers. They frequently caught said smugglers and called for their officer, a young self-important captain they didn't like very much—noticed the looks the two exchanged and the roll of their eyes when they brought him up—who would come with his selected goons and take whatever unlucky individuals they had in custody away to prison to await trial. It sounded like it was the same grim, self assured Moroccan officer we had seen on the other side of the mountains. We described him to them as best we could and they said that yes, that was probably him because this was his week to be on that side instead of with them, for which they were grateful. It seemed we had been right. We all have our Pogos to bear in life.

Shorty, because he was quick and witty, quickly became a favorite of the two and had them laughing as he imitated their beloved captain, swaggering and glowering in parody. I was laughing with them and wishing Shorty would knock it off so we could go when I happened to glance down. I nearly died on the spot.

There, in Shorty's right boot, was the hash pipe.

His pants leg had apparently ridden up as he got out of the car and was now firmly stuck behind the pipe stem, clearly exposing it and the top of his leather stash bag as they stuck out of the top of his cowboy boot for all the world to see.

I made a tiny whimpering noise as my life flashed before me, and my heart began to pound loudly in my ears. They were bound to see the pipe. Three full inches of stem were thrust upward and it looked like it might as well have had flashing lights and bells and whistles on it. They couldn't miss it. Termite had been right. We were doomed. Cow had been right. We were going to jail forever and ever. Maybe they would put him with Bubba The Buttfucker and not me. Cow was cuter than me. I would look lousy in a sundress. What was I going to do? I must have made another whimpering sound as I contemplated what had just become my immediate future because Cow, who had been laughing at Shorty's antics with the soldiers, glanced at me and following my gaze, focused on the three inches of doom that was stuck out of Shorty's boot. He made a sound that sounded a lot like the whimper I had just made. His face drained of color and became a pasty white. He looked at me and I looked back and it must have been like two trapped rabbits looking at each other to figure out how to get out of an ever-tightening snare.

Termite was sitting at a bad angle and hadn't seen what we could see just yet, but Shorty suddenly turned during a little tin soldier matching drill he was doing and Termite saw the pipe. To give him his due, he didn't squeak like Cow and I had done. The smile froze on his face and he immediately looked at the two soldiers, neither of whom had given any hint that they had seen the pipe despite being focused on Shorty. It was Termite who pulled our fat out of the fire this time.

He stood and stretched and began to thank our hosts, shaking hands and salaaming, which is a sort of classy half-bow in which the right hand touches the forehead, the lips, and the heart. Cow and I got the hint immediately and rushed over, joining in the fond farewells, shaking hands and salaaming as well. The soldiers protested that we should stay longer. We were brothers of the uniform. They were delighted at the company and especially pleased that Shorty had made them laugh. I took it that duty at this particular post wasn't all that pleasant and any diversion was welcome and I suspected that genuine laughter was rare. We tried to get Shorty out of the door with a minimum of contact with the two but he just slid between us and shook hands with them, much to our dismay and ever increasing horror. We then walked out together like one big happy family, Shorty striding between the two of them, shoulder to shoulder.

The short walk to the Falcon took a lifetime. Any second I expected them to shout and point those damn guns at us again after they saw Shorty's pipe. They had to see it. It was neon. It was huge, glistening like a barber pole with disco lights. It was shouting, "Hey, you! Yes, YOU! Here I am! Wooo hooo!," like a lone shipwreck survivor in a lifeboat shouting for attention. They would look down any time now and we would be screwed.

At some point, maybe in a past life or something, I had apparently done something that had given me a column on the credit side of the books. They never looked down. They never saw that damn pipe. We got into the Falcon. I was rigid with apprehension and acting like nothing in the world was wrong. So were Cow and Termite. We knew we had to pull it off because the least little thing, a slip, a bit of out of place behavior, would make them suspicious all over again. We should have won an Academy Award for that little piece of acting because all I wanted to do was fall down in place, flop like a fish, and cry.

Shorty, as usual, was completely clueless.

Termite started the car and just before we drove away we gave each of them a fifty durham note, which was worth about twelve or thirteen dollars at the exchange rate of the time. It was probably close to a month's salary for them, and they were very pleased with the unexpected gift. They waved as we drove away, and we waved back until they were finally out of sight.

We all breathed a heavy sigh of relief when we really felt safe and slumped down in our seats. Shorty looked at all three of us and finally picked up on the fact that something was wrong, The fact that I was blotting sweat from my face with my shirt-tail must have finally clued him in. "What?," he asked, glancing from one of us to another.

"Shorty...." I started to say.

"What?" he asked again, and I was over the seat and on him in a flash, my hands closing on his throat. "What? What?" he croaked as, babbling in anger, I began to strangle him.

They told me later that Termite nearly drove off the side of the mountain before he could get the Falcon stopped. And then it took both of them to pry my hands from Shorty's throat. I don't remember because I was apparently in a homicidal frenzy. I was embarrassed about it later and spent the rest of the trip apologizing to the nearly murdered Shorty, even though he had almost gotten us all put away in a dank Moroccan prison for a very long time with Bubba The Buttfucker and pals. Shorty was horrified when we found out what he had done and we spent days apologizing to each other in a genuine, pathetic sorrow fest, which Cow and Termite found hilarious. Especially since I had been the one to advocate Shorty's presence on the trip and had been a one man Anti-Shorty-Strangling Committee when Cow had suggested it in the first place. The bruises on Shorty's throat would take days to heal and he talked in a raspy whiskey voice for about a week.

We finally rolled through the gate at Bouknadel safe and sound. Fuzzy the donkey was standing in the second floor bathroom, patiently waiting for Flagg to take him back to Special Services. It looked like it would be a long wait because Flagg was passed out on the tile floor, snoring like a chainsaw and wearing nothing but his boxer shorts, cowboy boots and that ridiculous black cowboy hat.

There was nobody else around and no music playing anywhere, which was a bit odd, but we were tired and didn't really pay it much attention. We had sort of been expecting a hero's welcome but our fatigue outweighed our disappointment. We split up and headed to our rooms. Carlos was on boonies and Jerry the Juicer was snoring loudly. He and Flagg had probably been together, this being the result.

I had just stuffed a sock into Jerry the Juicer's open, snoring mouth and settled into my bed when my door opened and Brunner walked in, Shorty, Cro, and Freaky Deac behind him. I could tell by the expressions on their faces that something was wrong. My first thought was that someone had been killed and Henley flashed through my mind again.

It was almost that bad.

"Marshal," said Brunner, "Mouse has been arrested by Naval Intelligence Service for having classified documents in his possession. Drugs, too. They took him away tonight."

21

Mousetrapped

The news that Mouse, our loyal conduit to the inner workings of Major Malfunction's and now Meyers' little command, had been arrested by NIS pounded through me like the shock wave from a two thousand pound bomb. I had a hard time comprehending at first, "Mouse? Arrested?" was all I could say.

Cro nodded, "They came and got him last night, NIS and some MP's. They wouldn't tell anybody what it was about but Jerry the Juicer," he nodded at Jerry's sleeping form and did a double take at the sock in his mouth before continuing, "was Corporal of the Guard last night and overheard the NIS guy telling Major Malfunction that they had searched Mouse's desk and had found the documents in question, whatever that meant. He also said they found some dope. They came over here and searched Mouse's locker. I don't know what they found but they most likely found his personal stash if they searched his locker. Anyway, they took him."

"Took him? Took him where?"

"Probably to battalion at NTC. They have a brig of sorts there."

"Oh, man. This sucks. What documents? What are they talking about?"

Freaky Deac joined the conversation, "Don't know, cowboy, but Mouse is fucked."

"Well," I was nearly stammering, "what can we do?"

"Can't do nothin'," Freaky Deac and Cro shook their heads in unison. It is a grim truth of the military, especially the Marine Corps, that lower enlisted men have no voice, no control over their daily lives other than whatever tiny bits of space they are able to carve out, very often at their own risk. The desire to help Mouse was a powerful drive in me, but at the same time I knew we were helpless. The bitter reality of the situation danced in my mind like a vicious leprechaun, mocking me and my need to help someone who had been so loyal to us. No one could help Mouse but Mouse. I would just have to accept that.

There was only one problem. I didn't want to accept it.

"Is there any way we can find out just exactly what it was Mouse was supposed to have done that would warrant them carting him off?"

Brunner looked at me, "Marshal, you've got that look on your face. Get over it. This is way, way out of our league. This is the NIS, the Naval Intelligence Service for those of you—you in particular Marshal—who think we can fuck around with them the same way we do with Major Malfunction or Pogo. We need to stay away from this and let the chips fall where they may for Mouse." He raised his hand and cut short a protest from me. "Before you even go there, Marshal, we all love Mouse every bit as much as you, but get this…If the NIS gets even a sniff that you're poking around about this, they will do nasty things to you. You know about the Labrea Tar Pits, Marshal?" With that aristocratic deep-south accent of his he pronounced it 'tah pit.'

I looked at him like he was stupid, "Of course. What the hell does that have to do with Mouse?"

"They pull bones out of there, saber-tooth cats and wolves, lots of them, piles of them. What would happen is that they would see something stuck in the tar and they would all jump on it. They would all get stuck and eventually sink. Everybody, including the first one to get stuck. This is a tar pit. If we jump on, we'll get stuck and sink right along with Mouse."

He was right and I knew it. There was just something I had to find out and I would do it with or without their help. I had to do this just right, though.

"All right, all right. You're right. We'll just have to trust in the lawyers to help Mouse. Right now, though, I need some sleep. We had a hell of a trip."

"Yeah," said Cro, "We saw Shorty's neck."

There was brief snicker at this but the small attempt at humor couldn't cut through the gloom that the news of Mouse's arrest had brought to all of us. They said their good nights and drifted out the door. Cro was the last out but before he could close the door I caught his eye and gestured for him to come over. "Get Freaky Deac and come back. We need to talk."

****

Mama's was about the most popular nightspot in Kenitra for the American military people stationed there. There were others, the American Club, the Casablanca, Sunny's, and so on but Mama's had the décor, the right prices, and the very best looking bartenders I've ever seen anywhere. Some of these women had become very much a part of our daily existence in Morocco and had, in some cases, even attained an almost legendary status.

There was Fatima, tall and stunningly gorgeous in that classic Middle Eastern way—and way out of my league. It was rumored that Schmidt was having a torrid affair with her and we were all jealous. Even if it wasn't true we were jealous of the rumor. There was Big Khadija, not to be confused with Little Khadija who was further not to be confused with Cherry Khadija. Cherry Khadija was alleged to still be a virgin and looked the part with her huge dark eyes and innocent face, but I doubted the story. She may as well have been for all the attention she gave me, though.

Then there was the sly Zorah, a tiny fox of a creature who liked me. I liked her, too, but I knew better than to trust her one inch because she would steal the fillings out of your teeth if she had the chance. She'd worry if they were gold or not later. But we got along very well and she paid a lot of attention to me whenever I went to Mama's and even slipped me into her apartment from time to time to cement our friendship. She was just as beautiful as Fatima but in a smaller, different way and I liked the fact that she singled me out in front of the others whenever I was around. Not that I had any illusions that she didn't single someone else out when I *wasn't* around, but it was fun nonetheless. And then there was the sneaky red headed bitch Michelle, who would tell you how great you were while stealing your wallet. Last but not least there was Grand Canyon who, rumor had it, had earned her nickname. But I won't go there.

It was Zorah and Cherry Khadija who were keeping Cro, Freaky Deac and I company in Mama's three nights after I had received the news about Mouse. We sat in the dark bar and drank, anxiously glancing at the door from time to time. "What's the matter with you tonight?" Zorah asked after bringing me another Heinekens. I didn't like that beer but I drank it because I thought it made me look cool and sophisticated. "You don't like me anymore?" She was used to me slobbering after her at every opportunity. I was too distracted to be my usual hormone afflicted self this night, but I still flirted with her because I didn't want to piss her off. With women there's always tomorrow. Unless you piss them off, then maybe not.

It was early, only about seven, when the person we had been waiting for walked in. It was a tall thin black guy named Johnson, and he was Apache the dope dog's handler. And he also happened to be assigned to the MP detachment that was guarding Mouse.

He walked up to the table. Freaky Deac stood and they did the dap, then Johnson sat down. I gave Zorah a five, told her to get Johnson a beer and keep the change. This amounted to a four-dollar tip. I was extravagant because I needed to ask her to go away so we could talk. I reasoned that the tip would take the sting out of being dismissed, but based on the way she stuck her face in the air and flounced off I wasn't so sure it had worked. Right now, though, I had more to think about.

"Johnson, my man," said Freaky Deac, "this is Cro, and this is Marshal Dillon. They are righteous dudes." Johnson eyed us warily, then reached into his shirt pocket.

"Man, Deac, they better be," he said nervously looking around, "because they will bury me if they get wind of this." He handed Freaky Deac a folded piece of paper that he immediately handed to me under the table. I put it in my pocket even though I was dying to read it.

"Tell me what you know, Brother," said Deac.

"I got another of the brothers—you don't need to know who—who was assigned to watch your man to slip him your note. Besides that I don't know much else other than your man is telling anybody who'll listen that he was set up. Trouble is, ain't nobody listening. Nobody that matters, anyway. They got some cheesy little fuck of an Ensign assigned to him as his counsel. They're talking general court-martial."

I leaned back in the chair. A general court-martial is the most severe of all the judicial processes in the military. It would appear that Mouse's problems were great indeed.

"What exactly is he being charged with?" I asked.

Johnson drained his beer in swift gulps. He stood, obviously uneasy at being with us. "Espionage. And drug possession." He stood started toward the door, "Stay cool, Deac. And we're now officially even." With that he disappeared.

"Shit," said Cro, "espionage. They'll put him away for life," he said something else but I didn't hear. I was reading Mouse's letter.

Dillon:

I don't know who did it, but they got me good. NIS found the evacuation plans for Bouk, the defensive positions, personnel strength, and even ammo lists in my desk in a large envelope. There was some dope there, too. A chunk of hash and some little blue pipe with a glass bowl I'd never seen before. It wasn't mine. I've never even seen one like it. When they searched my locker they got what dope was really mine. They charged me with that, too. They've been grilling me day and night but won't believe me. I don't have much time, this MP's getting antsy. I didn't do what they said. Why would I? Who would do this to me? I don't know, but they're offering to lower the charges to something dealing with just being in possession of classified documents and the dope. That means a year in either Portsmouth or Leavenworth and a Bad Conduct Discharge if I plead guilty to those charges. If I fight it I run the risk of a general court for espionage, maybe twenty years, and a Dishonorable Discharge. My lawyer is recommending I take the deal. By the time you get this I will have decided what to do. Either way I have to tell you that it was an honor to serve with you guys. Tell them for me, will you? Gotta go.

Your friend,

Mouse

Wordlessly I handed the note to Freaky Deac who read it and handed it to Cro. After he read it he struck a match and held the note by a corner until it burned away, then dropped the remains into the ashtray in the center of the table. We all sat and stared at the embers as they faded.

"Man," said Freaky Deac, "who would do that?"

"I don't know but I hope he burns in hell, whoever he is," said Cro.

I just sat, silently nodding, not saying anything. I didn't need to. I already knew. There was a reason Mouse had never seen a pipe like that. It's because it was one of a kind. I had bought it in Marrakech and hadn't ever shown it to anyone. The last I had seen it Meyers had taken it from my locker during his aborted bust.

Meyers.

But why? As they sat and wondered who, I thought about why. I didn't have to wonder long, though. It was obvious. Mouse was our spy, our insider. He kept us apprised of what went on in Meyers Land as soon as he found out. He had also been the one who had talked to Major Malfunction and let him know that Meyers was out of control, that he was going to end up doing something really stupid that might cost the Major, and Malfunction had cut his vacation short. He had come back just in time to save his career and make a complete fool of Meyers. So, yes, Meyers had a reason. But, would he? Would he actually send somebody to jail just for a form of vicious self-satisfaction or revenge?

Then I thought about that something I had always seen behind Meyers' eyes and I knew I could stop wondering. Of course he would. He would get rid of Mouse any way he could. Right down to an anonymous call to the NIS about shady doings on the part of a certain company clerk. He would. And he did.

We left Mama's and moped toward the bus stop to go back to Bouknadel. I hadn't asked Termite to come along because I figured the fewer who knew anything about this the better. Therefore, no Falcon. Cro and Freaky Deac used the time to wonder who the rat was who had set up the Mouse. I stayed quiet and they attributed my silence to my grief over Mouse. I didn't tell them of my conclusions concerning Meyers.

We had almost reached the bust stop when, turning the last corner, we ran straight into Betti and Dani Robair and that pesky Rabbi Trosclair.

I had never told anybody at Bouk about my misadventure as a fake Jew. I figured that the old adage about the least said soonest mended worked real well in this situation. Right now this was a complication I didn't need.

"Shalom, Dillon," cried the Rabbi, like he hadn't seen me in years when in fact I had paid a visit to the Robairs only two weeks before and he had been there. There was nothing to do but play it out and hope for the best. Again.

"Shalom Rabbi!" I cried in return, "*Bon soir*, Beti, Dani!" There were hugs and kisses all around and a short bit of happy small talk and the usual questions, what had I been doing with myself, etcetera. I chose not to tell then I had gone to Ketahma and bought twenty pounds of hashish and almost had gone to prison for it. So I settled for asking them what in the world they were up to. They were out for an evening walk with the Rabbi. It was *such* a happy coincidence meeting me. Cro and freaky Deac stood back watching, bemused by the strangeness of the whole thing and by my conversation with the three in broken French. After a few short minutes I used them for an excuse to say goodnight, saying they were waiting for me and I must go and the appropriate goodbye noises were made.

They walked away, a happy chatting group. Cro and Freaky Deac watched them go. "Uh, excuse me, cowboy, but just who the hell was that?" asked Freaky Deac.

"Just somebody I knew when I was Jewish," I said, wanting desperately to avoid the subject.

"Huh?" said Cro.

"Don't ask because you really don't want to know," I said.

"Dillon, my man, sometimes I think you are one seriously throwed off motherfucker," said Freaky Deac.

"My friend," I said quietly, thinking of Meyers, "you have no idea."

22

The Legend of the Phantom Poet

A few days after our return from Ketahma the impact of the news of Mouse's arrest had been pushed into a safe place in the back of the other guys' minds. Life went on. I was not so lucky. I knew he had been ruthlessly set up and by whom. I became almost obsessive in my hatred for Meyers but I was careful not to show it. I stayed as normal as I could. I buried the five kilos of hash I had gotten from Farouk in the antenna field after sealing it in one of the five gallon steel drums we got our dog food in. I didn't tell the others what I did with it, either. They were curious but stopped asking after a while because I wouldn't tell them. They thought I was being a bit of a prick about it but that had to be all right. I had my reasons. Other than that things slowly returned to normal. I continued to smoke and party with the rest and gradually it began to fade, even in me. Then, finally, there came a distraction that made it easier to not think about Mouse in some jail cell somewhere. The Legend Of The Phantom Poet began shortly after he made his first mysterious appearance late that summer, and he caused quite a stir among the Dog Men. I was the one who was unfortunate enough to find the first poem. I say it was unfortunate because Alfie and some of the others naturally blamed me for the thing. I was the known reader, the bookworm of the group. I read everything from Batman to Steinbeck, Tarzan to Shakespeare, so naturally it was assumed that only I would leave a poem for the entire world to find. Despite my sincere protests of innocence I was saddled with the blame for the first poem discovered, and was accused of being the mysterious Phantom Poet.

It was one of those incredibly warm, clear nights. The stars were so thick and close that I felt like I could reach up with a net and scoop those diamonds out of the sky and put them in a bottle to keep forever. Argo and I again lay on Perimeter Road, him snoozing and raising his head occasionally to check out some small sound, and my head on his chest as I stared up at that clear sky. John Denver, Cro, and myself had relieved Carlos, Shorty, and Cow and were on Second Boonies. We had all split up to check our posts before meeting at the bunker to begin the serious dereliction of our duty together. I watched those stars twinkle and flicker, hypnotic in their beauty. A satellite hurled itself across the sky, clearly visible and, although I couldn't know it then, a harbinger of advances in technology to come. Technology that would one day make this place obsolete. I watched it until it disappeared from view, lost forever in the bright mass of the Milky Way.

Like an omen from a Norse god the most incredible shooting star I have ever seen suddenly tore across the sky so close to the earth that I could imagine I could hear the whoosh of its passage. It flashed a light that I thought illuminated the ground briefly it was so close. I sat up, thrilled at the rare and unexpected sight. That cosmic flare broke the spell of the stars so I got Argo up and we headed for the bunker to meet my two compadres.

I got there first. Cro and John Denver were nowhere in sight so after securing Argo to one of the old machine gun mounts I went on in to set up the candles. I lit three and distributed them evenly around the inside of the bunker then, as I started to go back outside to wait for John Denver and Cro, I saw it.

It was a poem. Someone had carved a poem in the hardened concrete of the rear wall of the bunker. It was painstakingly carved in a beautiful script and had four lines. Amazed, I picked up a candle and read it. It said:

> **Young birds dream of lightning wings,**
> **To flee the fears the daylight brings,**
> **In Moroccan sands a night bird sings,**
> **And Dog Men dream of Magic Things.**

It was beautiful. I was flabbergasted. Who had written this elegant poem, then taken the effort to carve it permanently into the concrete of the bunker? And carve it well. The flared, swirling script was as elegant as the poem, and carving it in the concrete had required rare skill. It had to be one of us, a Dog Man. Nobody else that we knew of ever came to this place. But, who? If any of the guys would or even *could* write such a thing he certainly never let on. Poets and poetry were not highly regarded by your peers when you are a young Marine. The Gods of Macho would not approve. Admitting to or being caught writing poetry could be socially disastrous in that testosterone laden world. And, furthermore, nobody had even hinted at having the skill to carve stone with lettering like this. I was still staring at the poem in wonder when Cro and John Denver entered the bunker.

I had been so absorbed in the poem that I hadn't even heard them come up. Cro entered with a blustery, "Howdy, Marshal!," and John Denver nodded in his usual conservative way.

"Look at this, guys," I said, stepping back and holding the candle so they could see the poem, like some archaeologist studying hieroglyphics in an Egyptian tomb. Cro peered at the poem, then read it out loud.

"That's pretty good, Marshal. Where did you come up with some shit like that?"

"Where did I.... I didn't! It's not mine! It was here when I got here just a few minutes ago," I was suddenly on the defensive without really knowing why.

"Sure it was, Marshal," John Denver said, "Are you one of those touchy-feely types, Marshal? Alfie keeps saying so, but I wasn't so sure...until now." They laughed, knowing they had me. I decided to take the high road.

"Look, you goons. I did not write this, nor did I carve it into the wall. Look, no tools. If I had I would tell you because whether you Philistines know it or not, that's pretty good work. If you'd read something besides Spiderman and the Hulk once in a while you might be able to recognize good stuff when you see it. Fucking pagans."

"Ouch," said Cro, "I'm wounded. Well, if you didn't write that crap, who did?"

"I have no idea, but I'm gonna find out just to prove to you barbarians that I didn't do it."

John Denver settled into a corner near a candle, "Well, you just do that," he said, "and I'll have you know that I do read other stuff and not just the Hulk and Spiderman." So saying he unzipped his coveralls and produced two comics, an Archie and a Superman, "See? I don't limit myself. And I'm not a Philistine *or* a pagan, I'm a Democrat."

Grumpily I settled in with them as they ribbed me about my sensitive side. That very next day all the Dog Men knew about the carved poem and a group at a time trooped off into the antenna field to see it. We even took a select few post standers out there to see it, Brunner and Freaky Deac among them. Nobody came forth as the author, not that I blamed them, even though everyone was intensely curious as to who that might be. I was still the prime suspect despite my denials.

I finally convinced all but a few that I was not to blame, and the hunt for The Phantom Poet, as whoever had written and carved that bit of rhyme was immediately and universally known, was launched. Opinions about who it could be varied, although because I was the known quantity, a reader, I was still number one on the hit parade of suspects. Actually, under other circumstances I wouldn't have minded taking credit for something I felt was as neat as that little poem because, besides the dreams I had that I never told anybody about, I thought it captured the unique magic of being a Dog Man very well in a few short lines. The cynical Alfie, with his ever sensitive style, persuaded me that I shouldn't even think about any association with the Phantom Poet as we sat in the kennel house the next day.

"Fuckin' pussy," his opinion, as always, was straight to the point, "Whoever wrote that is a fuckin' pussy. And maybe a faggot, too. Faggots write stuff like that, you know. Are you sure you didn't write it, Marshal?" He leered at me with that Alfie face that frequently made me want to punch his lights out.

"No, Alfie, I didn't write it. And that means that somebody else did. One of us. And it doesn't mean the Phantom Poet is a faggot, either. He was expressing himself like writers and poets do."

"Yeah, well, whoever the Phantom Poet is, he'd better stay away from me. Those sensitive types get on my fuckin' nerves," he picked up his dog gear and walked away muttering, "Faggots." I shook my head as I watched him walk away. He would be merciless to whoever was responsible for that poem should he ever be unmasked. I was glad it wasn't me, just because of Alfie.

The furor over the Phantom Poet finally died down as these things will and a few of the guys even eventually begrudgingly admitted that they liked the poem because it was about Dog Men.

A few days later the Phantom Poet struck again. A second verse mysteriously appeared, carved by the same hand, just below the first:

> **A rich man dreams of simpler things,**
> **While young girls dream of golden rings,**
> **The stars belong in Dog Man Dreams,**
> **For Dog Men dream of Magic Things.**

This time I couldn't be blamed because Cow and I had taken the train to Marrakech for the weekend and I wasn't anywhere around when it was discovered. I was reluctantly absolved of blame and the mystery continued. Who was it? Who was the Phantom Poet? Speculation, as they say, was rife. Again.

I had a watertight alibi this time. Even Alfie couldn't blame me for this one. He was disappointed, "I thought sure it was you, Marshal," he said, "But, since it's not, now I have to figure out which one of these other guys might be the faggot."

I had about enough of this, and of him, with his bullying ways and sneering attitude toward everything and everyone, "Maybe it's you, Alfie," I said, anger finally getting the upper hand, "Maybe you like writing little poems and blaming it on other people. Maybe you're the one everybody here should be looking at, not me. How about it, Alfie? Is it you, you little prick?" He jumped to his feet, fists clenched, and charged me. I met him halfway across the kennel house. We slammed together and went down on the concrete floor, grappling and punching. We rolled around together, each seeking an advantage and trying to get a solid punch in when hands grabbed both of us and tore us apart. I looked around. Schmidt had the struggling Alfie and Cow had me.

"Knock it off!," Schmidt said, "you two got problems take 'em somewhere else, not in my kennels! Understand? Especially not now. Right now we've got something else to worry about other than you two school girls in a bitch fight. And like it or not you two may need each other sooner than you think."

Something in his tone caused the two of us to forget our sudden fight and settle down. We looked each other, then at him and gave him our undivided attention.

"That's better. Now, listen up. As of right now we are on heightened security alert. No more games, girls. At 0300 this morning, Egypt invaded Israel."

23

The Incident That Never Happened

That night as we assumed our posts our entire outlook had changed. We had a tactical briefing that afternoon in the little theater by Major Malfunction, Pogo, and Gunny Favor in which we were given the scoop on the newest exchange of slaughter in the Middle East. It seemed that Egypt had swept across Israel's border with thousands of troops and tanks and Israel was presently fighting desperately for its life. The major power brokers, the U.S. and the Soviets, weren't involved yet, at least not militarily, but they could be any minute. And the U.S. had not won any friends among the Arab countries with its strongly pro-Israel stance.

That's where we came in.

Major Malfunction said that we had reports that attempts may be made by certain terrorist groups—including one called Black September—to disrupt communications in the Med, possibly by damaging or destroying our antennas. All leaves, days off and passes were hereby cancelled. The dogs would run four teams per Boonies instead of three. The post standers would begin to practice drills involving the evacuation of civilians to the coast, as well as what he deemed "reactionary squads" to come to our aid in case we ran into shit out there. Jets from Rota, Spain and from the Sixth Fleet would arrive within minutes or hours to provide air cover for any evacuation or any other "contingency" that may occur. The Dog Men were to return to the compound as soon as possible if the antennas proved to be indefensible.

We weren't fooled by that. There would be no returning to the compound for most of us out there. We knew that we would basically serve as early warning systems for the main compound. If we got into a firefight and they couldn't raise us on the radio it would be a batten down the hatches, close the gates, and circle the wagons situation. They would deploy the rest of the guys in a defensive perimeter to shield the civilians and squids and hold until the air power and the Marines from the Sixth Fleet arrived to help. It would be far too late to help the Dog Men by then. And the Moroccan Army may or may not come to our aid, and if they did, it would be a question of just how timely they would be. They were an Islamic army, after all.

That night, before we went out, all the Dog Men held our own little meeting. We knew we would be truly screwed if anybody came with the intent to do real damage to the base and brought enough force with them to do it. We resolved that, if any of us hit on anything, we would all come, no matter what. The four of us could not make any realistic difference in the defense of a perimeter but we could still help each other. For a while.

It was a very sober group that went out that night. Nobody smoked. The bunker would be a death trap so we stayed away from there. When I came on at midnight I eased my way into the antenna field with a whole new outlook on just how I was going to do my job. I remembered every little piece of my training, both infantry and K-9. I used the wind and the terrain like my life depended on doing it right because, well, it did. Looking back I'm still amazed that all that training stuck with me despite my complete lack of interest in accomplishing anything at all. I still remember most of it. When they say that the Marine Corps has a brainwashing system that would have made Stalin enviously write to the Commandant of the Marine Corps for 'how to' manuals, boy, they aren't kidding.

Argo was all business, too. He and the other dogs seemed to have picked up on our moods and were working like textbook examples of K-9 patrol. We swung from side to side, quartering our posts as the wind flowed and eddied around us. I could feel every change in his attitude, every nuance of his body language. He was telling me that there was nothing out there to bite, no bad guys, Boss. Yet.

After a couple of hours he alerted and by his poise I knew it was one of the other guys. I had come out that night with Cow and Blackie, Cro and Rolf, and Alfie and Mutley. I let Argo tug me toward the alert and eventually Cow and Blackie came into view, materializing out of the darkness. Argo and

Blackie eyed each other as Cow and I stood as close as we could without the two of them coming into contact, which would have had very bad results. "Anything?" Cow whispered.

"Negative," I replied in the same low hiss of a whisper. Nothing else was said. We looked past each other and out into the field, then drifted apart, each concentrating on the night.

It was like that for a week, then the slaughter that has become known as the Yom Kippur War came to an end with Israel beating the Egyptians and their allies silly. We worked the field intensely each night and I slowly became aware of a change that had taken place in me.

When I had first started as a Dog Man, the whole thing was a bit frightening. The night and the blackness and lack of vision that comes with it, the thought that there could be a bad guy out there who would kill me if he could, and the thought of things that may go bump in the night like the White Lady and the Turd Lake Monster.

I no longer worried about any of that. Somewhere, without even knowing it, I had smoothly slipped past the last stages of childhood, like a jet slipping past the sound barrier. I could see very well at night now, my eyes having adapted to my semi-nocturnal existence. Now *I* was what went bump in the night. I had once before used the simile of a werewolf when it came to the night tandem of me and Argo and it was never truer than now. I liked that comparison. All my night fears had slipped away. The night and the darkness were no longer threats. They were my friends and allies, and the darker the night the better. If there was a bad guy out there, he would have a problem if I found him.

At the close of the Yom Kippur War we remained unmolested by any terrorists except Meyers, who was in his glory as he prepared for The Last Stand. He held regular meetings and bored us to tears with war stories. Major Malfunction did not attend most of these and we suspected that he was as sick of Meyers as we were.

It was in one of those meetings that we once again bumped noses. Meyers had drawn out maps for the placement of the mortars he said we had in the ammunition bunker but that none of us had ever seen. His primary location for most of them was *right smack dab on top* of the two story barracks because, as he explained, it had a clear view of the surrounding area and a clear field of fire. It was clearly a tactical disaster in the making but he didn't ask anyone else their opinion as he laid out his plans for the gallant last defense of Bouknadel should the Berber hordes come a-screaming.

Then he made the mistake of asking if there were any questions.

I raised my hand. If there was anyone else in the room with a question they quickly decided that watching a show develop between me and Pogo would be much more entertaining than anything they could come up with. No one else raised a hand. Meyers, despite looking desperately around for some else to call on, had to call on me.

He looked at me, reluctance written all over his despicable Nazi face, "Yes, Dillon?"

"Sir," I said, sincerity oozing from my voice, "Can we assume that whoever attacked us would have their *own* mortars, or at least RPG's?"

He tried his best not to sneer at me, "Of course, Dillon. That goes without saying."

"Yes, Sir. Then, I have a question."

"Go ahead," the smug bastard said.

"Why would we place our mortars on top of the tallest structure in the area? I mean, wouldn't the barracks be something they would use to zero in their own heavy stuff? It seems that our mortars would be taken out pretty quickly if we put them up there instead of in pits." I could have added something about mortars being intended for ground use, not rooftop firing, but I left well enough alone at that point and shut up.

There was a murmur of assent among the assembled Marines, some of them combat veterans. Meyers didn't like it. His face reddened. He knew I was dead right but he would have rather gouged out one of his eyes with a spoon than admit it, "Private Dillon, I suggest you leave the tactical planning to officers and you just follow orders," he huffed.

I kept a straight face, "Yes, Sir," I said agreeably.

He called the company to attention then and dismissed us. It was clearly 'Dillon-1, Pogo-0'. I was heartily congratulated by many after we were safely out of Meyers' range.

Anyway, things gradually began to get back to normal. Our alert was cancelled and we went to our usual three dog team shifts. We had been so keyed up during the entire thing that we didn't let our guard down for a while and, as it turned out, that was a good thing. It probably saved my life.

Somewhere near the end of October Argo and I were once again on second Boonies, which was always my favorite shift. We had gotten the brushy, slightly hilly post where we had fought the bold little bull months before. We were completing our first sweep and were getting ready to head to the bunker to meet Carlos and Cow when suddenly Argo swung into the wind, his ears up, his eyes focused in the darkness ahead, and his body rigid. I dropped to one knee and looked between his ears, using them as a sight. It was a hard alert, and he was focused on the last antenna in the field, one that lay closest to Perimeter Road. By his stance and body language, plus the fact I could feel his tension through the leash like an electric current I knew this one could be hot. I drew my .45 and quietly jacked a round into the chamber. I stood and whispered, "Whatcha got, buddy? Whatcha got?" Argo quivered at the end of the leash and I knew he wanted to go, "Find him, Argo!"

He lunged forward, pulling me along. Normally I would have run behind him, allowing him to pull me at full speed but something about this urged caution. I slowed him down and pulled him back to me a bit, then suddenly, I could hear it.

There was a slight noise, a metallic, tapping sound from the direction of the antenna. I pulled Argo to my side and crouched, approaching the antenna quietly. When I was about fifty feet away I could see them.

Two dark forms were hunkered down inside the wires of the antenna. One was working with some kind of tool, making the tapping sound I had heard. The other was holding a shielded flashlight for the first and would raise his head from time to time, looking around. I waited just long enough to see if there were any others but nothing indicated that there were. The one that kept looking around convinced me that he was the only lookout. There a popping sound as one of the wires at the center of the antenna broke loose.

I pulled my seldom-used flashlight and with my pistol in one hand and the light in the other, I lit them up.

The world exploded.

They leaped to their feet as I yelled "Stop!" It was in English, not Arabic, but that command in that tone is understood under these circumstances in any language. They did not stop. The one who had been looking around grabbed a bag of some sort from the ground at his feet as the second one began to run.

I shouted, "Get him, Argo!," and let the leash slip from my flashlight hand. Argo focused on the runner and in a instant had hit him and taken him to the ground, biting hard on his legs and thighs. He began to scream and I started forward but the second one didn't run. He did the last thing I expected. I should have expected it, anticipated it, but I didn't. He pulled a gun from the bag and shot at me, spraying bullets wildly in my direction.

I saw the flash and felt the first round burn past my face about an inch away. I don't know where the rest went because I threw myself prone in the sand and was wildly firing back, the .45 bucking in my hand and sounding like a cannon in the night, huge balls of flame erupting from the barrel with each shot. I shot back four times and the second man melted in the darkness. I then leaped to my feet just in time to see the first man get to his feet and slam Argo to the ground.

There was a thud and a yelp from Argo, and he lay still as the man began to run again. "You bastard!," I screamed, and leveled the .45 at his back, but before I could fire there was a yellow flash from the corner of my eye and from nowhere the savage Blackie hit him like a freight train.

Argo was fearsome enough in his own way and could do damage in a fight, but he was nothing like Blackie. Nobody was. Blackie hit the man like an avenging demon and they went down together in a cloud of dust, then Blackie was back up and on top of him, roaring and ripping with his awesome power. I didn't see it all because I rushed over to Argo who was stirring, trying to sit up, but I could hear it well enough. The man's panicked shouts of pain quickly became screams of agony as Blackie began to savage him, biting and twisting with that massive head and using his weight as he began to rip the man apart.

Argo stood, apparently just stunned from having the wind knocked out of him when he was slammed to the ground. He began to lunge forward again, eager to fight. I got control of his leash and turned my attention back to Blackie as Cow came racing up, "Get him off, Cow!" I yelled, "He'll kill him!"

But Cow already knew that and was screaming, "Out! Out! Blackie, goddammit, OUT!"

But Blackie wasn't coming out for anybody. He was like a drunken Viking berserker gone mad, his only thought to kill. We both saw it. Cow lunged in desperately and grabbed Blackie's leash. Then, with all his considerable strength, he yanked Blackie from atop the now groaning, sobbing man.

Then, the worst thing that could have happened, did.

Blackie twisted after Cow yanked him off and without a moment's hesitation planted his feet and leaped dead into the middle of Cow's chest, knocking him off his feet. Cow went down with a thud, Blackie astraddle of his chest. Blackie's face was within inches of Cow's and he was growling savagely, his fangs exposed in an awful grimace. I could see blood glistening on his lips in the glow of the two dropped flashlights, mine and the bad guy's, that were still on.

This was bad. This was very bad indeed. Cow began to talk to Blackie in a calm voice, "Easy, Buddy, easy now, Blackie. That's my boy, that's a good boy." But Blackie wasn't listening. His yellow eyes glowed as he stood there, vicious and unpredictable, savage as a sabre-tooth cat.

I eased Argo over to the down man, gave him a sit command and told him,"Watch him!" As he began to stare at the man I draped my leash over Argo's back, then stepped away from him. If the man moved, Argo would be on him. But that was his problem. I had another priority.

I had to kill Blackie, and quickly.

I drew my pistol and put the sight just behind Blackie's right shoulder. Cow continued to try to calm him but I wasn't going to take the chance that Blackie would rip out his throat before I could react. I was squeezing the slack out of the trigger when, suddenly, Blackie just stopped. He just quit. Without warning he stopped growling and stepped off of Cow and sat, staring off into the night.

"Holy shit," was the only thing I could think of to say.

Cow shakily got to his feet. He looked at me still standing with my .45 pointed at Blackie and nodded, "Keep it right there for a minute." He picked up his leash and gave Blackie the command to heel, which he did without resentment. I could see headlights approaching and I knew the Corporal of the Guard and the reactionary squad were on their way. Cow walked back and forth with Blackie, giving him drill commands until they arrived. He responded like he was in afternoon training, his blind rage of moments before apparently forgotten. Carlos and Hasso, who had been on the far side of the antenna field, came panting up then.

The Corporal of the Guard, who happened to be Freaky Deac that night, got there with the reactionary squad in full war gear. Deac, a combat veteran, immediately deployed the squad in a perimeter around us and it was quickly evident he knew what he was doing. His commands were crisp and soon we were encircled in a tight perimeter of rifles, with Deac firmly in control. It was interesting to see him in that mode. A Navy corpsman was with them and he checked out the down man, exclaiming, "Oh, fuck!" when he saw his injuries.

We never found the second man but the next day we found a clear blood trail leading across Perimeter Road. Apparently I had been luckier than he had been and had hit him in our exchange of fire, which didn't bother me then and doesn't bother me now. The sonofabitch had tried to kill me, after all. We also found the bag he had been carrying. It contained some tools, some 9mm ammunition, and a quarter pound block of plastic explosive.

The mauled prisoner was turned over to the Naval Intelligence Service. The same guy who had arrested Mouse came out that very night with a couple of dark, shady looking characters from what was probably some branch of Moroccan Intelligence. They whisked him away in an unmarked panel truck and we never saw him again. From the looks of those guys I doubt if anyone did.

The next day the same little self important little jerk of a Naval Intelligence officer came back to Bouk to "debrief" us. We were told that this incident never happened, and that we were to be like Schultz on Hogan's Heroes. We knew nothing. And that anyone who divulged anything about that night could be subject to penalty for security violations.

That suited us just fine and even though he was trying hard to be mysterious and intimidating. We weren't intimidated but we just didn't want a confrontation with the clown. We wanted him out of our hair so we kissed his ass until he was satisfied and then he went away.

Argo developed a limp from being slammed that night and was on light duty for a month, which meant he didn't have to run the obstacle course, which he hated anyway. Blackie seemed to be fine, although Cow watched him closer than ever.

After watching Blackie's scary performance of the night, I was forced to once again agree with Alfie's assessment: If he had been born human, he would have been a dangerous psychopath.

Or maybe a war hero.

24

Bad Choices All Around

I would have been in a much better mood that Halloween if Argo hadn't tried to screw Rolf in the ass.

It was all my fault, mind you. Mine and Cro's. That's what I was mad about when it was all over. The lack of common sense used by the two of us that day was astounding and could have caused very bad things to happen to both of us.

He and I had kennel maintenance and feeding duty that day and we spent the afternoon scooping dog shit, cleaning runs, and getting very stoned at the kennels, and generally enjoying the day as much as two guys cleaning up dog shit could. It was warm and pleasant and when we finished we languished at the kennels for a while, reluctant to wade back into the hustle and bustle of the barracks.

Cro had let Rolf out and hung the "Loose Dog!" sign on the kennel gate so we could smoke in peace without fear of interruption from duty oriented busy-bodies of the type that infested the Marine Corps like Meyers or his eunuch Barney. Rolf had an even tempered, pleasant personality and was a favorite with us since you could actually approach him without losing digits or substantial amounts of blood. He roamed around while we did our work, then came and sat with us when we were finished. We smoked and talked, sitting in the warm grass. It was Cro who brought the subject up.

"You know, Marshal," he said, "I wonder if our dogs would run together?"

I had eased back and now lay flat, examining the sky. I looked up from where I had been marveling at a large cloud that seemed to have a striking resemblance to Linda Ronstadt, "What do you mean?"

"Well, they never seem to get aggressive with each other when we're on boonies. I'm just wondering if they could get along well enough to play together."

"I dunno, Cro. Might not be a good idea."

"Why not? Might be fun for them. And we have good control of our dogs. They won't get stupid."

It was those fateful words that got me thinking, yeah, why not? What can it hurt? We have control. If they start getting keyed on one another we'll just call them off and put them away back into their runs.

"Alright, then," I stood and dusted the sand and grass from my rear, "let's do it. It might be fun." I walked over to Argo's run. Argo saw me coming and was hopping and spinning, hoping I would let him out. I popped open the lock on the gate and he slipped out.

He ran around me for a couple of minutes before he and Rolf saw each other. Cautiously they approached one another, stiffly at first, then with tails wagging. They stopped and began sniffing one another in the traditional doggie way. No problems so far. Neither of them had an aggressive expression on his face and their tails wagged in an open, friendly fashion. Cro stood to one side beaming and said, "See? They get along just fine."

That's when Argo decided to screw Rolf in the ass.

Suddenly, without warning or indication of any kind that he had such notions in mind, Argo just jumped aboard Rolf started pumping for all he was worth. Rolf was dismayed and tried to pull away, but Argo had him firmly in a grip with his front fore legs. Rolf was a bit dumbfounded by this indignity for a second then became extremely resentful, and turned on Argo to express his displeasure. And the fight was on.

Talk about things going to hell in a hurry.

Suddenly the two big, very aggressive dogs were in a flashing, roaring fur ball of a fight. Cro and I, to put it mildly, freaked.

I began yelling," NO! NO! Out, Argo, out!" and Cro was yelling for Rolf to come out and heel. Neither dog paid us the least attention. So much for the much-vaunted control we had over our dogs. They mixed it up wildly, twisting and slashing at each other. If you haven't ever seen two dogs like this in a fight, you haven't really seen violence.

Neither dog had a collar or leash on and when Cro began dancing in a circle around them yelling, "Get your dog by the throat, get your dog by the throat!" I saw that that was the only way and I joined him, dancing crazily around the two wildly fighting animals, jockeying for position.

We finally saw an opportunity and with a silent count each of us reached in and grabbed our dogs by the throat at the same time and pulled them apart, holding their heads with both hands tightly against our bodies until we got them calmed. Finally calmed, the two dogs were once again responsive to us. As I held Argo I asked Cro, "Is he alright?"

"I think so," he responded shakily, "he's a little cut up on the back of his neck but it looks okay. How about Argo?"

I carefully examined Argo for cuts or wounds around his neck and shoulders. I didn't see any and was just about to breathe a sigh of relief when I turned his face toward me.

"Cro!" I cried, "Argo's eye's out!"

"What? Oh, man, we're goin' to jail!"

Argo's left eye was a mass of pink tissue. I really thought it was out for a second and then I realized that it was just a thin flap of skin from his eyelid that had been torn loose and was folded back in a weird way. But it sure looked like it was destroyed at first. When I realized that his eye wasn't out and wasn't damaged at all, in fact, I let Cro know. "Cro, it's not out. It's just a flap of skin."

"What?" He came over and saw for himself. "You asshole! I nearly had a heart attack."

The damage was very superficial and we had him patched up in no time. It healed quickly and well.

We were lucky. It would have been hard to explain how we had gotten our dogs injured this way. It was plainly dereliction of duty, or at least neglectful destruction of government property. By the time those dogs are mature they are worth many thousands of dollars including their training hours, food and veterinary care, and schooling. Not to mention the man-hours required to train and patrol with them. The government takes a very dim view of people who are careless with such valuable property. I could have explained having to shoot Blackie if I had been forced to in order to save Cow. I didn't think the Marine Corps would accept the fact that I had gotten my dog maimed because we had decided to let them have a little romp together, like poodles or something.

Meyers, of course, would have been orgasmic at the chance to slam me. Cro would have just been icing on the cake.

It was plainly a lack of common sense on my part and on Cro's. I was upset with myself more than anything, though. I'd gotten my dog hurt because I didn't use good sense. I was thoroughly disgusted with my little screw up as I walked back to the barracks that evening.

Cro was a little less worried about it. In fact he began bursting into people's rooms, clasping his hands to his face or raising them to the sky and yelling, "Argo's eye's out! Oh, Nooooooo!," then running away screaming, "What am I gonna DO?" He did that for weeks afterwards, too, casually forgetting that the whole damn thing had been his stupid idea in the first place.

Jerk.

So that was why I was cranky that Halloween. I was moping in my room and feeling sorry for myself the way I did when I had made a bad decision that I couldn't blame on anyone else. Carlos was out on first boonies and Jerry the Juicer was nowhere around. It was the perfect setting for misery. I had just settled into a deep-blue-genuinely-feeling-sorry-for-myself funk when my door flew open and my roommate, Jerry the Juicer, came in with Brunner, "Hey, Marshal! Riley's on Brownbagger's Row trick or treating for shots of booze!"

Riley was Jerry Riley, a post stander who had been transferred to Bouk from Sidi Yahia a few weeks before after being caught in bed with one of the senior Navy officer's eldest daughter. She had been eighteen, so they couldn't do anything to him in that area, and she wasn't married, but daddy was most pissed nonetheless, so the Marine brass quietly transferred Riley to Bouk in the best tradition of out of sight, out of mind.

Riley was a dark, lean Irishman who looked like a twenty two year old Errol Flynn, right down to the little mustache. He was a charmer, to say the least. When he was drunk, which was much of the time—he didn't smoke—he developed an Irish accent that I thought was a little much until I found out that it wasn't a put on. His parents had brought him to the states when he was seven and when he started drinking the accent began to creep back and his voice took on that mischievous Irish lilt, much to the delight of most female persons anywhere near puberty. Us, on the other hand, he annoyed tremendously, especially me.

He was a world class ass-chaser and had already focused on the buxom blonde daughter of CWO Fifer USN. We'd warned him that she was only seventeen and would certainly earn him a place in Portsmouth if he laid even one of his lecherous fingers on her stacked little juvenile frame.

It didn't help that she was a constant flirt with some of the guys at Bouk, or that she looked like a Bourbon Street stripper. Most of the crowd I hung with steered their boats well clear of those rocks, not needing the type of trouble that she would bring into an otherwise relatively nice existence. Termite put it well, "Seventeen will get you twenty." Enough said, as far as I was concerned. She was nice to look at, but distance lends enchantment, and I'd long since satisfied myself with leering at her from afar like everyone else.

Anyway, I lay on my bunk looking up at Jerry the Juicer as he babbled about how Riley was even now knocking on doors on Brownbagger's Row. When whatever person who lived there would answer he would say, "Happy Halloween! I'm trick or treating for shots!" And—they were giving him large glasses full of straight whiskey for Halloween, which he was merrily chugging down, then going on to the next house.

My reply was simple and reflected the depth of kinship I felt toward Riley, "So?"

"He's gonna get juiced and end up going to house to see, you know….," he held his hands out in front of his chest in the universally accepted sign for Big Hooters, "CWO Fifer USN will crucify him!"

"What has this got to do with me? I don't even like the fucker."

"He'll listen to you, Marshal. We tried to get him to knock it off but he wouldn't listen to us. Come on, Marshal. Give us a hand." Brunner evidently felt indebted to Riley because just the week before Brunner had been tripped out on acid and was wandering around the barracks in a daze. Riley had taped a sign to his back while he stood in the head watching his face change shape in the mirror. It said, "Hello. My Name is Tim. If you find me please guide me to my room." Brunner had a wire or two loose and viewed this as an act of kindness.

"All right," I sighed, "I'll talk to him but if he doesn't want to come the chips will just have to fall where they may. I will not attempt to persuade, cajole, or argue with him. I haven't taken my idiot shots this week. If he won't be reasonable, fuck him."

It didn't take long to find him. He was in the process of knocking on the door of Chief Warrant Officer Fifer, USN, who hated Marines.

I broke into a run, hoping to drag him away before the door opened but when I was still thirty feet away it swung open and Fifer's wife stood there, looking at Riley with her head cocked to one side, curious.

"Good evening ma'am," Riley slurred, his Irish brogue making him sound like a bit like the old drunk from *The Quiet Man*, "Er, Happy Halloween! My name is Riley and I'm trick or treating for shots." I could see him craning his neck to one side, hoping to get a glimpse of the object of his lustful, not to mention illegal, desires.

I expected her to start screaming and calling for Chief Warrant Officer Fifer, USN, Hater Of Marines to come and sweep this vermin away. I grabbed Riley quickly and began to make my apologies while trying to pull him away from the door but she raised a hand, and I stopped, puzzled, "It's okay, sergeant," she said, mistaking me for someone with some kind of authority, and her clear Irish lilt floated in the air, "it's quite alright. I'll give the man a shot, if it's a shot he wants. It's All Hallow's Eve, you know."

Riley swayed back and forth on the steps as she went back into the house. I was getting queasy just watching him rock back and forth. She returned shortly with a water glass filled almost all the way to the top with whiskey, "Irish whiskey," she said pointedly, as she handed Riley the glass.

"You're a saint ma'am. If I might ask, what part of the island are you from?"

"Derry," she replied with a delightful, impish smile.

"And I'm from Belfast," Riley said.

"Now that's fine. Bottoms up," she said, and to my amazement Riley tilted up the glass and drank it down like it was water. He finished the glass, wiped his lips on his sleeve and handed it back to her.

"You, my lady, are a saint," he repeated, and with that fell backwards like a post. He landed with a solid *whump*, his fall unbroken by anything except the ground. Riley didn't feel it though because he was out cold before he hit the turf. I looked around in alarm, still expecting her to yell at any minute. She just smiled, looked at me, and winked.

"My mother used to say, if you can't stop them one way, stop them the other. He wasn't far from the edge. I just gave him a wee nudge."

She was a class act. I thanked her for her patience and her kindness and signaled to Brunner and Jerry the Juicer. Those intrepid rescuers had been bravely hiding behind some trees nearby. With nervous looks around they slinked from their hiding places and came to my assistance. We attempted to get Riley to his feet, and had just succeeded in getting him between the two of us when Chief Warrant Officer Fifer, USN, drove up.

He leaped from his vehicle thundering, "What's going on here?"

Jerry, who had been supporting one side of Riley, snapped to attention and let his side go. I tried to hold on but if I had the limp Riley would have dragged me to the ground with him, and I didn't like him that much. I let him go and he crumpled like a boneless chicken. Jerry the Juicer just stood there blinking stupidly like someone had hit him in the face with a raw fish.

"I want to know just what you people think you're doing in front of my home with this drunk! Who's responsible for this?"

I just stood there because I really had nothing to say that would help anybody just now. When Fifer turned his glare on me I did what any red blooded American would do in this situation.

I pointed to Jerry the Juicer. After all, he had gotten me into this.

He turned the wrath of the highly ranked onto Jerry, "Well?"

Jerry began to stammer that Riley had been trick or treating for shots and….

Fifer was nearly apoplectic. He began to rage, promising that he would have us all court martialled for this, he would call Major Malfunction right now and he would….

And that's when she stepped in, "You'll do no such thing, Charles," she said in that lovely Irish accent, "The young sergeant here," she nodded at me and I didn't bother to correct her about my rank because that wouldn't have been prudent at that particular moment, "has everything in control, or at least he did until you came up shouting. Just let it go."

She looked at me again, "Can you get him home safely, Sergeant?"

"Yes, ma'am," I said, pleased to watch Fifer squirm but careful not to show it.

"Then please do so," and she took Fifer by the arm and led him inside, patting his arm like I did with Argo's head when he was upset or agitated.

That was my first real lesson that, sooner or later, we all meet our match. Even people like Chief Warrant Officer Fifer, USN. Like I said, she was a class act. I didn't know what Chief warrant Officer Fifer, USN, ever did to deserve a woman like her, but he was a damn lucky man.

I turned my attention back to the problem at hand, which was the limp and now snoring Riley and how to remove his carcass from the scene before any other unwanted attention came my way. I didn't try to stand him up this time. I grabbed him by the collar and began to drag him to the barracks, much to the alarm of Brunner and Jerry the Juicer.

Brunner was alarmed, "Hey, Marshal!"

"Stay the fuck out of my way," I snarled, and continued to drag Riley like an unwanted corpse.

. About halfway back Riley came to somewhat and started singing "And When I Die" and generally began having a good old time as I dragged him down the street, across the parking lot, and into the barracks.

Cow had seen me coming as I dragged him across the lot and he met me at the foot of the stairs. Together we heaved his worthless carcass up the stairs and into his room, where we dumped him without ceremony or care onto his bed.

We passed the remainder of that Halloween smoking and shaking our heads about the juicers as we coughed our lungs out with the acrid hash smoke.

Why would the juicers do that to themselves, we wondered?

25

Funeral for a Friend

Tragedy takes many forms. It is indiscriminate and can strike without warning. The Henley incident had been a tragedy, and so had the whole issue with Mouse. Tragedy wasn't done with us, however. He struck about a month later in another of his many guises. Personally, I didn't consider the issue all that tragic, but another of tragedy's qualities is that he is subjective. What is tragic to you may not be so tragic to me.

It was nearly Christmas again and a lot of the guys were making arrangements to go home, at least as many as were allowed according to the dictates of security. I was staying again this year, not minding the extra shifts. The thought of a bitterly cold, snowy Christmas spent huddled up in an Indiana farmhouse was too much to bear anyway. Everyone seemed to be in that happy mood that you are required to be in during Christmas, although for the life of me I could never figure out why that time of year should be any different from any other time of year. Guys were buzzing around, getting ready for their leaves when we got the word that tragedy was once again in our midst.

J.R. died.

The snuffling little creature Timmy Brunner set such store by had, as the song said, he up and died.

Timmy was devastated. He had been set to rotate back to the states permanently in just a few days and had already made himself a padded box, complete with holes, to smuggle J.R. back home with him, I assume to live happily ever after. He was distraught.

Carlos shook his head, "He'd went through all that and it never occurred to him that J.R. would just up and die."

"It also never occurred to him to find out just how long hedgehogs live in the first place," I reminded everyone in the room. This might have been pertinent information before long term plans involving the critters were made. I didn't think it would have been tactful to bring that up to Timmy right then, though, so I didn't.

Disasters of this magnitude will bring out the best in folks, especially during the holiday season, you know. Cro, our psycho shaman, organized a funeral for the little rodent. Our Seabee pal Sunshine, who was a fine carpenter and always eager to participate in anything bizarre, designed and built a dazzling little coffin. It really was fine craftsmanship, considering it was for dead vermin.

I was careful not to laugh or poke fun at the whole thing while Timmy was around. While I had genuinely detested the snuffling little J.R. for some reason that I could never quite put my finger on, Timmy was my friend and I would do nothing to hurt him under any circumstance. Sneering at his little pal's corpse right now would have been extremely upsetting to him. Even Alfie laid off, much to my surprise.

So, that was how I found myself as part of a funeral procession for a damn hedgehog. Flagg got Fuzzy from Special Services and hooked him up to a little cart that was used to haul kids from Brownbagger's row around the base on weekends. I considered kids another form of vermin at the time so to me it was an appropriate conveyance. Termite, John Denver, and Cro decorated the cart with lettuce and stuff like that they had spirited from the mess hall. Someone decorated Fuzzy with his usual white sailor hat, which he seemed to like. And then we all put on our dress blue uniforms for the funeral, as if a general had died, or a Playboy Playmate, or someone equally important to us.

The coffin was placed on the cart and, with about thirty Marines in dress blue uniforms following, it made its slow way to the antenna field, with Cro, still in his jelaba and staff, leading. Someone had found a tiny American flag somewhere and it was draped across the shoebox-sized coffin. The new guy on Post Two, a sharp Brother named Jones who had adapted well to Bouk culture in a few short weeks, snapped to attention and whipped up a sharp salute as Fuzzy passed with his charge.

A hole had been dug earlier by Shorty and Jerry the Juicer just outside of Post Two. We were amazed that the two of them actually managed to get it done without slicing off anything important with the shovels, but they did. The bizarre little procession stopped there and stood in formation as Cro gave a sermon that said something about hedgehog heaven, and how J.R. was this or that, but I didn't hear it.

I was busy trying not to burst into laughter, which is inappropriate behavior at funerals.

So we buried the little varmint there in the antenna field. When we had all come to attention and saluted the thing one last time, we walked back to the barracks. Chief Warrant Officer Fifer, USN, passed us on his way to Oz with some other Navy officer in the car that we didn't know and probably wouldn't like anyway. They returned our salutes as we passed, staring at Cro and Fuzzy. As they drove away we could see Fifer talking animatedly and shrugging a lot, no doubt trying to explain us and the sailor hat-wearing donkey to his visitor.

When we got back to the barracks we got out of our dress blues, then got stoned in honor of J.R.'s memory (as if we needed an excuse) in that order.

Timmy was with us in the room and was slowly recovering from what I was beginning to fear would become a full-blown psychotic episode over the death of vermin.

I was standing at the window, staring out across the street toward the snack bar and theater while they all talked behind me, trying to get Timmy out of his funk and not doing very well at it.

"Come on, Timmy," I said, "snap out of it. You're starting to worry me."

He groaned and put his face into the pillow.

"Is he all right?" asked Freaky Deac.

"Other than the fact of him being in a full blown psychotic episode over a varmint, yeah, I think he's okay." Timmy groaned into the pillow again.

It was getting dark and chilly outside, and I was getting good and stoned, "You know, Deac, I was just thinking, I saluted a hedgehog today. A dead hedgehog. I can die happy now because my life cannot possibly get any more bizarre than that. I have peaked out."

I turned to the window as Freaky Deac laughed and said, "You are one throwed off motherfucker, cowboy." Then I saw what had to be an hallucination.

Across the street was the little strip that contained the two-lane bowling alley, the snack bar, the exchange, and the little theater where Pogo had set up his successful failure of an ambush. Behind it was Brownbagger's Row, the street of housing for the officers and senior enlisted. CWO Fifer USN's house was directly to the rear of the little theater. It was white and two storied, the second story sticking up past the theater. It was flat roofed in the Middle Eastern style and the second floor was surrounded by a narrow ledge. And standing there, perched on that ledge just outside of one of the upstairs windows, was Jerry Riley.

Naked.

I thought, *no way. I don't see that.* I walked slowly away from the window and sat down in one of the chairs in the room that wasn't being occupied by a stoned hedgehog mourner. Sitting for a few seconds thinking about your sanity will make you want to check the things that made you wonder about yourself at least twice. So I walked back to the window and peeped through the blinds again.

There he was, all right.

He held a pair of boots in his hand but other than that, there wasn't an article of clothing anywhere near him. He looked pathetic standing there in the dark, clutching his boots. It was obvious he was praying that someone from the shopping strip wouldn't look up and see him there.

I had to bring this to someone else's attention. But…. who? The answer, at least to me, was obvious. Everyone, of course! "Hey, guys! Check this shit out!" Some opportunities in life are not to be missed.

It was a time of great joy. Two minutes after I notified the guys in the room with me about Riley's plight the word spread like the wind and every off duty Marine on the base knew about it. Every room in the barracks that faced Brownbagger's Row soon had a crowd at the windows.

Normally we would have been scrambling to help one of our own who was in such a predicament but we knew how he got there. And he had been warned by us many times before, "Riley, you'd better leave that little bitch alone," Cro had told him.

"Yeah," said Cow, "she's sixteen. You're gonna get yourself in a world of shit if you don't back off. You'd be safer handling plutonium."

"No sweat," said the cocky Riley, "I'm safe. And anyway, you fuckers are just jealous she's not fucking any of you." He obviously didn't listen, but that was okay. We didn't like him that much anyway.

We stood at various windows, pointing, laughing, and making rude and uncharitable comments.

"Is his face turning blue?"

"Look at him. He looks like a trapped rat."

"Man, that cold isn't very flattering to guys who don't pack much gear to start with."

"Yeah. I though he said he was a stud."

"No, I think you misunderstood. He said stub, not stud."

"Oh."

Freaky Deak shook his head, "It's a damn shame what nature has done to that man. He should cover that little thing up before he further embarrasses himself and the rest of the Caucasian Persuasion."

They all nodded sadly in agreement. What could they say, with Wee Willy Winkie over there as living proof of the inequities in life. I, however, felt it was my duty to protest on behalf of the Persuasion. "Hey," I objected, "that's not necessarily representative, you know." Freaky Deac looked at me, "You hung, cowboy?"

"Like a fucking plow horse," I assured him.

He threw his head back and laughed, "One throwed off mother*fucker*."

There was some sympathy offered, but not much, especially from me because it was obvious to us what had happened. Riley had waited until CWO and Mrs. Fifer, USN had left the base on some mission or errand then, through some pre-arranged system of signals, he had slipped into their home for a rendezvous with their large breasted, small brained daughter. The two hormonally driven individuals had been in the midst of a tryst when CWO and Mrs. Fifer USN had arrived home. Quite unannounced and unexpected, obviously. Riley had made a quick exit through the girl's window as he heard the footsteps of doom approaching, somehow neglecting to take his drawers with him.

We watched him for a while before the debate about just what to do about this started.

Shorty was a bit concerned, "It looks like he's freezing."

I took as sympathetic a stance as I was going to, "Fuck him. He's an idiot."

"He was warned not to fuck around with that," said Termite.

"I say let nature take its course," voted Cow.

"Yeah," I added, "it's the natural order of things. He's diluting the gene pool anyway." That was soundly seconded by almost everyone in the room. Even Timmy had withdrawn from his funk long enough to agree with me.

"Yep," he said, then buried his face in his pillow once more.

Shorty was not giving up, though, "He's still one of us. If he stays up there long enough somebody else will see him and either Pogo or CWO Fifer USN will get him. We can't let that happen, can we?"

We groaned in unison. "I hate it when he's right," said Cow.

Even I had to agree that despite the fact that Riley was a greasy creature even he shouldn't be fed to the likes of Meyers or Chief Warrant Officer Fifer, USN.

Since Shorty was so concerned it was decided that he should play rescue ranger. Shorty eventually took a pair of his coveralls over and stuffed them in a bush behind CWO Fifer USN's house. When it looked like the coast was clear Riley dropped to the ground and retrieved them, then beat a hasty retreat to the barracks. He was much humbled by the experience.

It turned out that our assessment of the situation had been correct. He had been in the midst of, well, in the midst of the girl, actually, when CWO Fifer USN shouted that he was home, and had begun walking up the stairs to see his darling daughter. Riley had just enough time to make a dive for the window, grabbing for his clothes and boots on the way. He snagged his boots, but missed his clothes. With time running out he made it out the window just as CWO Fifer USN opened the bedroom door and walked in to see his little angel, who was now cleverly pretending to be ill to explain why she was in bed and all covered up so early. When CWO Fifer USN went for Mrs. Fifer USN to come to her aid, she managed to stuff Riley's clothes under her bed. The concerned parents then closed and locked the open window to prevent the cold night air from further injuring their daughter's health, leaving Riley no further access to his clothes or to room temperature.

Riley, now trapped like the rat he was anyway, hesitated just a bit too long before deciding to drop to the ground and attempt to hide in some bushes until further plans could be sorted out. "Being naked on a ledge can confuse you," he told us later. He waited a bit too long because just as he had made up his mind to risk a drop, then scuttle into foliage to regroup, the sliding glass door directly beneath him slid open and CWO Fifer USN exited and casually lit up a rather large cigar. And sat on his patio peacefully smoking that cigar as Riley quivered and turned blue twelve feet directly above him, his gonads rapidly shrinking in the December cold to the humiliating dimensions observed by all of us as we pointed and laughed from our rooms.

CWO Fifer had just finished his cigar and went back into the house when Shorty came around the corner, hissed once to get Riley's attention and stuffed the coveralls into a bush. Shorty then executed a tactical withdrawal, leaving Riley to his own devices from that point on.

Alfie, always on the offensive, asked, "Hey, Shorty. If you were so concerned about that dumbass why didn't you stay and help?"

"I didn't want to be seen with a naked guy in the bushes," Shorty explained.

"Oh," said Alfie. We understood.

Riley managed to drop to the ground without being caught, quickly put on the coveralls and came to the barracks, where we pounded him senseless with humiliating insults. Having your genitals being pointed to and laughed at, even from a distance, can be a humbling experience. He couldn't have heard us but he knew what we were getting at.

The whole thing had a cheering effect on me, and even helped Timmy shake off the blues over the untimely death of his varmint.

I reflected, as I dozed off that night, that the day had turned out all right after all, despite being forced to attend a funeral and salute something I probably would have just flushed.

26

Meyers' Final Cut

Change is a vicious little bitch who works with or without your command and very often works against your wishes. But she works whether you want her to or not. Gradually things were changing at Bouk. Some of the guys were rotating back to the world and new guys were arriving. Timmy Brunner, Rock, Freaky Deac, John Denver and Jerry the Juicer all went home within weeks of one another. I was sad to see these guys go, especially Freaky Deac. I would miss his racially charged humor and his constant, tongue in cheek criticisms of the Caucasian Persuasian. We gave each of them a dazzling, smoke filled send off. Even Jerry the Juicer consented to lower his standards and smoke with us. New guys were arriving to take their places but those of us who remained mostly ignored them. They weren't family yet.

Carlos rotated a month before Christmas. He and I had grown close over the past year, our long evening talks had whiled away many a lonely hour, both in our room and on Boonies. I learned to respect him despite his ethnocentrism, or maybe because of it, and I missed him badly after he left. Some new guy took his place as my roommate, a dippy idiot named Stafford who I never bothered to speak to. He was an interloper, an intruder on the sanctity of my room. I inherited Carlos' stereo when he left and I took to playing lots of Led Zeppelin, Black Sabbath and Uriah Heep (and anything else that would make him think I was an off-the-deep-end radical) whenever Stafford was around with the volume at a level that made reasonable conversation impossible. He tried several times to be friendly but I made it obvious I wasn't interested. After being snubbed repeatedly he just gave up and steered well clear of me, which suited me fine.

Cow, Termite and Cro had all applied for extensions, all of which got approved so they didn't rotate when their dates came up. Their rotation dates came and went and they stayed at Bouk, another year in Morocco with their dogs safely in their future. I resolved to apply for my extension a month prior to my rotation date just like they did. Those things were usually granted without difficulty. The Corps figured it was easier to just keep the people there instead of having to send new ones all the time so if they wanted to stay, let them. I was under the assumption that the brass would have no real reason to deny it and it would be granted in the same automatic fashion the others had.

I was wrong.

About a month before I was due to rotate I filled out the necessary paperwork and submitted it through Major Malfunction's office. We missed Mouse badly because he had been a good friend and a constant source of priceless information, but he was gone and had been replaced by some little guy with glasses who Meyers immediately browbeat into absolute cringing obedience. We quickly named him Igor because of his continual fumbling attempts to please his master. We and began to try to pull him into our circle so that we could stay up with Meyers. A tame company clerk is a good thing to have, but Igor was very afraid of Meyers and steered clear of us. Consequently we steered clear of him because we were concerned that he just might funnel information the opposite way, to Meyers. Igor received my paperwork and promised it would be on Major Malfunction's desk when he got to the office in the morning.

I left the office feeling certain that I would spend another year with my dog and my friends. The first real friends I had made in my cocky little life.

I had Second Boonies again that night. Argo and I spent a foggy shift lurking in the antenna field, looking for bad guys. We hadn't had any problems since the night of The Incident That Never Happened, but I never let my guard down after that night. My one concession to the totally relaxed days prior to the slaughter in the Middle East was to crawl into the bunker once in a while with the guys, relax for a bit, and get lightly stoned as a social courtesy. We would discuss things like the number of new guys arriving all the time to replace members of our old crew, and how none of them could possibly be as cool, as good, as skilled, etc., as our guys had been. Often our gaze would fall upon the poem etched in that intricate hand in the concrete of the back wall of the bunker. It had gone from being a cosmic joke to being a revered artifact of good times, except with Alfie, who still insisted that it had been the work of a closet homosexual. Often our conversation would turn to the eternal speculation about just who the Phantom Poet was. Since no more mysterious rhymes had popped up anywhere we were convinced it had been one of the guys who had rotated back to the world and that we would never know the identity of the real author. After debating the world shattering importance of things like the Phantom Poet's identity, I would then crawl back out and hit my post again.

I was sleeping well the next morning when Igor knocked on my door and informed me that Major Malfunction wanted to see me, pronto. Thinking that he was just sending for me to tell me that my extension would be approved, I casually slid out of bed, got dressed, and plodded off on the direction of the company office.

When I walked through the door to the company office, Igor gave me a slightly quizzical look that made me a little uneasy as he went into Major Malfunction's office to announce my arrival. Meyers had been seated at his desk when I entered but he got up and left as I came in. He only glanced at me once. It was a curious, sideways glance, but before I could start to analyze it Igor stepped out of the inner office and told me that the great man would see me now. As Meyers put his hat on and stepped outside I heard him start whistling the Marine Corps Hymn. A dark sense of foreboding stole over me like a dark blanket.

Very uneasy now, I walked into Major Malfunction's office, centered myself on his desk and from the position of attention said, "Lance Corporal Dillon reporting as ordered, sir."

"At ease, Dillon," I shifted to that position. He reached onto a pile of papers and picked up my extension request. "I see you requested a year's extension."

"Yes, sir."

He leaned back in his chair, "Close the door. Well, Dillon, I'll come right to the point. I never got this request. Lieutenant Meyers apparently intercepted it before it got to my desk. He denied it in the comments section before sending it on to CMC. Whether you get extended or not is ultimately their decision, but they almost always follow the Commanding Officer's recommendation. They denied your request, Dillon."

I wasn't sure I heard right. Denied my request? There must be some mistake. "Sir?"

"I'm sorry, Dillon. For some reason Meyers took it upon himself to send your request on without my review. I asked Meyers about it and he said he feels that you are a disrupting influence here. He thinks you are the leader of some faction, some group of troublemakers. I haven't seen anything that would make me think the same thing, but what is done is done. Your request is denied. Sorry. Any questions?"

Any questions? *Any questions?* Damn right I had questions. I could feel the pulse pounding in my temples as a rage toward Meyers built. "Sir," I managed to choke out, "can you fix this? I…"

"No, Dillon, I can't. CMC has spoken. It's over. I'm very sorry. For what it's worth I've reprimanded Lt. Meyers. I know that doesn't help, but it's the best I could do for you."

I stood there like someone had hit me in the face with a board. Slowly it started to sink in.

Meyers had won. And had I lost without firing a shot.

I simply stared at him and said, "Thank you, Sir."

"Personally, I think you've done a fine job, and your actions that night in apprehending that saboteur were exceptional. I'm putting a letter of commendation in your service record book. Fill out a dream sheet and I'll do what I can to help you with that."

I stood there blankly, the absolute hopelessness of the situation sinking in.

"Unless there's something else, Dillon, that will be all."

"Yes, Sir," I brought myself to attention. I did an about face and headed for the door.

"Dillon?" Major Malfunction said.

I stopped, but didn't turn around. "I really am sorry," he said.

I just nodded.

On my way out I picked up the dream sheet from Igor. A dream sheet is a form on which you select three duty stations when you are due for orders. You fill it out and submit it up to some lofty perch in the Marine Corps structure, and somebody gets to decide just where you will be sent next. If you get incredibly lucky it just might be one of the three you requested. Or maybe somewhere in the same hemisphere, anyway. That's why it was called a dream sheet. Because you may as well be dreaming if you think you'll actually get anything you specifically ask for in the Marine Corps.

But I had other things on my mind right now. I had less than a month and I would be leaving. Leaving the friends who had become my family and worse, leaving my dog.

I felt a lump building in my throat as I thought about it as I went looking for the crew and I resolved right then and there that no one here would ever see me cry over this issue. What was done was done. There was nothing I could do to change it. I would take it like a man when it came. And in the mean time, I would enjoy myself as much as I could in the time I had left.

I found Cow, Termite, Cro and Alfie at the kennels. They took the news hard but then we all got good and stoned and had a great time filling out my dream sheet. They wanted me to put places like Australia, Tahiti, Cancun, and a special request for assignment at a nude beach in Florida Termite knew about. Which were all great ideas but the Corps, being rooted in reality, requires that you fill out the form with three mainside duty stations. I'd already spent a lifetime at Lejeune, so I picked three stations in California, several thousand miles away from Lejeune. Camp Pendleton, El Toro Air Base, and MCRD San Diego were my three choices. Surely I would get lucky and hit on one of them. If I had to leave Morocco, a California beach complete with California girls seemed like a reasonable consolation prize.

I went about my business as casually as possible, and spent as much time with Argo as I really could without seeming weird. I was trying to live each minute with him to the fullest. I didn't even want to tie him outside the bunker when I'd meet whoever I was on boonies with so I didn't really spend too much time there despite repeated invitations. The guys understood and didn't take offense at my seeming snub of their good intentions.

Then, one night about two weeks after learning that my extension had been disapproved, Cro and Cow came and found me and Argo at our spot on perimeter road. We were lying there as usual. I felt Argo raise his head and stiffen, then relax. He kept his head up, though, looking toward the center of the field. I could tell it was a Dog Man he was alerting on so I didn't even get up. After a few minutes I heard them approach, their dogs leading them to me and Argo.

"Hey, Marshal," whispered Cro softly. After my battle with the two saboteurs we were much more careful when we were in the antenna field. One tends to contain oneself after 9mm rounds whistle past one's face. "You gotta see this."

"What?" I asked.

"Come on," Cow said, "It's in the bunker."

"What is?"

"Just come and see," Cro said with a touch of impatience.

I stood and Argo stood with me. I'd humor them, then maybe they'd leave me alone. We trudged to the bunker and I reluctantly tied Argo outside. They had obviously already been there to set up for the nightly dereliction. Three candles were burning and the inside of the bunker was bathed I their warm yellow glow. "Okay, guys, what's the deal?" I asked as I stepped inside.

"Look," said Cow.

He nodded toward the back wall. There, below the first two verses of the poem was a third verse. It was written in what looked to be charcoal and hadn't been carved into the concrete like the other two verses had been. It read:

At dawn the light wakes with gentle touch
A dreamer who to sleep's mantle clings
While in that sleep he's learned so much
For Dog Men Dream Of Magic Things

"It's different from the first two," Cro said, staring at the poem.

"Yeah," Cow agreed, "I wonder why he didn't carve it."

"Maybe somebody else wrote it," I said.

They both turned to me and gave me that accusing look, the same look I had gotten when the poem first appeared. "Don't even start," I told them.

That night I dreamed of that poem and what it meant to me, to all of us, the Dog Men. When I woke that morning my pillow was damp, and Igor was knocking on my door.

When I opened it he looked down at the floor, obviously hoping I wouldn't kill the messenger.

"Your orders are in, Marshal," he said.

27

Revelations

Camp Lejeune! Camp fucking Lejeune! I felt like pounding my face on the floor when I saw that. There would be no consolation prize of bronze California beauties. No beaches. No anything that had anything to do with how I had filled out the dreamsheet. There would be humidity, boredom and great big giant mosquitoes. Mustn't forget the mosquitoes. I was ordered to report to Second Marine Division at Camp Lejeune. Again! I had just come from there. There was absolutely no justice in this world. Fate was crapping all over me and there was nothing I could do about it. Less than nothing. I had filled out their stupid little dreamsheet in the hopes of never seeing Camp Lejeune ever, ever again. But there it was, in Marine Corps black and white. Lejeune. Jesus! And to top that off I was going back to Second Marine Division, which enjoys the reputation as being one of the most hardcore infantry units in the world. I hated that stuff.

Well, this just sucked.

I was sure Meyers had his paws in there somewhere. He was a cunning bastard and as we had found out, completely ruthless. I was convinced that he had set up Mouse, and now he'd gotten his vengeance on me for whatever ills he felt I had brought into his life. He had somehow made sure I would not get anything near what I had asked for. I tried to find out just how he had screwed me but I met a brick wall. His lab assistant Igor wasn't talking. Mouse was long gone, serving the year in Leavenworth he had pleaded to, and Igor was way too whipped and timid to give me any inside scoop or help me in any way. Spineless little creep.

Anyway, I had less than a week to get ready. I stuck to my promise to myself that I wouldn't show the guys how much this bothered me. Oh, they knew I was upset alright, but not nearly just how upset I really was.

The final night of boonies came quickly. As usual, Argo and I took Second Boonies, along with Termite and Nero, and Cow and Blackie, which was fitting. They were closer to me than anyone had ever been before in my life. We walked all night, smoking and talking and laughing, not caring whether or not we were seen or heard by anyone. If a bad guy with intent had been out there we would have been screwed but we didn't care. Something special was about to end, something like I had never been a part of before in my life. And never would again.

Since it was my last night we decided to smoke in the bunker one more time. We piled in, stoned and laughing. Cow lit a candle and automatically my eyes went to the poem as they always did. This time, though, there was a surprise.

Someone had carved the final verse into the concrete beneath the other two. The words flowed in the same fine script as the other verses.

"I'll be damned," was all I could say.

Shorty and Cro, two of the original crew, slipped out into the antenna field and joined us at the bunker for a while, then slipped back into the compound. I climbed on top of the bunker where Alfie had told me the story of the White Lady and watched them disappear into the night. It seemed like a perfect metaphor.

That morning, as the sky began to lighten and the truck carrying the post stander for the Post Three tower wound its way to the tower behind Oz, signaling our relief, I walked slowly into the kennels, finishing my watch for the last time. I took the heavy collar from Argo's neck as I put him into the run. I started to drop to a knee and hug him to me, then I thought, not yet. It's not goodbye, yet. I had until five that afternoon before the Navy transport van would arrive to take me to the airport at Casablanca, so I patted him like I did every other time and stepped out of his run, locking it as I left.

Cow and Termite stood back and watched, waiting until I had finished my morning ritual before stepping up. We walked to the barracks together and talked a little more, and I eventually went to my room dropped off into a light sleep. I dreamed of the White Lady again, only this time she wasn't flying over the sand of the antenna field. She just stood there in an early dawn looking at me with sad eyes, then faded as I watched, the rising sun coming through her ever more transparent form, until she disappeared altogether.

I never dreamed of her again.

I got up with just a couple hours to spare that afternoon. Cow, Termite, and Shorty helped me pack. Shorty seemed to be taking this whole thing harder than I was despite the fact I had nearly killed him once with my bare hands. He wouldn't hang around as I got ready to leave. He hadn't applied for an extension and would be leaving himself in just few days and I guess he saw my departure as a harbinger of his own.

When it was almost time I walked to the kennels. The guys all stayed at the barracks because they knew that this had to be my time. Mine and Argo's.

I walked slowly to Argo's run and let myself in. When he saw me coming he began to prance the way he always did, and I knelt and drew him to me, holding against my body. For almost a year and a half I had fed him, groomed him, trained him, and depended on him like I had depended on nobody else in my life. We had walked together and played together. We had fought together against beast and man and won together. He was loyal to me the way no human had ever been, and I was loyal to him as I had never been to anything, human or otherwise. He had fought for me without a second's hesitation, and I for him, battling that brave little bull and those never identified bad guys together. And winning gloriously. Together.

And now—it was over.

I fought down the lump in my throat. It was time to go. This would do no good. I squeezed him to me one more time and whispered, "Go get 'em, Argo," then, releasing him, I stood. He had that intelligent, curious look in his eyes and was giving me that "What now?" look of his as I let myself out of his run. I couldn't stand it anymore, "Bye, buddy," I said and turned, walking to the kennels gate. I didn't look back until I out of the kennels and had walked through Post Two, back into the main compound. There, I stopped for a second and turned around for a last look at the kennels. I could just see Argo in his run, sitting, staring after me and I turned back around before I started to cry, and headed for the barracks.

I would not cry, not here.

The guys were gathered around, all the old ones and some of the new that we had allowed into our inner circle the way I had eventually been allowed into another inner circle in another time. They had already carried my bags to the transport van, which sat like a gray cancerous lump across the street waiting for me. They lit a bowl up as we said our goodbyes; all of us making promises to get together that would never be kept, as is the nature of those things, although we were sincere as we made them that day.

One by one I said my goodbyes. Termite and Shorty shook my hand and hugged me. Cow said, "What can I say, man? You're my brother," then he hugged me too, nearly crushing my ribs as he did so. Alfie and Cro were nowhere to be seen. I didn't expect Alfie to be there, but I was disappointed that Cro wouldn't be telling me goodbye. I finally said my last goodbyes and slipped out of the door, wanting to walk to the van alone. I would not let them see me cry.

Dusk was beginning to settle as I reached the van. I sighed and put one foot in the door, then a voice from behind me said, "Dream's over, Marshal."

It was Alfie. He came from behind the van and now stood with his head cocked to one side, looking at me strangely. I turned to him and said, "Yeah. Yeah, it is."

"Mine too, soon. Three weeks. I'm at the end of my extension. They won't grant another one. My dream will end then, just like yours is ending now."

Something in his voice, or something he said, caused me to look at him sharply. There was something there I couldn't quite pull together, something he wanted to tell me, but he wasn't coming out with it. Then it all came together for me.

"It's you isn't it?"

He looked at me, expressionless.

"You're the Phantom Poet, aren't you?"

He grinned a crooked little grin, looked around conspiratorially, and said, "Yeah. It's me. Don't tell anybody."

"I think I knew it, sort of. Hey, wait a minute! You mean to tell me that after all that bullshit you put out about that poem and whoever wrote it, it was you all the time? You asshole! We even got into a fight over it!" His grin widened, and I went on, "Why didn't you take credit for it? It's good. I mean, it's not Tennyson, but it had style."

"The first two verses—or the whole thing?"

"Well, the whole thing."

"I can't take credit for the whole thing. I just wrote the first two verses. I didn't write the third one. I just carved it in. By the way, that third verse wasn't bad, Marshal."

I smiled and looked at the ground, "Figured me out, huh?"

"It wasn't hard."

"Where did you learn to carve stone like that?"

"My old man is a stone cutter in El Paso. So was his. It's the family business, has been for generations. I was raised doing it. I got the tools from Sunshine before he left and bribed him to keep shut about it. I slipped out into the antenna field during the day to carve it. The guy at Post Two thought I was just going to the kennels."

"Why didn't you take credit for the poem? It could have given us a whole new insight to Alfredo Morales."

He sighed, "That's just it, Marshal. People leave you alone when you're an asshole. Or when they think you are. They don't expect too much because they think what you've got to give is limited. And they think you won't give it anyway," he shrugged, "It's easier. Not like you."

"Me?"

"Yeah. You like going around and having people think you don't give a shit, that you're this cool guy with a don't-fuck-with-me attitude. People see right through you. People like me, anyway. You're one of the good guys, cowboy. That's why those guys always came to you when they needed something. Those guys know how much it's tearing you up to leave here, man. And as long as they know you got something to give, they're gonna want it. That's why that asshole Pogo disapproved your extension, and why he tries to screw you every chance he gets. I see through him, too. He has a bad heart, and he hates you. Because he knows you're clean, man, inside, like he'll never be. And he hates you for it. But he left me alone. Why? Because I'm just an asshole, so I'm no threat to anybody. So everybody leaves me alone. I got my extension."

"Why did you decide to write a poem of all things?"

"I have a degree in English lit. The old man insisted on it in case I ever wanted to do something with my life." He saw the look on my face, "You aren't the only one here who reads, Marshal. I just didn't want anyone to know."

I stood there, staring at a side of Alfie that he had hidden very well indeed. He went on, "I knew you liked the poem. That's why I tagged you with it. So nobody would even think to look my way. We all wear masks. Even you. Especially you. Only yours is transparent. Mine's not. It covers a lot of my real face. Like I said, it's just easier. And now, your Dog Man dream is over. Mine too, soon."

"Yeah, but it's been good," I said, and he reached over and I shook his hand for the first time ever, and the last, "Real good."

He reached up with his other hand and squeezed my arm as we shook, then dropped it and stepped back, "Yes it has, *amigo*. Take the dream with you, Marshal. I will. It's too good to ever forget. Oh, and, hey....I'd really rather you didn't tell anybody it was me that wrote the first part of the poem. Or about the degree. I have an image to live down to, you know."

I barked a short laugh, "I won't, Alfie. Your secret's safe with me."

With that he turned around and walked quickly away. I got into the van. The squid driver was giving me an odd look until I said, "What the fuck are you looking at?"

He said, "Nothing," and started the van. As we started to pull out the windows of the barracks opened and I could hear wild shouts of, "So long, Marshal!" and cowboy yips and shouts coming from the guys. They faded as the van turned toward Post One. We completed our final security check by some dress blue wearing new guy at Post One I hadn't bothered to get to know and were just pulling off of Bouknadel for my last time when the driver said, "What the fuck?" and sharply jammed on his brakes. There in the middle of the road stood Cro, arms upraised. He wore his *jelaba* and carried his staff. As we watched he lit up a bowl and approached the van and began to blow smoke on the hood, then went to all four sides of the van and repeated the ritual, finally stopping again at the front, where he tapped the ashes from the pipe onto the hood of the van. He then made eye contact with me, nodded, and when I nodded back he tapped the staff on the ground and raised it high in a salute, then walked away, back onto Bouk and out of my life forever.

The driver, who was a squid and couldn't understand, was a little shaken,

"What was that all about?"

"Don't worry about it," I told him, "You've just been blessed. It worked once before. Now, go."

The van pulled away from Bouk and began the journey down the long side road to the main highway. Evening was turning into night as we finally reached Mohammed V. I turned to look at the lights of Bouk one last time and could see the red helix tower lights thrusting their way skyward, and I knew that somewhere close to them some Dog Men were on First Boonies, their dream not yet over, as mine was.

As the van pulled onto the highway I put my hands into my face and, not caring who saw me, I cried.

28

Loose Ends

I'd been back at Lejeune about two weeks when I got the letter from Mouse. I read it a half dozen times before lunch, and a couple more after. It said:

Dear Dillon,

I found you through the base locator system. I thought you would like to know that my conviction has been overturned and I'll be out of here by the time you get this. It seems that Lt. Meyers was caught sending five kilos of hashish home from Morocco in a footstool, an ottoman sort of thing he pulled the stuffing out of and stuffed with hash. Can you believe it? Somebody tipped off the Des Moines police who then called NIS. He was arrested right after you left Bouk. He denied everything, of course, but during the questioning he admitted he set me up. Whoever tipped them on the dope tipped them about that, too. I still don't know why he did it for sure and it doesn't matter. I'm soon going to be free. I want to thank you for everything you tried to do. It didn't work, but your heart was there. Good luck, Dillon.

Mouse

"Dillon! Are you gonna lean on that rake or use it the way God intended for shitbirds like you to use it?" My new platoon sergeant, another in a line a fools I was forced to suffer gladly, said. A couple of my fellow shitbirds laughed at me silently behind his back and pretended interest in raking as he exercised his authority in my direction.

"Okay, Sarge," I said. *You fucking idiot*, I thought.

I folded the letter, put it back in my pocket, and began to rake the pine needles that had fallen on hallowed Marine Corps ground, whistling the Marine Corps Hymn as I worked.

"Catchy tune, ain't it, Sarge?"

****

After the Dream

Dillon: Finishes his four years in the Marine Corps without ever rising above the rank of lance corporal, which suits him just fine. He vows never to become an authority figure like those he detests so much or to assume a leadership role of any type. At the time this novel was written, he is a decorated career police officer in Indianapolis, Indiana. His rank is Captain.

Termite: Last seen on a Harley somewhere west of Reno, Nevada.

Freaky Deac: Stays in the Marine Corps. Retires in 2000 after a career spanning 34 years. His last six years is spent as the Sergeant Major of the Marine Corps, the highest enlisted post in the Corps. To the day of his retirement he enjoys terrorizing second lieutenants and does so as only a Sergeant Major can.

Cro: Starts his own church, the New Age Church of Holistic Medicine. It grows into one of the most popular cults in America, rivaled only by L. Ron Hubbard's Church of Scientology. It is currently under investigation for promoting the use of smokable cures to a wide variety of illnesses.

Cow: Never gets that teaching degree. He starts his own kennel, White Lady Kennels in his home state of Connecticut, and breeds his own line of German Shepherds. His line is one of the most sought after in the country.

Shorty: Goes back to school and gets that engineering degree, then goes even further and gets his Doctorate in the aero-space field. He currently works for NASA and is involved in the Mars probe missions, two of which have disappeared. There is no truth to the rumor that he was involved in the Challenger project.

Timmy Brunner: True to his word he goes back to Alabama and lives off of his parent's largesse. He is currently still doing so, his only complaint being about the longevity that is common in his family.

Alfie: Senator Alfredo Morales (D), Texas. Becomes a power in the Senate and is known and respected for his rough and tumble political tactics. He also becomes a respected novelist and historian.

Carlos: Becomes a curator in the Rock and Roll Hall of Fame, where he pays particular attention to the Carpenters exhibit. His oldest son is a well known songwriter.

Chaplain's Assistant Greaves: Becomes a leading televangelist, developing his "Caddy For Jesus" motto into a mega-million dollar slogan. Comes under investigation for fraud and sexual misconduct but before the investigation is complete he is killed when an "electrical device" he was using while in bed with a transsexual prostitute short circuits and electrocutes him. The type of the device was not released. The transsexual prostitute survived and is currently suing his estate.

Mouse: After his experience at the hands of the military justice system he gets his law degree and spends a career fighting corruption in and out of the legal system. In a strange twist of fate he is selected as a special investigator into corporate embezzlement at high levels. He investigates and obtains an indictment on:

Meyers: Becomes an executive with a huge corporation after successfully hiding the less than illustrious end to his Marine Corps career. After being indicted in what is referred to by investigators as the "Pogo Papers" (no one outside of the prosecutor's office ever knew why) he disappears with a large amount of money and his secretary. He is currently on the FBI's 10 Most Wanted List.

The End

Printed in the United States
126420LV00003B/168/P